T0162073

# FRESH FIELDS

ALSO BY

PETER KOCAN

Novels
*The Treatment*
*The Cure*
*Flies of a Summer*

Verse
*The Other Side of the Fence*
*Armistice*
*Freedom to Breathe*
*Standing with Friends*
*Fighting in the Shade*

Peter Kocan

# FRESH FIELDS

Europa
*editions*

Europa Editions
116 East 16th Street
New York, N.Y. 10003
www.europaeditions.com
info@europaeditions.com

First Publication 2007 by Europa Editions

Library of Congress Cataloging in Publication Data is available
ISBN-13: 978-1-933372-29-7

Kocan, Peter
Fresh Fields

Book design by Emanuele Ragnisco
www.mekkanografici.com

Printed in Italy
Arti Grafiche La Moderna–Rome

This project has been assisted by the Australian Government through
the Australia Council, its arts funding and advisory body.

Australian Government

Australia Council
for the Arts

# CONTENTS

*Community, kinship, roots?*
*It was the essence of your situation*
*that you had no such connections.*
*You were, if you could bear it, ideally free.*
—SAUL BELLOW

*. . . those who knew the old order only as a broken promise,*
*yet who took the promise more seriously*
*than those who merely took it for granted.*
—CHRISTOPHER LASCH

# 1. ARRIVAL

There were three of them. They had just got off the night train from interstate and were walking along the platform to the ticket barrier. The woman was in her mid-thirties and she held by the hand a boy of seven. Following them with the two suitcases was a fourteen-year-old youth. He kept several paces behind, as though to distance himself from whatever was happening.

"Will Dad come after us?" the boy was asking worriedly.

"No," the woman said. "I've told you."

"Why won't he?"

"Because he doesn't know where we are."

"What if someone tells him?"

"Nobody knows where we are except us."

The boy did not look convinced. The youth did not feel convinced either. All night on the train, sitting upright on the hard seat, he had been going over it and over it in his mind. They'd left quickly with only what would fit into the two suitcases, and it would have been two or three hours before Vladimir got home from work. By the time he'd found them gone they would already have been miles and miles away on the train. But what if they'd accidentally left some clue? The youth had racked his brains, trying to think what clue they might've overlooked. Or what if Vladimir had come home early? What if he'd seen them pull away in the taxi with the two suitcases? What if he was on the next train right behind them? The youth had a continuous urge to look over his shoulder. From behind came a shout, but it was just a railway porter skylarking.

They went through the ticket barrier and came out in a huge echoing hall. There were signboards and kiosks and trolleys loaded with luggage. The woman led the boy to the middle of the hall and stopped. The youth followed and stopped a few paces away and put the suitcases down and stood beside them.

"Are you hungry?" the woman asked, coming across to him. "We could get some sandwiches."

"I don't care," said the youth.

"We should have a bit of something."

"I don't care," said the youth again. He was looking at the ticket barrier they'd just come through. They were standing in plain sight of it. He wanted to move away from the exposed position, but to suggest this might sound as though he was taking an interest.

"What kind of sandwiches would you like?" the woman asked him.

"I don't care," he replied without looking at her.

"I won't be a minute then," the woman said. "Mind your brother while I'm gone. Explain to him that we're safe now. Can you do that?"

The youth shrugged.

"I wish you'd try to be a bit helpful," the woman said and went off towards a kiosk.

The youth stood beside the suitcases and watched the ticket barrier. The boy watched a string of trolleys being pulled along by a little tractor.

"I got cheese and ham," the woman said when she came back. "Look, there's a seat." She led the boy to the other side of the hall and sat down with him and began unwrapping the sandwiches on her knee.

The youth followed with the suitcases and sat down a little apart from them. The woman leant across and offered him a sandwich. He shook his head. She put the sandwich down in his lap anyway. He was actually very hungry, but was getting more and more tense. They were still in plain view of the ticket barrier and every time a heavily built man came through the youth felt a clutch of apprehension. Why didn't they go from here? Why didn't they get out of sight? The phrase "criminal stupidity" came into his head. The woman's behaviour was "criminal stupidity" and the sandwich poised ridiculously in his lap seemed to sum it all up.

He felt suddenly enraged. He wanted to shriek at her: "You stupid bitch! Don't you care if Vladimir comes raging through the ticket barrier any moment? Don't you care if he starts bashing you up?" It was alright for her, he thought bitterly. If Vladimir appeared and started bashing her up she could cower and scream and everybody would feel sorry for her. And it was alright for the boy. He was just a little kid and no-one would expect him to do anything. But the youth was fourteen, almost a man, and a man is supposed to be able to stick up for his mother. But the youth knew he could not do anything. He'd never been able to. The very thought of trying to fight Vladimir drained his strength away and made him feel sick.

"The first thing," the woman was saying, "is to find somewhere to stay for a night or two. In the morning we'll get the paper and look for a proper place to live. And then I'll look for a job."

"Will I have to go to school?" the boy asked.

"Of course."

"What if Dad comes to the school?"

The woman stood up and crumpled the sandwich papers into a bin.

"There's a Travellers' Aid booth over there," she said. "They can advise us about accommodation." She led the way across and went into the booth. The youth threw his untouched sandwich into the bin and followed with the suitcases and stood near the door. He heard the woman telling someone that they hadn't much money and needed somewhere cheap for a night or two. This would normally have made the youth cringe with embarrassment, but now he just stared blankly away and told himself that he didn't care, that he wasn't involved.

The woman emerged with a piece of paper and said she'd been given an address and that it wasn't far. They crossed the big hall again and went through an archway and came out into the sun. They stood gazing at the tall buildings of the city, and at the traffic, and at the unfamiliar-seeming people in the streets.

"Look!" said the woman in a moment of sudden gaiety, holding her arms up in a gesture that seemed to take in the whole city and great distances beyond it: "These are fresh fields for us! *Fresh fields!*"

THE SHANGRI-LA Private Hotel was a doorway between two shops. They booked a room for the night. The room had a double and a single bed, and the window looked out on an alley and the backyards of the two shops. The woman said she wanted a couple of hours rest and lay down on the double bed. The boy cuddled down beside her. The youth sat on the edge of the other bed and looked at them and at the room and at the two suitcases. He was too tense to rest. If he'd been alone he might've had a cry to let some of the tension out. Instead he got up and went to the door. As he went out he heard the woman murmur that they'd go for a nice meal later.

It was about midday then and the traffic was heavy in the street and the footpath was crowded. The youth turned left out of the doorway of the Shangri-La and walked along, staying close to the shopfronts. He held his elbows tucked in and took care not to meet anyone's eyes. Looking anyone in the eyes always made him feel uncomfortable. He didn't see the need for it anyway. Keeping your eyes to yourself was just part of minding your own business. The youth kept along the one street so as to be able to find his way back easily. He was hoping to come to a park or open space where he could sit apart and think. He couldn't think properly with other people near, couldn't lose himself in reflection the way he needed to. The youth liked to mutter his thoughts to himself to hear what they sounded like in words. Whenever he went too long without some private thinking-space he became off-balanced and anxious, as though all sorts of dangerous complications might be building up unnoticed. Only by continually thinking could he keep things under control.

He was pondering this when he stepped off the footpath at an intersection and a bus swerved round and nearly hit him. The driver bawled abuse. The youth retreated to the kerb and stood there shaking. He heard girls giggling and thought it must be because of him. He dared not look around.

He managed to get across the intersection and hurried on through the crowd. He was afraid the girls were still behind him, so when he saw a shop doorway set back from the footpath he stepped into it to let them go by.

It was a gun shop. There were racks of rifles in the window and on the wall behind were medals and flags and badges and some Nazi armbands and a German steel helmet. The youth looked at the helmet and began to feel calmer, for it had reminded him of Diestl. Diestl was a character in a war movie he'd seen. There were many other characters in the film, American and French and Yugoslav, but only Diestl had struck him deeply.

In the film the war is lost for the Germans. Diestl's unit has been smashed up too many times to be put together again, and no-one is taking proper charge anymore. So Diestl is making his own way through the French countryside, his wounded arm held stiffly at his side, his tunic ripped and dirty, his Schmeisser sub-machine gun slung from his good shoulder.

Diestl knows very well that the war is hopeless, but he will never surrender. It isn't Nazi beliefs that keep him going. He has no beliefs anymore. And he hasn't any personal ties either, for all his friends are dead in the fighting and all his family in the bombing. Diestl has had every feeling burnt out of him except for a sort of grim pride that will make him determined and dangerous until the moment he goes down. Maybe "pride" was the wrong word. The youth didn't know what the right word was. All he knew was that the scenes of Diestl limping like a wolf or an outlaw along the roads of a ruined and hostile world answered something deep in him.

The youth left the doorway of the gun shop and went on. But now he didn't care about keeping his elbows tucked in or avoiding people's eyes. He stared straight ahead with a blank hard expression. He let his left arm hang stiffly and he imagined the solid weight of the Schmeisser slung from his other shoulder.

There was a big ornate church on a corner. It had open space around it and benches set under trees. The youth limped to one of the benches and slumped down and made a motion as if unslinging the Schmeisser and laying it beside him. He stared at the traffic and the people, a grimace of contempt on his lips. After a while he let the Diestl mood slip off. It wasn't good to stay in it too long. It would start to break into fragments and lose its effect.

The day was turning cool and cloudy and a breeze sprang up and rustled the leaves of the trees. That cheered the youth. Coolness and clouds and rain and wind always suited him better than broad sunlight. He thought of walking on to see more of the city, but realised that he was very tired and hungry. He decided to head back. He crossed to the opposite side of the street and began walking in the direction of the hotel. Drops of rain fell.

There were cinemas on that side of the street and the youth paused outside each one to look at the posters and the advertisements for coming attractions. One of the cinemas had what looked like a rude film showing. The photos outside were of girls wearing nighties, or romping on beds, or taking showers with their bodies vaguely visible through wet shower curtains. As the youth was looking at these he noticed an usherette watching him through the glass doors of the foyer. She probably thought he was perving at the rude photos. He hurried away and would have worked himself into a rage, except that the rain was falling nicely now. He let the rage drift away. When he passed the gun shop again and thought of Diestl he knew the usherette didn't matter. He grinned as he thought how Diestl would make the bitch smirk on the other side of her face.

When he got back to the Shangri-La the woman and the boy were waiting to go and eat. They left the room and looked for a nice cafe, but the ones they saw were either too grubby or too expensive-looking. The rain had set in too, and they didn't feel like searching too far. So they bought fish and chips and took them back to the room and ate sitting on the beds. The woman had a bottle of sherry in one of the suitcases and she poured some into a plastic cup and sat against the bedhead sipping it and eating chips. She offered the youth some sherry and he took a couple of mouthfuls. The boy wanted some too and the woman allowed him a sip so he wouldn't feel left out. The woman began to talk again about the future. They would find a proper place to live and she would get a job. The youth and the boy would go to school. With a bit of luck they'd soon be having a lovely new life.

The youth said nothing. It had come to him with peculiar clarity that these hopes and plans truly didn't involve him. He had a fate of his own in which dreams of a lovely life did not figure. He did not know yet what the fate was, except that it was somehow related to the image of Diestl limping down that lonely road towards a chosen end in the ruined world.

THEY FOUND a flat in a suburb called Ashvale about twenty minutes by train from the centre of the city. The flat was one big room with a kitchenette. There was a patch of scrubby weed at the back, and an old rusted car. The boy loved the car and would sit in it for hours, jiggling the steering wheel and making engine noises. There was only a double bed in the flat, but the landlady lent them a single mattress so the youth could doss on the floor. The landlady was very fat and wore a dressing-gown and slippers at all times. Her name was Mrs. Vetch, but she insisted on being called Ida. "I'm not formal!" she'd say.

They were cold the first night because they had only a travelling rug they'd brought with them and a couple of thin blankets lent by Ida. Next day the woman went to an op-shop run by the Salvation Army and bought blankets as well as cups and plates and saucepans and other kitchen things. She saw a cheap radio and bought that too. They began to feel cosier then. The woman cooked meals in the kitchenette, and they'd sit eating, drinking tea and listening to the radio.

Ida often came into the room. She did not knock but just loomed in and sat down. "How you managin', lovey?" she'd ask the woman. Then she'd suggest a cup of tea and a talk. "Life's grim without a chinwag," she'd say. "And besides, I'm not formal!"

The woman told her a little about Vladimir and Ida spoke of her own late husband. "My old bugger never laid a hand on me! Didn't have the nerve! Knew I'd cut his bloody throat one night!" And Ida assured the woman that she'd deal with Vladimir if he ever showed up. "I'll send him packin', don't you worry!"

Their money was almost gone and the woman looked in the classifieds every morning for a job. She wanted something like a housekeeper's position where she'd have flexible hours because of the boy. Ida advised her to go to Mrs. Hardcastle's employment agency in town. So the woman went to Mrs.

Hardcastle's and had her name put on the books. There was a problem at first because the woman did not have references, but Mrs. Hardcastle said it was okay, that she knew an honest face when she saw one. The woman mentioned this in passing to Ida that evening and Ida rushed off and came back with a biro and a sheet of paper and declared she would write out a reference there and then. It took up the whole sheet of paper and Ida went to fetch another sheet and filled that one up too with large scrawling writing. It was all about how Ida would Swear on a Stack of Bibles and how she wished she'd be Struck Dead if it was Any Word of a Lie. "Don't thank me, lovey," she said when she gave the woman the scrawled sheets, "I'm not formal." The woman said she was very grateful. When Ida had gone she put the reference in a drawer and left it there.

The woman got a job in a shirt factory and the boy was put into the school at Ashvale. The youth should have been enrolled at school too, for he was still under the legal leaving age, but the woman said they could let it slide for the time being. That suited the youth fine. Each morning he would walk the boy to the school gates and leave him there. Then he wandered the streets. He worked out a number of routes for himself. He liked to have familiar routes he could follow without fear of being surprised by anything. That left his mind free. He was seldom bored.

Ashvale was a suburb of quiet residential streets, not posh, but not slummy either. Some of the streets were lined with trees, and here and there were grassed areas with kids' swings and monkey bars. The main shopping centre was near the railway station and the youth spent part of each day there. He loved shopping centres. A shopping centre was the one place a person could loiter as long as they liked without anyone caring. And shop windows were interesting. It didn't matter what was in them. The youth looked at hats and refrigerators and chocolates with equal interest and in the same spirit that a visitor from another planet might look at them: they were items of this world and their uses and meanings and associations could be mused on endlessly. People were interesting too, as long as you could just watch them without being involved. The youth had favourite benches where he could sit and watch people.

The best position was outside a ladies' hairdressers. From a bench there the youth could see into the salon. There was a big indoor plant just inside the window and this gave the youth the feeling of being comfortably screened but without blocking his own view much. Three girls worked in the salon but the youth liked watching one in particular. She was slim and had beautiful legs and long auburn hair. Most days she wore her hair in a single plait down her back.

The youth could tell she was special by the way she behaved with customers. She was always friendly but without being pushy or silly like the other two. The way she worked was different too. She didn't skylark like the others but carried on calmly, doing one thing properly and then moving on to the next. When the salon door was open the youth heard snatches of talk, mostly from the two silly girls. He learnt that the special one's name was Polly. Seeing Polly every day began to be very important.

Polly mostly ate her lunch at an open-air section across from the salon where some tables and chairs were set up. She usually sat with her beautiful legs crossed, reading a book and making little circular motions with one foot. The youth loved the way she sat and would steal lingering side-on glances at her. Once he walked over close enough to see the title of her book. It was called *For Whom the Bell Tolls*.

One day Polly came out of the salon and went to cross the street. She paused a moment at the kerb right beside the youth. He tried to look the other way. "How are you today?" he heard her ask. He looked around and saw she was smiling at him. He felt stricken, as if he'd been caught in the act, but managed to mumble, "Good, thanks." Polly smiled again and crossed the street.

He avoided the area for a couple of days. But it was too hard to go without seeing her. So he drifted back to the bench and she gave him a smile and a nod another few times.

Apart from the shopping centre, the youth's favourite place was a park a few streets off. It had a shady avenue of big old trees, and a pond, and a sports field. The youth went there every afternoon on his way back to pick up the boy from school. It was lovely at that time of day, with the light gleaming on the leaves and the breeze ruffling the water of the pond. Sometimes he saw a man in a tatty brown coat near the public toilets on the other side of the sports field. One day the man wandered across and sat down near him. The youth stared straight ahead.

"Just waiting for some friends of mine," the man said. His voice was quivering.

The youth said nothing.

"Funny couple," the man said. "Specially him. Always, um, wanting me to massage his, um, privates."

The youth said nothing.

"I don't suppose you'd like me to, um, massage *your* privates?" the man asked.

The youth tried to think exactly what "massage" meant and what "privates" were.

"That's alright," the man said, after a long pause. "No harm in asking, is there?"

"S'pose not," said the youth, still not sure what the question had been.

"You don't mind that I asked?"

"S'pose not."

"Academic question, really, as most things are," said the man. He made as though to give an offhand sort of laugh, but it came out like a groan.

The youth gave him a cautious glance and saw that his face was very pale, and that he was drawing his tatty brown coat around him as though he was bitterly cold, and that his hands were shaking. The youth began to worry that the man was ill and might collapse. And he had a feeling that he was upsetting the man somehow. He thought he should go. Anyway, it was time to pick up the boy from school.

"I have to go . . ." he started to say.

"No, no, I'll go," the man broke in, getting up hurriedly. "I'll leave you alone. There's no problem. One is harmless, you know. Completely." His voice quivered away almost to nothing.

He seemed to want to say something more, but then turned and walked quickly away.

Sometimes there were spoiled moments, like if the youth had to alter his familiar route because of a barking dog in someone's yard, or if some woman watering her garden gave him an odd look. Such things would send him into the beginnings of a rage, but mostly he was able to let the enraged feelings float off. As long as he had plenty of time and space to himself he seldom needed the Diestl mood. By the time he had to collect the boy from school he usually felt relaxed enough to face the evening cooped up inside the flat.

The youth had made a corner for himself in the flat by pulling the wardrobe out at right angles to the wall so that when he lay down on his mattress he was well hidden. He could lie there and fondle his pillow and think about Polly. He had a reading lamp and some *Women's Weekly* magazines to browse through. There was the radio. He felt cosy enough. The woman always came home tired from the shirt factory and after she'd cooked the meal she didn't have the energy to do anything but sip a few quiet sherries. Only the boy was restless in the evenings.

They had been at Ashvale a couple of months. The stove in

the kitchenette didn't work properly and the woman was fed up with it. She mentioned the problem to Ida. Ida replied that the previous occupant hadn't complained. After that Ida wasn't so friendly. She still sometimes came into the flat to ask, "How you managin', lovey?" But it had a different tone and she didn't stay for a cup of tea and a talk. And then one evening the boy was playing on the old car at the back and someone came and told him to leave it alone. And then Ida asked them to keep their radio turned down because it was disturbing the rest of the house. The woman replied that the radio was always kept low. Ida said something about "airs and graces." The woman asked why the boy had been warned off the old car. Ida said something about "little brats."

A day or two later, news came from Mrs. Hardcastle's agency about a job. It was assistant manageress of a guesthouse in a suburb called Bankington. Accommodation was provided. The woman gave Ida notice that she was leaving and Ida said, "Good riddance!"

On the day they left they were putting their things into the taxi when Ida came to the front door and yelled that they'd damaged the stove and must pay for it.

"Malarkey!" said the woman.

"I'll have you up in court!" Ida shouted. "Just see if I don't! I know your kind! You're a flighty bitch! And I'll say it to your face! I'm not formal!"

"Not *normal*, you mean!" the woman called back as the taxi pulled away.

THE NEW place was a three-storey building with balconies and turrets. The front door was painted a pale yellow and there was a sign saying Miami Guesthouse. There was a courtyard where the taxi pulled in. They noticed a small dark man with a spotted bow-tie, talking earnestly with another man who looked unhappy. The small dark man was spreading his hands appealingly as he talked, and now and then he'd touch the other man's sleeve as though to soothe him. They unloaded their things and the woman paid the taxi, and then they went inside to the reception area. They were met by Mrs. Stott, the manageress. She told them that Mr. Stavros would be there in a moment to greet them. He was just sorting something out with one of the guests. Mr. Stavros was the owner, she explained.

The small dark man with the bow-tie came in from the courtyard. He looked very neat and clean and smelt like perfume. He spoke with a soft musical accent. Mr. Stavros told the woman that he liked to have a happy staff and that he hoped she would be happy with them too. The woman asked about accommodation for the youth. Mr. Stavros smiled that it was not a problem, that they had many rooms. Mrs. Stott would see to everything. Then he looked at his watch, spread his hands appealingly and hurried away.

"He's always like that," said Mrs. Stott, smiling. "You can't pin him down for a minute."

She took the woman to show her the room she and the boy were to have. It was just off the reception area, near Mrs. Stott's own little suite. Then she led the youth along a series of passages and up some narrow stairs. The further they got from the reception area the shabbier it became and the mustier it smelt. The youth was shown a tiny room on the third floor. It was part of a larger room that had been partitioned off with a thin ply wall. There were two single beds and two wardrobes, and these took up almost the whole space. There was a bare light bulb and no window. "You'll have it to yourself at the moment," said Mrs. Stott. She pointed to a faded and curled slip of paper taped to the wall. "Mealtimes etcetera written there." When she had gone the youth sat on one of the beds and looked around the room. It would suit him fine, he thought, as long as it was his alone.

The woman's duties were to attend to the reception area and

the phone switchboard after hours and at weekends, and generally assist Mrs. Stott. There were two other live-in staff, a cook and a cleaner.

The Miami Guesthouse was really four separate houses, each divided into as many rooms as possible, and linked to each other by a back lane. The dining room was in one of the other houses and at mealtimes the lane was filled with a straggle of guests going back and forth. The first and only time the youth tried the soup he truly thought they'd served up the dirty dishwater by mistake. Then the main meal came and he realised the soup hadn't been an accident. After that the youth ate with the woman and the boy in the staff tea-room. There were often angry scenes in the dining room and at the reception desk. Few guests stayed longer than a week, but that didn't matter. The whole operation was based on a constant turnover.

The youth liked it at the Miami. There were always things happening, always different people. It might be two New Zealand girls on a working holiday, or a bloke down from the bush in moleskins and a wide hat, or a family from interstate. The youth heard all the staff gossip and knew everyone's business, but without being personally involved. And because he seemed vaguely part of the staff he was often asked things, like where the bus stop or the post office was, so he began to get the hang of being conversational with people. It was like having a grandstand seat at the parade of life.

The best thing was that he had his little top-floor room to himself. He could retreat up there when he chose and lie on his bed with his *Women's Weekly* magazines, or he could cuddle his pillow and think about Polly. He went back to Ashvale once on the train and sat again on the bench outside the salon and looked through the window. But Polly wasn't there. Maybe she was off that day, or maybe she'd left the job. Anyway, it didn't seem the same at Ashvale and the youth did not go back after that one time. In a sense it didn't matter if he never saw Polly again. He had the image of her to focus on when he needed it—like when he was alone in his room, or when he daydreamed himself into other places and other times and needed to picture the beautiful girl whose lover he was.

One night about ten o'clock the youth heard shouts from downstairs. It did not sound like an angry guest demanding a refund. The youth went to the top of the stairs and got a faint whiff of smoke. As he went down the stink of burning got stronger and he saw people in their nighties and pyjamas gathered at the door of the staff tea-room. "It's alright," Mrs. Stott was telling them. "It's under control." The youth looked into the tea-room and saw someone lying on the floor under a blanket. There was smoke circling from a little room like a cupboard which opened off the tea-room and which had belonged to Beryl, the cook. One of the guests was in there, pouring water on the mattress from a plastic bucket. The youth found the boy beside him. "Where's Mum?" the youth asked.

"Ringing up," the boy replied.

The woman came from the switchboard and pushed through into the tea-room and told Mrs. Stott the ambulance was coming. Then she knelt beside the figure under the blanket.

"Just take it easy, Beryl," she kept saying. "Just take it easy." The figure under the blanket was shuddering violently.

"Someone fill this up for me," said the guest with the plastic bucket.

The woman looked over and saw the youth and motioned him to take the bucket. The youth filled it at the sink and handed it back to the guest and watched him pour the water carefully on those parts of the mattress that were still smouldering. There were burn marks up the wall beside the bed, and photos and other personal things were lying broken and jumbled on the floor. The youth filled the bucket a couple more times, trying not to look at the figure under the blanket. The shuddering had stopped and there was just the smell.

Mr. Stavros arrived as the ambulance men were carrying Beryl out on a stretcher. He went out with them and then came back and examined the burnt room. He was serious-faced but calm and businesslike and there was something in his manner that made the youth think that maybe Mr. Stavros had seen many bad things in his life and had no sense of drama about them anymore. Then he noticed that Mr. Stavros was glancing sharply at him. A moment later he noticed it again. He wondered what was wrong. His mouth felt stiff and tight and he realised he was grinning. Maybe he'd been grinning the whole time. He tried to make his mouth straighten to normal but the grin stayed. He put his hand to his face and pretended to be stroking his upper lip reflectively. Mr. Stavros glanced sharply at him again and the youth knew that Mr. Stavros knew he was still grinning behind his hand. The youth went up to his room and lay on the bed. After a long time his mouth began to relax and he could stop grinning.

Next morning he heard that Beryl had died in the ambulance.

IT WASN'T long after that the youth got a room-mate. His name was Sal and he was about twenty, thin and dark and quietly spoken. When he was shown into the room he apologised for intruding and said he probably wouldn't be staying long, so the youth made an effort to be friendly. They gradually began to talk and sometimes had good conversations. Sal talked mainly about girls. Each evening he would spruce himself up and go out to clubs and dances. Next day he'd tell the youth about the girls he'd danced with or kissed. At first the youth tried to appear knowledgeable, as though it was all familiar stuff to him, but after a while he let the pretence drop. It was easier then. He could ask questions. How does one approach girls? What does one talk to them about?

"Do you know any girls at all?" Sal asked.

"One," said the youth, anxious not to appear too pathetic. "Her name's Polly."

"How often do you see her?"

"Not much now. We had a sort of love affair, but it wasn't sex."

"What's she like?"

So the youth described Polly. He described how they used to meet every day for lunch and sometimes for a picnic in the park, or sometimes for an outing to the pictures. He explained that Polly was very religious, that in fact she wanted to become a nun, so of course it had never gone beyond just holding hands and a brief kiss once in a while.

One evening the youth confided that he'd like to have sex with a girl just once, to find out what it was like.

"Trouble is," said Sal, "when you've had it once you want to go on having it."

This impressed the youth deeply, and chilled him. He'd thought of sex as something he might have just a couple of times in his life if he was lucky. But if Sal was right, if having it once meant being a slave to it . . . No, the youth thought bitterly, he had no intention of being caught like that.

He thought of Diestl. There was a scene in the film where Diestl shelters for the night in an old barn. A beautiful French girl is by herself in the farmhouse nearby. She comes to Diestl just before dawn and kneels beside him in the straw. She is so lonely, she tells him, and frightened by the war. All she wants is a little tenderness. Diestl stares up at her with his cold blue eyes and says nothing. He has his knife ready to kill her if she makes a false move. The girl creeps away again. Then Diestl gets up to leave in case the bitch is alerting the partisans. He limps away down the road with the Schmeisser at the ready and his shadow long behind him, and the girl watches from the farmhouse window as he fades into the distance. The youth felt he understood that scene now. He must be cold and remote like Diestl, needing nobody but himself, scorning the trap of sex.

The youth was reading a book about the rise and fall of the Nazis. Or rather he read the first few chapters and the last few. The stuff in between was mostly about policies and strategies and it bored him. It was the Nazis as underdogs that appealed to his imagination, Nazis relying on their own hardness and will, battling first to win the streets from the Reds and come to power, and then battling at the end as the overwhelming might of the world bears down on them.

ONE NIGHT the youth was reading on his bed while Sal smartened himself at the mirror. Sal asked what the book was and the youth held it up for him to see. Sal said something about Jews.

"I don't know any Jews," the youth said.

"Yes you do," said Sal. "I'm a Jew. So is Stavros."

The youth looked at him in surprise. He wondered if the sight of the book had offended him. But Sal kept on combing his hair and brushing his jacket the way he normally did. He didn't seem bothered.

"What do Jews actually do?" the youth asked.

"I don't know," said Sal. "I'm not a practising Jew."

"But what made Hitler want to . . . you know . . ."

"Kill them?"

"Yes."

"Search me. Ask Stavros. He was in the camps."

Sal waved his hand and went out.

The youth would have liked to ask Mr. Stavros about the camps and the war and everything, but of course there was no way of doing that. Besides, the youth had felt a coldness in Mr. Stavros. Several times since the fire they'd passed each other and the youth had muttered hello and had only got a blank look. It was noticeable because Mr. Stavros was still affable and smiling with everyone else. Except perhaps the woman. He seemed a bit cold towards her too.

One evening the youth was sitting by himself in the staff tearoom. He had a packet of crayons belonging to the boy and was idly making designs on a drawing pad. He began to do a big swastika. It was turning out better than the other designs he had tried, so he kept on with it. When he had the outline right he filled it in with black. He left a circle of white around the centre and finished the background in red. It looked good, a complete Nazi flag in the correct colours. It had dramatic power. Just then he heard someone coming and he turned the pad face down on the table. Mr. Stavros stood at the door. "Just doing some drawing," the youth said awkwardly. Mr. Stavros came across to the table and turned the pad over and looked at it. Then he turned it face down again and went out without speaking.

The next day the woman told the youth she wanted to talk to him seriously.

"What do you want to do?" she asked when they had sat down.

"How do you mean?"

"With your life, your future. You appear to have no interest in going back to school, so what do you intend doing?"

"I don't know," the youth replied blankly.

"Well you'd better start thinking about it. You can't go around in a daze forever."

"I'm not in a daze."

"Aren't you? You're giving a pretty good imitation of it then. Who do you think pays for your room and board here?"

"I don't know," he replied. It had never occurred to him that these were being paid for.

"I do, of course," said the woman. "But I have your brother and myself to keep, as well as you, and this job might not last much longer. You have to start taking responsibility for yourself. That's all I'm saying."

"What should I do then?" asked the youth in bewilderment.

"You could look for a job, for one thing."

The youth felt as though he'd been told to fly to the moon.

"If you had a job you could support yourself. You could rent a room somewhere."

"Where?"

"Somewhere nearby. There are lots of rooms for rent."

"What's wrong with here?"

The woman looked at him.

"Mr. Stavros doesn't want you here anymore."

The youth stared away.

"Look," said the woman, "I've rung Mrs. Hardcastle and made an appointment for you tomorrow morning."

The youth said nothing.

"Well," the woman asked, "what do you think about that?"

"I don't know," said the youth.

The woman got up.

"You've got your whole life to get through," she said brusquely. "So you'd better smarten your ideas up!"

MRS. HARDCASTLE was a thin woman seated behind a desk. She wore a fox fur round her shoulders. The fox's head was still attached and rested against her bosom, the mouth drawn back in a snarl and the beady glass eyes seeming to glare across at the youth. Mrs. Hardcastle was flicking through a card index.

"And your dear mother is well?" she asked without looking up.

"Yes," murmured the youth.

"I like to think of my clients as one big happy family," Mrs. Hardcastle said, still not looking up.

The fox glared unblinkingly.

"And now you're part of our family too."

"Yes."

Mrs. Hardcastle stopped flicking the cards and looked closely at one of them. "What about the lure of the land?" she said, toying with the card. "Mr. Coles wants a station lad. Sheep property, near Balinga. Start ASAP."

"Yes," murmured the youth, wondering what "ASAP" meant.

"I'll telegram Mr. Coles then."

"Yes."

"Why don't you phone me this time tomorrow and I'll tell you the arrangements."

"Yes."

"And give my best to your dear mother."

"Yes."

Mrs. Hardcastle did not look up as he left, but the fox watched him to the door.

## 2. The Lure of the Land

The youth was to meet Mr. Coles at the stock and station agents in Balinga at two o'clock on the Wednesday.

He got to the main city station early, bought his ticket and then sat in the hall of the interstate and country trains, the same one he and the woman and boy had stepped out into a few months before. He had one small bag and a little money that the woman had given him in addition to his fare.

He kept going to the big board where the arrivals and departures were displayed, to check and recheck the departure time and platform number of his train. He kept feeling in his pocket to make sure the ticket was still there. And he kept touching his bag to make sure it was still beside him. Each time he checked these things he felt in control for a minute or two, but then anxiety would rush over him and he would have to recheck it all again.

The youth looked at the scores of people in the great echoing hall. They seemed to know what they were doing, where they were going, how to look after themselves in the world. He tried to draw courage from them, but it was pointless. He knew he was not like other people. When the time came to board his train he put himself into the Diestl mood. He limped along the platform, imagining the Schmeisser against his shoulder, then got into a compartment by himself and sat staring blankly ahead until the train began to move. Then he let the mood slip off because he knew he would need it later and didn't want to use it all up.

After about an hour the train left the suburban sprawl and climbed into the mountain range to the west. The tracks ran along the tops of ridges and through deep ravines and there were tremendous views. The grandeur of it all began to excite the youth and he opened the window and leant out to get the wind in his face. He felt like a boy in a storybook, going forth to seek his fortune.

But the exhilaration wore off and the train came down onto great flat plains. Station by station they got closer to Balinga and the youth's fear grew and whirled inside him until he felt sick. He forced himself to alight at Balinga and found his way to the main street of the town.

The street was very wide and there were utilities and Land Rovers angle-parked along it. He walked down one side until it started to peter out into paddocks, then he walked the whole length back on the other side. He could not find the stock and station agency. The town hall clock was already showing a couple of minutes past two. Mr. Coles would be waiting. Back where the youth had first entered the main street there was a big sign: STOCK & STATION AGENT. He realised he had looked at that sign before, and even read the words, but had not comprehended them. The woman was right. He *did* go around in a daze. He needed to smarten his ideas up. He paused a little way down the street from the stock and station agents, trying to make himself feel like a keen young lad with smart ideas. Then he went into the place and told the man at the counter that he was to meet Mr. Coles there at two.

"Who?" said the man. "Oh, yeah. He might be in sometime today."

The youth went back outside and looked up and down the street. He tried to keep his shoulders braced and his expression keen. About two-thirty, a burly man in a wide-brimmed hat came across the street towards him. He tried to meet the man's eyes keenly, but the man walked past. There were several others during the next couple of hours, and the youth had put on his keenest look each time, but none of the men took any notice of him. The last of them to go into the stock and station agency had been an elderly-looking man with a ginger moustache and brown boots with leather leggings. He had pulled up in an old truck and gone inside and was still there. The youth had used up all his keenness by now. Shadows were starting to lengthen along the street and he was trying to think what he'd do if Mr. Coles never came. He did not have enough money for the train fare back to the city.

The gingery man emerged with a coil of wire across his shoulder. He flung the coil onto the tray of the truck and then turned back into the doorway.

"Give a hand, lad!" he said brusquely.

"Pardon?" said the youth.

"Come on, lad. We're late as it is!"

The youth helped carry half-a-dozen more coils of wire out.

When all the coils were on the truck the man got into the driver's seat and the youth stepped back on the footpath to watch him go.

"Hop in, lad!" the man called. "Hop in!"

"Pardon?"

"Hop in, lad! Time's getting on!"

"Um, would you be Mr. Coles?" the youth asked.

"That's it, lad!" The man leant over and swung the passenger door open and revved the motor at the same time. The big old truck engine was painfully loud.

The youth got in and they drove along the main street.

"Got any kit, lad?" Mr. Coles asked, shouting over the noise of the engine, and glancing at the youth's one small bag.

"Pardon?"

"Got boots, hat, overcoat?"

The youth shook his head.

"Better get some," said Mr. Coles.

They turned a corner and pulled up in front of an army disposals store.

"The lad needs kitting out," said Mr. Coles abruptly to the man inside. "I'll be back shortly," he added, turning and going out before the youth could tell him that he didn't have enough money to buy anything.

"What do you need?" the store man asked.

The youth mumbled that he didn't have enough money, but the store man didn't catch it.

"Boots?"

"Um, I think so."

The man began pulling piles of elastic-sided boots off a shelf and told the youth to try some on. In a few minutes a pair of boots and a hat and a khaki overcoat were neatly parcelled on the counter. The youth stared at the parcels. What would the store man say when he found out his time had been wasted? And the wrapping paper and string had been wasted too. What would Mr. Coles say?

The store man was out of sight at the back of the shop. The youth began to edge towards the door. He would run for it and get back to the city somehow. Then he saw Mr. Coles crossing the street towards him. He had a sudden idea. As soon as Mr. Coles entered, he would blurt out: "I've just remembered my mother is sick and I have to go home," and then he would dash out the door and along the street and out of sight.

But when Mr. Coles came briskly in, the youth could not bring himself to speak or move.

"All set, lad?"

"All set, Mr. Coles," said the store man. "Will it be cash or cheque?"

Mr. Coles gave the man a cheque.

The youth sat with the parcels on his knees as the old truck roared and rattled along the dirt road. It had got dark. Mr. Coles did not speak to the youth but kept shouting at the truck. The gears did not seem to work properly and whenever Mr. Coles had trouble changing up or down he'd yell, "Come on, come on, you blasted swine of a thing!" The youth shrank back in his seat and stared at the dirt road in the long shaft of the headlights. A kangaroo leapt across the road in front of them. "Get the blazes out of it, you damned brute of an animal!" Mr. Coles bellowed.

They pulled up at a gate. There was a sign on it: DUNKELD. Mr. Coles told the youth to open the gate. He got out and fumbled blindly with a chain-and-peg attachment. He finally undid it and held the gate open while the truck went through. He refastened the chain-and-peg, stepping into a big blob of something as he did so.

"Gate secure, lad?" asked Mr. Coles as they drove on.

"Um, I think so."

"Better to know so, lad. Absolutely basic thing. Always secure a gate behind you. Got that?"

"Yes."

Mr. Coles gave an audible sniff.

"And another thing: avoid the blasted cow dung!"

The homestead was down in a valley. As they descended a long bumpy hill the youth saw the house lights getting closer and heard dogs barking. Because of the bumpy slope there were a lot of gear changes, so the truck needed a great deal of yelling at. Finally they rattled to a stop.

"I'll show you your quarters, lad. You'll want an early night."

Mr. Coles led the way across an expanse of deep sticky mud. The dogs were still barking and he shouted, "Settle down, you blasted brutes of things!"

The dogs went quiet.

They came to a big shed. It was dark and musty-smelling and the youth could just make out the shape of a tractor parked inside. Mr. Coles led the way in past the tractor and fumbled with a doorknob. There was a tiny separate room. It had a small window through which a trace of moonlight came. Mr. Coles reached in and flicked a bare light globe on. The youth saw a camp bed with some folded grey blankets on it.

"Early start tomorrow, lad," said Mr. Coles. He went back out and the dogs began barking again. The youth heard the blasted brutes of things being told to stop their damned ridiculous nonsense.

The youth sat on the camp bed. It was rickety and wobbled under his weight. He leant forward and put his hands around his knees and looked at the little room. It was empty except for the bed and a battered little wardrobe with its door missing. The walls were lined with some kind of three-ply, but the joins and corners were only roughly done and there were many small gaps. The dim light from the room spilled out through the open door into the larger part of the shed and showed the huge wheel of the tractor caked with mud.

He had deliberately not used the Diestl mood, but now he let himself go into it. After a few moments he made the motion of unslinging the Schmeisser and laying it on the bed beside him. He leant back against the wall and let his limbs go limp and his eyes go into a blank stare—like someone in the last extreme of tiredness, like someone who since early dawn has been trudging alone through a wrecked world. For a long time he stared blankly through the door at the huge muddy wheel. He no longer minded that he felt cold and hungry, or that there were rat-like scuffling noises in the shed, or that his life was a charred ruin. After a while the youth closed the door and unfolded the blankets and lay down under them fully clothed and with the light still on. He wanted to try to go to sleep while in the Diestl mood, for he was afraid of how bad things would seem when it began to wear off.

"HOY! YOU in there!"

The youth seemed to be hearing a voice.

"Hoy! You in the shed!"

There came the sound of something like a stone hitting the side of the shed. The youth scrambled off the bed and opened the door of the room and looked out. In the wintry light he saw a middle-aged woman standing some distance away at the edge of the muddy area. He saw her lob a stone at the shed and heard the tinny sound of it hitting.

"Yes," the youth called timidly.

"Come on!" the woman called back. "Get cracking! Mr. Coles has jobs for you to do. He's already been up for hours."

The youth half-registered that there was something a bit shrill about the way she spoke, and that she held herself away from the mud as though it disgusted her.

"Breakfast is on the table in the kitchen," the woman said, then turned and began picking her way back towards the house.

The youth straightened his clothes and combed his hair. He wanted to wash his face but didn't know where there was a tap. He went out of the shed and sank to his ankles in a patch of mud. The mud was very cold and clinging. As he plonked his way through it, trying to keep his balance, he came into sight of the dogs chained near the house. They began to bark at him. He reached the house and followed a concrete path through some flower beds to a back door. He was out of sight of the dogs now, but one of them kept up a steady barking. From somewhere on the other side of the house came Mr. Coles's voice telling the damned cur of a thing to settle down.

The youth was at the back door trying to scrape some of the mud off his shoes with a twig when Mr. Coles appeared.

"Ah, there you are, lad," he said. Then he noticed how muddy the youth's shoes were. "Um, better not tramp any of that mud inside on Mrs. Coles's floor. Just slip your shoes off before you come in, there's a good lad."

Inside the door was an alcove with coats hung neatly on

pegs and a row of pairs of gumboots. Beyond the alcove was a kitchen. It was quite poky and dark and there was a big black old-fashioned stove that took up nearly one whole end of the room. A small table stood against the wall and on it was laid breakfast for one—a bowl of cereal, a plate with scrambled eggs on it, and two slices of toast with a little jar of marmalade. And there was a pot of tea. The scrambled eggs and the tea had gone nearly cold, but the youth was so hungry he hardly minded. As he ate he looked through the window over the kitchen sink at the hills rising in the distance. Then he noticed a framed photo on the wall above him. It showed a wide, shallow-looking river with gum trees along it, and under it were printed the words: "The Banks of the Burracoola."

The youth felt cold. It was that clammy coldness you get when you've slept in your clothes, then thrown your blankets off, then gone out hurriedly into the morning air—that feeling that your body doesn't know what temperature it is supposed to be and so can't adjust itself.

From somewhere in the house came voices. A woman was complaining about something and Mr. Coles was trying to reassure her. The youth could tell that much even before he could make out what was being said.

"And I suppose I'm to go fetching the help out of bed every morning and in all weathers . . ." The voice had the shrill tone.

"Of course not, dear . . ."

"Honestly, you'd let people impose on you till kingdom come!"

"Well, it's only the lad's first day . . ."

"Oh, I'm sorry. I hadn't realised we were running a holiday home for total strangers."

The woman's voice had begun to get a tremor in it, and Mr. Coles was murmuring to her about not getting over-emotional.

"Don't start that!" the woman snapped. "Just don't!" There was the sound of a door slamming.

The youth had finished eating when Mr. Coles came into the kitchen. He seemed a bit distracted.

"Well, lad," he said. "We'll go across."

The youth had no idea what he meant by that.

"Damn it all!" said Mr. Coles, as though forcing his mind onto matters at hand. "We should've fitted you out with some gumboots in town. Just didn't think!" He pointed to the row of gumboots in the alcove. "See if any of those might fit you for now." He went back into the other part of the house.

The first pair the youth tried on were too big, the second pair a bit too small.

"How are they, lad?" Mr. Coles asked, coming back and pointing to the too-small pair the youth still had on.

"Okay," said the youth, anxious to please.

"Righto then."

Mr. Coles led the way out and went along the path in the direction of the shed. The youth followed, trying not to hobble because of his toes being scrunched up. As he passed one of the windows of the house he saw the curtain move and a woman's angry face peer out. Or maybe it was more upset than angry.

First Mr. Coles explained to him about feeding the animals. That was to be his daily task. At the other end of the tractor shed from the youth's tiny bedroom was another separate room. Mr. Coles called it the saddle room because there were saddles and bridles hung up on racks on the wall, but it also contained bins of wheat and pollard and oats and chaff. Mr. Coles showed him how to take a bucket and scoop up such-and-such an amount of this for the chooks, and such-and-such an amount of that for the pigs, and this much of the other for the horses. The pigs, for instance, got eight scoops of pollard mixed with water and stirred into a thick mush, with food-scraps from the house added into it. Mr. Coles showed him how to use an old bricklayer's trowel to mix with. The youth listened to all the instructions and tried to fix them in his mind.

"Got that, lad?" Mr. Coles would ask after he'd explained each thing.

"Yes," the youth would answer, having no idea what he'd just been told.

"Hope so," said Mr. Coles. "We had to let the last lad go because he didn't listen to what he was told. Went off half-cocked all the time. Ended up feeding *wheat* to the horses instead of oats! Damned *imbecilic* thing to do! Could've killed the poor beggars!"

The youth tried to look amazed that anyone could make such an error. Even in his helpless whirl of confusion, part of his mind was working clearly. He was thinking that if he just got through these few minutes, and waited till Mr. Coles left him for a moment, he would grab his belongings from his room and walk quickly away over the nearest rise and disappear.

"Well, lad," said Mr. Coles, "that's the drill. If you're unsure about anything, any time, *ask*. I never mind a lad *asking*. Just don't go off half-cocked. That's what I can't abide! Do we understand each other?"

"Yes," said the youth.

"Righto then, let's see you prepare the feeds."

Mr. Coles supervised him through it and the youth felt slightly reassured. It had gone from being a whirl of confusion inside his head to an outward set of moves and actions that he could probably get the hang of and do routinely.

After the feeding chores were done Mr. Coles milked the two cows, with the youth looking on to get an initial idea of it. Milking was to be another of his daily duties. "The trick, lad, is to keep her soothed and happy," said Mr. Coles as he leant his head against the cow's flank and directed a steady stream of milk into the bucket. Just then the cow whipped her muddy tail across the back of his neck and he yelled furiously at her that she was a blasted brute of a thing and had better stop the damned nonsense.

"Done any welding, lad?" Mr. Coles asked a bit later.

"No."

"A vital skill when you're on the land. You'll soon pick it up. A keen lad will pick most things up."

The youth tried to put a flicker of keenness on his face, but he felt too clammy and unwell. The exertion of the feeding chores had got him sweating and now he had cooled again.

They went into the main part of the shed beside the tractor and Mr. Coles began to fiddle about with some welding gear. There were bits of broken metal from a plough or something and he was trying to weld them together. He didn't seem to expect the youth to do anything, except hand him tools now and then. The youth gazed out at the mud and the drizzle. The shed was dim and cold, with a smell made up of metal and petrol from the tractor, grain and chaff from the saddle room, and a particular fetid odour which the youth thought was the smell of rats.

Every so often the welding gear did not do what Mr. Coles wanted and he would yell at it that it was a blasted swine of a turnout and not worth having on the place. The youth had got used to the yelling and was starting to be able to hear it without a clutch of fear in his stomach.

The youth needed to go to the toilet, but did not know where it was. When he finally asked, Mr. Coles waved his hand vaguely. "Just go round the side of the shed, lad." The youth went round the side of the shed in the drizzle but could see no toilet. The dogs saw him and began to bark. Mr. Coles called out to him to let Dolly off the chain. The youth hobbled across and looked at the three dogs. One was a big yellow thing that barked more savagely as he approached. The second was brownish and seemed to follow the lead of the big yellow one. The third was a nice black-and-white collie. She stopped barking and began to wag her tail cautiously as he approached. "Dolly? Are you Dolly?" the youth asked her. She wagged harder and looked up at him with soft intelligent eyes. He unfastened her chain and they went back to the shed. Mr. Coles slapped and patted Dolly and the dog wagged and twisted her body and made little swooning sounds as though being in Mr. Coles's presence was the sweetest thing that ever could be.

"Um, I couldn't see the toilet," the youth said.

"Ah," said Mr. Coles, realising that the youth didn't just need to pee. "There's the old outside loo of the house for you to use. Up the rise at the back. But try to be quiet, lad. Mrs. Coles might be having a lie-down."

The rain had got harder, so the youth went to his room and put on his new army disposals greatcoat. It felt stiff and heavy, like a coat of iron. He trudged through the mud, sinking deep with every step and having to pick his feet up carefully lest he step right out of the gumboots, tight as they were.

The loo was an old upright wooden dunny on the slope about twenty paces from the back door of the house. A big bush grew up against it, the leaves pressing round it on two sides, shielding it a little from sight. There was a horseshoe nailed above the door. Inside was a flat seat with a hole above a big tin container. In the corner was a bucket of sand and a drum of disinfectant. On the back of the door hung a hand-printed notice in capital letters: SPREAD SAND AND DISINFECTANT AFTER EVERY USE. WE DON'T WANT THE SMELL AT THE HOUSE THANK YOU! It was signed with the initials "C.T.C." The youth knew that Mr. Coles's first name was Howard, so they weren't his initials. Instead of toilet paper there were squares of cut-up newspaper skewered on a piece of wire. The youth wrestled the skirts of the greatcoat up and undid his other clothes and sat. Then a thought struck him and he got up hurriedly. He peered down through the hole. He could see no movement there. The youth knew vaguely that snakes went to sleep in cold weather. He wondered whether they chose dunnies to sleep in, and how much disturbance it took to wake them up. He sat again.

Up there on the slope a wind was blowing and it made the branches of the bush rasp and grapple against the dunny walls. The mournful sound of it was quite soothing. The youth read some of the squares of newspaper. There were bits of information about wool prices and cattle sales, and ads for sheep-dip, and stuff about export prospects for dried fruit. It was interesting enough. The youth found most things interesting when he could be alone with his thoughts. There was a sudden extra whoosh of wind against the side of the dunny and a cold rush of air came through the space under the door. The youth got the clammy, unwell sensation again and shivered.

He remembered a scene where Diestl is in Russia and the autumn of 1941 is beginning to wane. He is trudging back from the latrines, hunched over in his greatcoat, and he steps in a shallow puddle of water and hears something—the tiny crackling sound of the film of ice that had formed on the surface of the puddle. Diestl's heart sinks as he realises how close the winter is, and how bad it is all going to be. The youth had thought what a beautifully simple and profound moment that was in the story. Just after that Diestl's unit is suddenly transferred to Yugoslavia to fight partisans. It is very nasty, fighting partisans in the Yugoslavian hills, but sometimes there's a lull and then Diestl and his pals can sleep under a proper roof at night, and have proper rations. They can even sit around in village inns drinking wine and flirting just a tiny bit with the waitresses. Of course you can only sit around in the villages if you are in parties of at least half-a-dozen or so, and you are all fully armed. You can only flirt with the waitresses as long as you understand that you and they are only pretending, that the partisans are their friends and relatives and that they might be partisans themselves when they aren't serving the wine and exchanging the flirty half-smiles with you. You have to be aware that the only reason the wine isn't poisoned, or your vehicle wired to blow up, is that everyone understands about reprisals and about the official ratio stipulated by the highest authorities. Ten-for-one is the ratio. Diestl has seen an instance of this ten-for-one rule being enforced and he hopes very much that nobody will do anything to provoke it again in his unit's area. But even taking all those things into account, it is like a rest home compared with being in Russia. Diestl feels guilty that he has been spared from going through the worst of it in Russia and even applies for a transfer back there.

Yes, thought the youth: maybe it is better to go through the worst of it. Then you don't have to feel guilty that fate has given you an easy ride. That idea had helped the youth a lot in difficult moments. It had helped him get off at Balinga when every nerve of his body had wanted to stay safe in the train. Diestl's story was full of profound ideas. You could study it your whole life and still not cover all the ideas that were there.

A loud thud on the toilet door startled him. "Coming!" he called, hurriedly finishing up and adjusting his clothes and the greatcoat. He opened the door.

Mrs. Coles was standing halfway down the slope with a large stone in her hand. She had a sort of scared look, as though she would turn and bolt back to the house any moment.

"What are you doing there?" she demanded. "Why are you so long there?"

"Just using the toilet," he called back.

"Twelve minutes!" she cried, her voice going shrill.

"Pardon?"

"I can tell the time! Don't think I can't!"

The rain was plastering her hair and her mouth was working in an odd way. The youth began to feel frightened. What if Mr. Coles came along now and saw her looking so upset and him right there? It might look as though he had done something.

He started to walk away across the slope, away from the plastered hair and oddly twisted mouth, but then realised he hadn't spread sand or sloshed antiseptic in the dunny. He turned back, but Mrs. Coles gave a peculiar little screech and waved her hands as though to shoo him off.

"I forgot to spread the sand," he called, his heart thumping.

She continued to wave her hands and make little screeching sounds. He turned away again and went as quickly as he could back through the mud to the shed.

"I thought you might've fallen in, lad," Mr. Coles said, glancing up from the welding.

The youth did not mention the incident.

THEY WENT for long periods without speaking. The youth didn't mind. It left him free to think his own thoughts. But it was also a drawback at this early stage because it meant he wasn't getting the signs and clues he needed. The best thing was if the other person rattled on while you just put in a word now and then to encourage them. The Diestl story had taught him that. "Yes, I remember you," the beautiful Yugoslav girl says when he happens to bump into her a week or so after he and a bunch of his pals had drunk wine at her tavern. "You're the man who speaks one word to hear a hundred." She explains that this is a local proverb, but that it fits Diestl exactly. The youth often thought of that scene. It was a lovely moment because they only have a smattering of each other's language and you can see the communication happening in their eyes and their hand movements and the way they hold their bodies in relation to each other, rather than through what's being said. And it was sad because you know that if they hadn't been on opposite sides in the war they'd have had a love affair. It was poignant, too, in a way you only understand later, for it shows how sensitive and sweet Diestl was back then, before that side of him got burnt away.

The youth decided to ask a few offhand questions. He would use the knack of being social that he'd picked up at the Miami. So he asked how many acres the property had, and how many sheep were on it, and where the name "Dunkeld" came from, and things like that. Mr. Coles answered readily enough and didn't seem to mind expanding on certain topics. He explained, for instance, there were twenty-five hundred sheep at the moment but that the place could carry four thousand if there was a bit of Improvement done. Mr. Coles put an emphasis on the word "Improvement" whenever he said it and the youth got the feeling it was an issue. So he asked what sort of Improvement the property needed and that kept Mr. Coles rattling on for quite a while.

The youth found out that Mr. Coles wasn't the owner of Dunkeld. He was managing it for a big city businessman who'd bought it three years ago. Jimson, the chap's name was, and he made his money importing luxury Italian cars. Mr. Coles sounded a bit fed up with Jimson. "I said to him, when I agreed to come down from Burracoola: Just give me the proper support and I'll have the place on its feet in five years!" He had pushed the welding mask back up on his head and was glaring out at the mud. He muttered something about the "blasted dozer," put his mask down and went on working. After a few minutes the youth asked what sort of a place Burracoola was, and Mr. Coles told him about the small property of his own that he had there, and which he'd neglected these past three years for no other reason than to help Jimson out.

In the middle of the day there came a couple of hollow clanging sounds from the direction of the house. "There's lunch," said Mr. Coles. He put the welding gear down and led the way across. The youth hobbled behind, his toes really hurting from being so scrunched up in the gumboots, but his mind alert and wary.

The table in the kitchen had a meal laid out on it under a clean tea-towel. There was a portion of shepherd's pie with peas and carrots and cauliflower, some jelly and custard, and a pot of tea. The thought suddenly came to the youth: *What if she's poisoned it?* But then he reflected that it was a case of eat it or go hungry, and he told himself that a bullet either has your name on it or it doesn't.

So he sat under "The Banks of the Burracoola" and ate the food and listened to a vague murmur of conversation between Mr. and Mrs. Coles as they ate somewhere further inside the house. Mrs. Coles's voice sounded plaintive and Mr. Coles's sounded as if he was trying to jolly her along, but there didn't seem to be anything really wrong. He heard Mr. Coles call her Clare. That fitted with the initials C.T.C. on the sign in the dunny. Once or twice Mr. Coles called her "Clarey" in a fond voice. "Scary" was more like it, the youth thought, and began to giggle softly. Then he got a mental picture of her rushing in with an axe, and that helped him stop giggling. When he'd finished eating he went back across to the shed and sat patting the collie dog until Mr. Coles came over.

The afternoon dragged by. The youth was losing the last of his alertness and beginning to feel clammy and unwell again. He wanted to ask if he could go into his room and lie down, but couldn't pluck up the nerve. He wished he could just curl up in a corner like Dolly. When the evening dark began to come on, Mr. Coles went back to the house and left the youth to do the feeding.

The youth racked his brain to remember the exact routine, and the amounts, and hoped he was doing it fairly right. The difficult part was feeding the pigs in their big enclosure down in the corner of the home paddock. There were five of them, large and black, and they came bustling and oinking to the fence as soon as he approached. They would not wait for him to pour the food into their trough, but shoved their snouts up and jostled the bucket as he tried to get it over the railing. The big snouts came very close to his hands and he was afraid of being savaged. The jostling, and his fear, made it hard to pour the mush cleanly. Most of it ended up on the pigs' backs or on the ground. The youth had never been this close to pigs before and it shocked him how big and pushy and frightening they were. The pigs made him understand Mr. Coles's habit of yelling at things. The youth felt like bellowing at the blasted brutes and swines to stop their damned bloody nonsense.

Feeding the horses and cows was much nicer. He would fetch a sweet-smelling bale of hay from the stack, cut the wire that held it together, break the bale up into several bits and then spread them so that the three horses and two cows could all have a nibble without crowding each other too much. The youth was also a bit scared of the horses and cows at first, in case they might bite or kick, but none of them seemed to want to do anything bad. One of the horses was enormous, some kind of draughthorse. It approached and sniffed at the youth. Mr. Coles had told him you can tell if a horse is in a bad mood by seeing whether its ears are laid back. This horse's ears were upright. He lifted his hand carefully, ready to snatch it away if he had to. The horse stood calmly while he stroked its nose. The breath from the big nostrils was warm on his hand.

After a few moments the horse backed gently off and went to join the others at the hay.

"You there, lad?" Mr. Coles called from near the shed.

"Yes."

"Shower at the house, lad, before dinner. You'll need to step lively. It's almost on the table."

The youth fetched his towel and went across. Mr. Coles showed him through to a bathroom. It was lovely being under the hot water, feeling the long day's cold and damp being soothed away. There was a cake of flowery-smelling soap and he lathered himself up with it. But then the hot water began to give out and he had to rinse himself off as quickly as he could. He dried himself and dressed and opened the bathroom door. Mrs. Coles was standing there with a mop in her hand. She gave him a dark intense look and strode past him into the bathroom and began running the mop across the floor in angry swipes. The youth went out to the kitchen.

He could hear Mr. Coles telling Mrs. Coles that she needn't mop the bathroom. Mrs. Coles's voice came back angry and sharp. Then Mr. Coles said he'd mop it himself if she wanted it mopped, and that she should sit down and relax. Again came the sharp and angry voice: "Scrubbing! That's what it needs! Scrubbing from top to bottom! Will you do that? Will you? No! What do you care if the house is *filthy*?" Her voice had gone shrill and Mr. Coles's voice became very soft and soothing. The youth thought he heard low sobbing. He finished eating and left the house.

The drizzle ran down the window of his room and the dampness of mud and rain seemed to penetrate everything. The youth sat on the rickety camp bed with one of the blankets round his shoulders and his back against the wall. He thought of his room at the Miami and how nice it would feel to be there now, lying back cosy and warm on his bed with magazines to read. He had only brought one of his magazines with him. It had been hard leaving the others behind, but he'd had to pare his things down to what would fit in the little bag.

He fished the magazine out. It was a copy of *Home Weekly* with a picture of Grace Kelly on the cover and a story inside called "Monaco's Fashion Queen." The article was all about the clothes Grace Kelly wore to balls and banquets. The youth wasn't very interested in the clothes, but he really liked looking at Grace Kelly. He loved the cool, poised way she gazed out of a photo at you. She was sort of remote, and yet gave the impression of being friendly and sensible too.

For a long time he examined the photos of Grace Kelly in her ball-gowns and diamond tiaras, and gazed into the blue eyes in the cover photo. Her poised self-containedness made him feel a bit more poised and self-contained himself. The youth had learnt that there were times when he needed a different kind of consolation from the sort Diestl gave. This other kind came from pictures of certain women, and from Grace Kelly more than anyone. He had a secret name for her. He thought of her as Sweetheart.

The youth lay down with the blankets and his greatcoat over him. He tried to ignore the rat-like scufflings he could hear in the shed. He drifted to sleep thinking of a lovely blue-eyed woman it was utterly safe to be with and who understood all your yearnings. At some point in the night he imagined that he heard voices, and the dogs barking, and a car engine starting up.

# 3. Horseman

"How ya goin'?" said a voice behind him.

The youth had just stumbled out of his room, afraid that it was quite late in the morning and that he had overslept and was going to be in trouble. He looked around and saw a man sitting on a horse. The man had a battered leathery overcoat on and was leaning forward on the horse's neck. He looked completely relaxed, as though the horse was as comfortable to him as a sofa.

"Clem Currey's the name," drawled the man, holding out his hand.

The youth shook hands and said who he was.

"Yeah, Coles said ya came day before yesterdee."

"Yes."

"How ya findin' it?"

"Alright," said the youth. He wondered if Clem was from the neighbouring property. "Do you know what the time is, please?" he asked.

"'Bout half past eight," Clem replied.

Shit, thought the youth. "I'd better go," he said, pointing across at the house.

"Nobody there," said Clem. "They're in town."

"Sorry?"

"Coles's missus went crackers durin' the night. He had to take her in to get her seen to. Might not be back for a coupla days."

The youth looked blank.

"It ain't the first time it's happened. It's just a matter of gettin' her into town so the doctor can give her a needle or some-thin' to settle her down. Anyway, Coles rang me up and said to let ya know they was gone and that ya to come to my place for ya meals and that."

"Um, okay," said the youth, trying to take it all in.

"If ya want to go and do ya feedin', I'll do the milkin', and then we'll go."

So the youth fed the animals while Clem milked the two cows in the milking yard just across from the shed.

"Ya can ride Gypsy, if ya like," said Clem. "Do ya ride, at all?"

"I never have," the youth replied.

"Ah well, ya might as well have a go, if ya like."

Clem got a bridle from the saddle room and went across to where the three horses were at the hay the youth had just put out for them. He went to slip the bridle on the big one that looked like a draughthorse. It took a little time because the horse kept turning away whenever he lifted the bridle towards her.

"She's a cunnin' old bugger," said Clem. "She's twenty-two years old and knows all the tricks."

Clem got the bridle on her and tethered her outside the saddle room. He combed her back a little, and explained that it was to make sure there were no burrs under the saddle to make her sore. Then he saddled her. He showed the youth how she took a deep breath just as he went to tighten the strap under her belly.

"I told ya she knows all the tricks," said Clem. "And fair enough, I s'pose. I'm not keen on havin' me belt too tight, either."

When the mare was saddled and ready, Clem said that they might as well get moving. The youth went to his room and put on his new boots and hat and threw his greatcoat over his shoulder. Back outside, the mare looked enormous.

"Don't be scared of her," said Clem. "She's cunnin', but she won't get outa hand. All this old girl wants is a quiet life."

The youth wasn't convinced.

"I'll give ya a leg-up," said Clem.

The youth found himself on the mare's back and for a moment thought he would pitch straight over the other side, but he got a desperate grip on the saddle and on the mane. He swayed there trying to get his balance. The ground looked a long way down.

"I'd better lead her, if ya like," said Clem. "That'll let ya have ya hands free to hang on till ya find ya balance."

So Clem walked ahead, leading his own horse and Gypsy, and the youth clung to the mane with both hands, bobbing and swaying and trying to grip with his knees. They paused beside the barking dogs and Clem let Dolly off her chain. Then they went slowly towards the gate out of the home paddock.

After only a few moments in the saddle the youth's hands and knees ached from the effort of trying to grip and stay upright. The lurch of the mare's movement began to make him feel seasick. He told himself that if he could make it to the gate he'd be okay. Meanwhile, Clem was explaining the art of falling off horses.

"The trick's to hit the ground in a relaxed frame o' mind. And to try not to fall under the hooves if possible, 'cos the horse might sprain a fetlock when he's steppin' on ya. Apart from that, it's as easy as fallin' off a log. In fact it's a fair bit easier, 'cos a log usually won't start buckin'."

They reached the gate and went through.

"Well," said Clem, looking up at the youth, "I reckon ya must be a born horseman. Ya sure ya never rode before?"

The youth nodded.

"Well, that's amazin'," Clem said, and swung himself onto his own horse with a single fluid motion. "I'll keep on leadin' Gypsy, if ya like. Just gettin' ya balance is enough to learn at the moment. Handlin' the reins can come later."

They rode slowly through another paddock towards the

next gate. At times the old mare slowed so much that she was hardly moving.

"Ya need to let her know who's boss," said Clem.

"I think she already knows," replied the youth grimly.

"Give her a bit of a spur with ya heels," Clem advised.

The youth tried but could not relax the grip of his knees enough to get any purchase for a spurring motion.

"Never mind," said Clem. "There's no hurry. Ya doin' real well. A lot of blokes woulda fallen off by now."

The youth fell off.

"That was good," said Clem when the youth had confirmed he was okay. "Ya hit the ground *relaxed*, like I said."

The youth got up and brushed himself off and after several attempts managed to get back into the saddle. They rode on.

"That was real good," Clem said. "Gettin' straight back on like that. It shows her she can't bluff ya. That's the main thing. Same with those pigs. I noticed ya was lookin' a bit dubious when ya was feedin' 'em."

"I'm worried they might bite," said the youth. "*Do* they bite?"

"They can do," replied Clem.

"Mr. Coles told me about a farmer who got eaten by his pigs. He had a heart attack while he was in the pen with them. All that was found of him later was his wrist-watch. Is that true?"

"Nah," said Clem.

"It isn't?"

"Nah."

"That's a relief, then."

"It was a *pocket*-watch," said Clem.

They came to the top of a long rise and saw the country spread out. There were steep slopes and shadowed gullies, and rows of hills stretching into the distance, looking more pur-plish-blue the further away they went. There was a lot of old felled timber on the hillsides and it showed stark and white.

Great shadows of clouds moved across the landscape. The youth felt the same kind of exhilaration as when he'd looked at the grandeur of the mountains from the train. But then he had to refocus on just keeping upright in the saddle.

On a long bare ridge stretching below them was a group of buildings. There was a small house with a windmill whirling beside it, and another narrower structure nearby, and further along what the youth recognised as a shearing shed with a set of yards. They went through a last gate and plodded down the long ridge. A couple of dogs tethered near the house began to bark.

"Gladys said she'd have a bit of late breakfast ready for ya," Clem said, "and a good strong cuppa tea."

They came up to the front fence of the house and Clem languidly swung down off his horse and looped the reins of both horses over the fence. The youth sat for a few moments trying to untense and unclench himself enough to slide off. But as soon as he tried to move he found his muscles wouldn't obey him and he lost his grip and fell in a heap at the mare's feet. She lowered her head and gave him a look, as if to say: *Another point on the board for me.*

A woman in a yellow flowery apron came out of the flyscreen door onto the verandah.

"There's a cuppa tea made," she said. "I saw youse comin'."

"Thanks love," said Clem.

The youth got up off the ground and followed Clem in at the gate.

Gladys Currey held her hand out to the youth and said, "Pleased to meet you." They shook hands and she led the way inside.

It was a stark place with bare floorboards and hardly any furniture. Gladys poured them a cup of tea and then set to stirring something in a saucepan on the stove. Clem told her that the youth had just had his first ride on a horse and was doing real well, having got the measure of old Gypsy. Gladys gave the impression of being quietly pleased and impressed by this, as though she hadn't just seen the youth in a heap on the ground. She asked him a bit about himself. Where was he from? Did he have any brothers and sisters? The youth sat on an unsteady chair and answered while he tried to get his aching muscles to untense. Gladys served up baked beans on toast for him. She and Clem began talking about Mr. and Mrs. Coles and when they might be back from town.

The youth was able to observe them while he ate. He realised that they were probably quite old. Clem's hair—when you saw him without his hat—was almost white. It was hard to judge the age of grown-ups, but the youth decided Clem must be at least forty, and Gladys much the same. They both looked worn and threadbare, like the stony ridge they lived on and like the meagre dwelling with floorboards unsoftened by any mat or rug. It dawned on the youth that the Curreys were very poor.

CLEM WAS saying something to Gladys about "digging out" under the shearing shed. The youth did not know what this meant. Gladys asked Clem what he reckoned about it, and Clem replied that the stuff would be hard as a rock, but that they'd better have a go if it was what Coles wanted.

"He's the boss, I s'pose," Clem concluded, in a resigned tone.

"Yeah," said Gladys, in the same tone. "You probably better have a go at it, if that's what he said to do."

The youth could tell how conscious they were of not being their own masters in life. He realised that the Curreys weren't next-door neighbours but employees on the place, like himself.

"Well," said Clem after a while, "we might as well do a bit, if ya like."

"Okay," said the youth at once, to show he'd go along with whatever Clem thought best.

He had cottoned on to the way Clem never *told* him to do anything. It was always put as an idea, as something you could do *if you liked*. Clem hated bossing anyone about. Putting it as an idea left a person with a bit of dignity, as though they were doing the thing because they felt like it, or to lend a mate a hand, not just because of being a mug battler with no choice.

They got a pick-axe and a shovel and went along to the shearing shed. Clem explained that they were to dig out a layer of earth from under the shed. This layer of earth was rich with all the years of sheep droppings that had fallen through the slat floors of the holding-pens above. This enriched earth made good fertiliser. Anyway, said Clem, Coles wanted it done.

They got under the shed. It was too low a space to stand upright in, so they bent on their knees. This meant they were trying to use the pick-axe and shovel from unnatural postures which didn't allow any swing or purchase. The earth felt damp and cold but was packed so hard that trying to break it up was like trying to break up concrete. After a few minutes Clem said it was time for a "blow." They came out from under the shed and sat with their backs against one of the yard fences and Clem rolled a smoke.

The youth learnt that the Curreys had been on Dunkeld ever since Mr. Coles had come to manage it for the rich city businessman. Clem had been working on another property in the district and had a run-in with the owner, a Mr. Izzard, and had chucked the job in. Because of that he'd been available when Coles was looking for a station hand. "Coles and old Angus Izzard weren't too keen on each other from the first day they met," said Clem. "Too much alike, I s'pose. So my havin' had a run-in with Izzard was a recommendation as far as Coles was concerned."

The youth asked about Mrs. Coles. Had she always been peculiar?

"Mad as a cut snake from the start," said Clem. "But I had

nothin' against her till I saw the airs and graces she put on, specially with Gladys. Gladys took her measure quick smart."

When he'd finished his smoke Clem said that they could have another bit of a go, if they liked. So they went back under the shed and tried to break up a little more of the packed earth. Again they quickly became exhausted in the cramped space. They came out and Clem rolled another smoke. Dolly came and sat with them and the youth stroked her head and soft coat. The youth said what a nice dog she seemed. "Yeah," said Clem, "she's a real good little workin' dog." Then he added grimly: "She's clever enough that even belongin' to Coles hasn't ruined her."

They forced themselves to go back under the shed for another stint, and when they stopped for their next break Clem was in the mood to tell the story of the bulldozer.

"When Jimson bought Dunkeld he had this grand vision of bein' a big-time grazier and one o' the landed gentry, and Coles egged him on. Jimson had never been closer to the bush than Pitt Street, and didn't know a sheep-run from a hole in the ground, so he gave Coles a free hand to do whatever he thought best to improve the place. Coles kept sayin' that in five years he'd have it lookin' like a *park*. That was the big thing, to have it lookin' like a *park*.

"Well one day Coles went out and bought this bloody great Caterpillar, this bulldozer, that the shire council was gettin' rid of because it was a clapped-out piece o' junk. But Coles paid top price for it—thousands and thousands of Jimson's money— and had it trucked to the property as if it was God's gift to the place. The idea was that the dozer would clear all the felled timber that'd been lyin' around on the slopes for the last sixty-odd years. But the dozer never did a proper day's work of clearin' because it was forever breakin' down, and Coles was forever forkin' out Jimson's money to pay for new parts and for specialist mechanics to come out. Of course, it was a lucky thing that the dozer *was* a dud, otherwise somebody woulda got killed when it rolled over, seein' as how most of the property is too steep and treacherous for any dozer to operate on.

"Well, Jimson might not have known the first thing about the bush, but he knew about money and he knew that Coles was wastin' heaps of it. Now Coles isn't the kind of bloke who'll admit he's made a galah of himself, so he keeps insistin' that the Caterpillar's a great investment and it'll be a real goer as soon as a few little problems are sorted out.

"So this day Jimson drives up from the city in one of his flash Eye-tie cars. A *Maserati*, I think it was, one o' them racin' cars that's worth its weight in friggin' diamonds. *And* he's got his new girlfriend with him that he wants to impress, and she's a fashion model or somethin', done up to the nines. Anyway, after they have lunch, Coles decides to show Jimson and the girlfriend how good the dozer is so he jumps on and starts her up and goes roarin' around the home paddock, churnin' the ground to buggery. I seen this meself, because me and Gladys happened to be drivin' past along the top of the hill just then, on our way to town. Suddenly the controls jam on the dozer, like they was always doin', and it's headin' towards where the Maserati's parked. Well, I s'pose the whole thing only took about ten seconds, but I can see it now like it was happenin' in slow motion. Coles is wrestlin' with the levers and shoutin' at the dozer at the top of his voice that it's a bastard swine of a thing. Jimson is jumpin' up and down and yellin' and wavin' his arms like he's got a goanna up his trousers. The girlfriend is leanin' into the car to get somethin', and she looks up and starts screamin' and scramblin' to get out. And Mrs. Coles is at the side o' the house doin' a sorta mad shriek. And the dogs are all barkin' too.

"Well, I thought the Maserati was gone for sure, and the girlfriend with it. The blade o' the dozer is about twenty feet from the driver's-side door when Coles gets control again and stops. By then Miss Australia's flung herself away and is face down in the mud and the cow dung. That's the last we saw. We went below the crest o' the hill then."

Clem took a long last drag of his butt and flicked it away.

"Gosh," said the youth, deeply impressed.

"Yeah," said Clem. "As I say to Gladys: No matter what happens now, we've got that to remember."

"How long ago was it?"

"'Bout a year. Jimson hasn't been up since. He's lookin' to sell the place. Even if it hadn't been for the other things, the tussock would've given him second thoughts about bein' a Pitt Street grazier."

"What's the tussock?"

"Serrated tussock. It's a noxious weed. This place is startin' to be riddled with it. See that line o' yellowy-green at the edge o' the paddock over there?"

"Yes."

"That's it. It spreads across an area and takes it over. Sheep won't eat it. Nothin' will eat it. Nothin' will kill it either, except bein' dug right outa the ground clump by clump. That's another grudge Jimson's got against Coles. He reckons Coles should've warned him about the tussock at the start, before it got a grip on the place."

"Why didn't he?"

"I don't think Coles knew much about it. It only really started spreadin' down from the north a few years ago. Nobody round here was too worried. Same around Burracoola where Coles comes from. Anyway, Jimson was led to believe that Coles knew everythin' there was to know about runnin' a property and would turn this one into a showpiece. I bet he wouldn't mind stranglin' whoever it was told him that."

They went back under the shed and worked hard for another hour or so, but managed to shift only a tiny amount of earth. Clem was getting fed up. He declared that this "digging out" was a ratbag idea, and typical of boss cockies who wouldn't know whether their arse was punched or bored.

"Another one of Coles's Caterpillars," the youth said.

Clem was struck by that and chuckled.

Gladys came across from the house to see how it was going and Clem told her what the youth had said. Gladys liked it too.

"I've just been tellin' him about that day," Clem said.

"Poor girl," said Gladys, picturing the scene. "I felt sorry for her. Must've *ruined* her clothes."

The youth was starting to feel at ease with the Curreys.

Gladys made them a nice lunch. Afterwards they tried to dig a little more, although their arms and knees and backs were aching so much it was difficult even to wield the implements. Then Clem slapped his thigh and declared he was jacking up.

"I'll tell Coles we did what we could but the stuff is just too hard to shift. And how does he expect anyone to get a proper whack at it when they're bent double? And what's the benefit of it? To have a few bags of fertiliser for the homestead garden?"

He said this firmly but calmly, like someone who has thought it through and is ready to stick by his decision. It seemed to the youth that the digging out offended Clem because it went against some basic rule of economy of effort, and that in turn was bound up with the issue of people's dignity. Poor people's dignity, at least.

They spent the afternoon repairing some broken bits of railing in the sheepyard fence. Clem went about it in the same calm and precise way he had of getting on or off a horse, or rolling a smoke. He seemed to quietly coax the tools to do what he wanted and to caress rather than manhandle the new bits of railing into place. It was the opposite of Mr. Coles's way of barging and blustering at things.

Gladys was hanging tea-towels on a line at the back of the dwelling and they flapped in a fresh breeze, and so did Gladys's flowery yellow apron. The blades of the steel windmill beside the house whirled with a clean metallic sound. The youth thought how much fresher and nicer it felt here on this bare stony ridge than back at the other place. Clem suggested the youth might prefer to sleep in the shearers' quarters that night.

In the fading light they rode back to the homestead to do the feeding.

Again Clem led old Gypsy by the reins so that the youth could concentrate on staying in the saddle. He went the whole way without falling off, but collapsed in a heap again when dismounting. Still, he felt he was making progress.

They did the feeding. It was almost dark but the sky had cleared a lot and you could see some stars. The youth went to his room in the tractor shed to get a few things to take back with him—his toothbrush, the old flannelette shirt he used as a pyjama top, his magazine with Sweetheart on the cover. Clem had gone across to check that the main house was secure. The youth stood for a minute or two in the dank room, lost in a thought. Then he turned and saw an enormous rat crouched beside the tractor wheel. The rat looked at him with a beady stare, and the youth stared back. He gathered his nerve and made a sudden move, flinging his arms out, thinking this would make the rat run away. But it stayed put. The youth began to feel scared. He wished he had a big stick to defend himself with.

"We can get goin', if ya like," said Clem, squelching into the shed from the mud.

The rat had gone.

They rode back to the ridge and the meal that Gladys was making. As they rode, the youth tried to put everything out of his mind except the high clean windy stars above.

THE COLESES stayed away for three weeks. They'd gone back to their own property at Burracoola. The place needed some seeing-to, Mr. Coles told Clem over the phone.

"I s'pose that means she isn't comin' out o' the mad state too easy this time," Clem remarked.

"It's very sad," said Gladys. "I admit I don't have much time for the woman, but it must be awful for her."

The youth thought how Mrs. Coles had looked when she'd stood in the rain near the dunny, her hair plastered and her mouth twisting so oddly and her hands making helpless gestures. He told the Curreys about it, and that he'd not mentioned it to Mr. Coles.

"Ya did right to keep quiet," Clem replied. "He don't appreciate anythin' bein' said or noticed. We've learnt that, ain't we, Glad?"

"Yes," said Gladys earnestly to the youth. "Best to keep well outa other people's troubles. Unless they're your own people and they're dependin' on you."

THE YOUTH practised riding every day and was in agony from saddle-soreness. But he had his balance and was learning to use the reins and to urge the old mare forward with his heels. Even then, it wasn't easy to get her to do what he wanted.

"That's because she knows you ain't wearin' spurs and can't give her a good jab," Clem said.

The youth would've liked a pair of spurs. Clem wore them and they jingled nicely when he walked. With his spurs on, and his worn leather coat, and his hat at an angle, and his economical way of doing things, he was the very model of a Horseman. A true Horseman wasn't just someone who rode a horse. It was someone who had a Horseman's attitude to the world. One of the reasons Clem had hated the digging out was that he'd had to take his spurs off. The cramped space meant you had to sit back on your heels a lot, and with spurs on you'd stick yourself in the backside. The youth sympathised with the idea of a Horseman's dignity. It was disgraceful to expect a man like Clem Currey to grub about in the dirt! How right they'd been to jack up!

The youth would wake each morning in the neat room in the shearers' quarters and go out and douse his head under the tap of the water tank. Then he'd sit on the little verandah of the quarters and look out at the morning sky and at the play of light across the hills and gullies. He would hear the birds' calls and the baaahs of sheep. Then there'd be a good hearty breakfast about seven-thirty, with Clem and Gladys talking about local goings-on. They'd both been born in the district, and their parents before them, and they knew everything about everyone.

There was always a program called *Country Calling* on the radio at breakfast time. The youth loved it when they gave the weather forecasts for the entire state and ran through the names of the various regions one by one. These names made the hair on the back of his neck stand up, for they were packed with possibilities. You didn't know what the possibilities *were*, exactly—that was why the yearning was spiced with a slight touch of fear—but whatever they were, they were brought nearer just by hearing those names said aloud. The youth's favourite of all was the High Plains. He imagined what a fine thing it would be to have it said of you, "Oh yes, he was a great Horseman. He rode the High Plains with Clem Currey!"

After breakfast they would ride over to the other place to do the feeding and milking. Clem was teaching the youth how to milk. If you did it as expertly as Clem you got two lovely strong squirts of milk going into the bucket almost without any pause. At first the youth struggled to get any milk out at all. He was squeezing the teat with his whole fist rather than getting the downward ripple motion of the fingers. You could tell from the cow's reaction if you were doing it wrong. She'd seem twitchy and irritated and would turn her head in the bails and look at you as if to say: *What's the problem? What are you playing at?* But then the youth got the hang of the downward ripple and the milk began to flow. "Ya got a real knack for it," Clem told him. "Just like the ridin'."

With the Coleses away the milk wasn't needed for the homestead, so they gave it to the pigs.

"I notice ya still a bit nervous round them pigs," Clem remarked one morning.

"Yeah, a bit."

"Ya need ta show 'em who's boss," said Clem.

"How?" asked the youth.

"Try givin' 'em a whack with that bloody great trowel ya got. They're smart buggers, pigs. They'll get the idea."

So the youth took to leaning over the fence and hitting them on the back with the trowel when they were crowding the trough and not giving him room to pour the mush. It worked. A whack or two with the flat of the trowel would make them flinch back long enough to let him pour cleanly. But the effect wore off in a day or so and they were back to crowding him. He tried using the edge of the trowel. It worked much better. A whack of the edge and a pig backed right off. And they didn't lose their fear of it. After a few days of using the edge of the trowel he hardly had any more trouble and only needed to give a whack now and then, when a pig came within reach, just as a reminder.

After nearly a fortnight the youth could manage the milking as well as the feeding, and felt more secure on horseback. He went by himself each morning to carry out the chores, then back to see what Clem was doing.

The day might be taken up with fixing a fence, or repairing a saddle, or maybe taking the tractor and trailer out on the slopes to cut a load of firewood with a chainsaw. Clem did everything in his graceful style. Watching him, you'd never have guessed how tricky it was to work the tractor on the slopes or how dangerous a chainsaw could be.

The youth understood that Clem never expected any machine to get the better of him, any more than he expected to meet a horse he couldn't ride. It wasn't a case of being arrogant. Clem was the least arrogant person the youth had ever met. It was just that if you honed and practised particular skills every day of your life, and took a pride in them, you were entitled to expect that they would serve you well. The other thing was that he never panicked.

The youth began to wish he could smoke thin hand-rolled cigarettes the way Clem did. And wear spurs. Those two things seemed to him the height of "panache." Panache was what Grace Kelly had, according to the article in the magazine. She wore her clothes and jewels with "a panache envied the world over." It was a lovely word, though the youth wasn't sure how it should be pronounced. He said it in his mind as "pan-at-chee." Yes, Clem had "pan-*at*-chee."

So did Gladys. Gladys was like the female version of him, with a similar way of looking and speaking, a similar way of doing things with a light, expert touch. Her "pan-at-chee" was summed up for the youth in the way she'd looked that day she was hanging tea-towels on the line and the breeze was blowing them, and blowing her yellow flowery apron, and moulding her blue cotton dress to her body in a way that showed how strong and shapely she was, even at her age.

It was nice in the evenings at the Curreys' place. After the meal the youth would help wash and dry the dishes and put them away. Then they'd sit around the kitchen for an hour or so, with the fire going in the big old stove and the radio on quietly in the background. Gladys would knit and Clem would fiddle with some bit of mechanism that needed taking apart, or maybe he'd sew a bit of saddle gear or something. The kettle would be simmering and Gladys and Clem would chat quietly. Now and then they'd bring the youth into the conversation by explaining something—like how Dave Dawson, who ran the general store in Burrawah, was the son of Charlie Dawson, whose brother Stan hadn't been the full quid. So the thing about it was that you never mentioned old Stan in front of

Dave Dawson, because he was sensitive about having an uncle who was a bit off.

"Mind you, though," said Gladys, "old Stan was the only one o' the Dawsons that anybody ever liked."

After they'd had enough tea the youth would say goodnight and go over to the shearers' quarters. Being outside in the cold air would brace him and he would not want to go to bed just then, so he'd wrap a blanket round his shoulders and sit on the verandah and look at the night sky. Dolly would come and put her head on his knee and get some patting. Then she'd lie beside his chair and keep him company till he went inside.

THE DAYS were cold but mostly fine, with an occasional whooshing surge of rain across the landscape. The sky was full of great tumbling banks of cloud, and the sun kept coming out from behind them to light up the land in flashes of gold.

The work they'd been doing—feeding, milking, repairing odds and ends, getting firewood—was what Clem called "pottering."

"Bit of a holiday for us," he'd say, "seein' as we're just potterin'." Or he would get up from breakfast and walk across to the door with his spurs jingling, put his hat on at the angle he liked and drawl: "Ah well, we might go and do a bit o' potterin', if ya like."

One day Clem wanted to ride out to one of the furthest paddocks to check on the sheep. The paddocks all had names, and this one was called "Pies." At breakfast Clem had said to Gladys that he wanted to "see the sheep in Pies" and the youth had got a mental picture of rows of enormous meat pies made out of the Dunkeld flock.

They rode away from the house, past the shearing shed and along the ridge to the first gate, which led to the far reaches of the property. They had their overcoats on, and Clem had a saddlebag with sandwiches and a billy for making tea. Dolly was with them, and one of Clem's dogs, a kelpie called Tess. Tess was so thrilled to be off the chain and going somewhere that she was out of her mind for a minute or two at the start. But she calmed down and trotted along with Dolly at the heels of Clem's horse.

After the first gate they descended a long track into a gully, then went along beside a swift-running creek and then up another slope. The ground was rough and strewn with old dead timber and full of rabbit holes. They settled into single file, with Clem in front, the two dogs behind him and the youth at the rear. He was getting the hang of keeping old Gypsy going along at a steady pace.

Here and there they met bands of sheep that scattered at their approach. Tess got a bit crazed again and went streaking off to turn them on one flank or the other. Then, not hearing any shouted instructions from Clem, she'd stop and look back with ears pricked and every hair alert, as though asking: *What should I do? What should I do? What? What? Huh? What?* Getting no response, and seeing Clem riding on, she'd sprint back and fall into step with Dolly at the horse's heels.

They went down into another gully and followed another creek for a while. The air was damp and the vegetation lush, and everything smelt somehow more green. It was like another world down in the deep gullies, exhilarating but so dank and cold that you felt you should not stay too long lest it seep into you. On the opposite bank of the creek was a fence. It was ramshackle and covered here and there with undergrowth.

"That's Wondina," Clem called over his shoulder and waved a hand at the fence. "Angus Izzard's place."

It was hard to hear him over the sound of the rushing water.

They came to strands of wire so loose they were dangling near the ground. Clem dismounted, crossed the creek on some protruding rocks and began to adjust the wire with the pliers he carried. The youth dismounted to ease his backside, and stood patting the mare's neck and looking into the under-growth. This was a place for sprites or fairies, he thought, or the ghosts of swagmen, or maybe pygmy head-hunters with poison darts. At any rate, it was a long way from the Miami Guesthouse.

Clem came back across the creek.

"Somethin's come through that fence just lately," he said. "One of old Angus's prize bulls or somethin'." That'll send him off his head. He'll prob'ly accuse Coles of pinchin' it, and want to take him to court. He's a great one for takin' people to court, old Angus. Or threatenin' to, anyway."

They remounted and rode up out of the gully and along the steep slopes. There they discovered what had come through the gap in the fence. A mob of eight Wondina cattle was graz-ing along a hillside. Clem decided to drive them to the nearest connecting gate between the two properties and put them through.

The dogs at last had some proper work to do. When Clem called "Bring 'em up! Bring 'em up!," Tess went streaking off to nip and dodge at their heels. Dolly worked more calmly, her ears pricked in Clem's direction to hear instructions. Clem had said that normally you wouldn't work another man's dog, in case you confused it about who it was supposed to obey. But it didn't apply to Dolly: "If she was gonna get confused she'd've died o' confusion long ago." Coles, he said, was hopeless at working a dog. He always lost his temper and bellowed a lot of contradictory commands. "Dolly's the brains o' the outfit, when she's workin' with Coles."

They did a miniature cattle-drove with the eight steers and it tested the youth's new riding skills on the rough hillsides. He had to turn the mare this way and that, making feints to dis-courage a steer when it tried to break back or to one side. Gypsy was surer-footed than she seemed.

"Well, we've prob'ly saved Coles a bit o' aggravation," Clem said when they had finally put the steers through a gate and back onto Wondina.

They rode on to a river. It was a real river, wide and deep-looking, and formed a boundary of the property. Clem declared it was time for a cuppa. They dismounted near the bank, beside a big warren of what Clem said were wombat holes. Clem filled the billy from the river while the youth gathered bits of stick and leaf. They weren't very dry, but Clem said that didn't matter. He would demonstrate a bushman's trick of making a fire out of damp materials. He built the sticks and leaves into a pile, then reached into his saddlebag and with a flourish drew out half-a-dozen little cubes in red paper. They were Little Demon Fire Starters that people used to light barbecues in their backyards.

"What were you expectin'?" Clem asked, seeing the youth's face.

"Dunno exactly. Maybe that you'd rub two wombats together or something."

They boiled their billy and made tea and sat on the bank and watched the water flowing past. Clem rolled three of his thin cigarettes and lit one of them. He remarked that there were interesting caves up-river. They were called the Abernathy Caves because an escaped convict called Abernathy had discovered them way back in the early days and used them as a hide-out. "We can go and have a look at 'em sometime, if ya like," said Clem. "Not today though. It's a bit far." They stayed silent for a quarter of an hour, sipping tea, the cigarette smoke wafting up, the dogs settled beside them and the horses standing nearby with their reins on the ground.

"Would you like to have your own property?" the youth asked.

"Be nice, wouldn't it," Clem replied, lighting the third of the cigarettes.

"Do you think you might one day?"

"Nah, mate. It don't work that way. Not for the workers. The squatters and bosses have got the system all tied up. You get born into ya property, or ya somehow get rich enough to be a Pitt Street cocky, like Jimson thought he wanted to be."

"Reckon you could make a go of Dunkeld if it was yours?"

"Make a go of *any* place if I set me mind to it." He blew a long slow stream of smoke. "Ah well, we ain't done *that* bad I s'pose, me and Glad. We got the house paid off. Means we always got a roof over our heads, anyway."

"Where's your house?"

"In Burrawah. You'll have to come and see it sometime. It ain't too grand, but we're doin' it up gradual like. Well, Gladys is, mostly. Glad likes to have things nice. It was a struggle at times, keepin' the payments goin'." But we done it. We're boss in our own house, me and Glad. We've got our own roof to put over our heads, and that's what we always said we'd have, no matter how long it took."

The youth tried to picture the Curreys' house in Burrawah. He imagined a storybook cottage with a green picket fence, flowers at the front, a crooked chimney, a brass knocker on the door and all neat as a pin. It was nice to think they'd got a place like that, that they'd achieved their dream.

"And what about *you*?" Clem asked, emptying the dregs of the billy and scuffing dirt over the remains of the fire. "How are ya likin' life in the bush?"

"I didn't much, at first. But I'm liking it alright now."

"Takin' to it like a duck to water, I'd say," said Clem as they remounted. "Fair dinkum. Ya doin' real well."

The youth felt as if someone had pinned a medal on him.

They looked at the sheep in Pies and Clem declared they were putting on condition and that it was a good thing to have had a bit of a ride out to see them. "Better than potterin', eh?" he said. The youth agreed, even though his backside felt rubbed raw. They left Pies and turned toward home. They

would return a different way, Clem said, so the youth could see
more of the property. "Might be able to show ya a wedge-tailed
eagle, if we're lucky."

The ground rose steeply again. They got back up to where
they could see the country spread out and the hills going away
in the distance. The river was right down below them now.
They came towards a cliff edge and Clem pointed. A great
brown bird was gliding up in their direction. You could see its
wings flexing and tilting as the bird controlled its approach.
Tess ran to the edge of the cliff and barked at it. Then the bird
disappeared below their line of sight. "That's the wedge-tail,"
Clem called above the brisk wind that was blowing. "There's a
pair of 'em live on a ledge there."

When they got to a more sheltered spot they boiled the billy
again and ate the sandwiches Gladys had made. From where
they were they could see the cluster of buildings on the ridge.
The youth could make out Gladys's washing flapping on the
line. They felt cold, even with their coats on. They decided to
go back the shortest way and have a good warm beside the
kitchen stove.

As they came up the ridge towards the shearing shed they
saw Mr. Coles's blue ute. He came from round the corner of
the shed as they rode up.

"Hello Clem," he said. He didn't acknowledge the youth.

"How ya goin'?" said Clem, leaning forward on the horse in
his relaxed way. "How's the missus?"

"She's good, thanks."

"Good."

"I notice there hasn't been much done under the shed."

"The diggin' out?"

"Yes."

"Well," said Clem calmly, "it wasn't worth the time and
effort. The ground's so hard we could've hacked away for six
months and hardly made a dent in it."

"So you decided not to do what I'd specifically asked you to do."

"I made a judgement about the best use o' time and energy."

"We need to discuss this," Mr. Coles said.

"Righto," said Clem. He swung off the horse and handed the reins to the youth. "Just tie him up in front o' the house for me, mate, will ya."

The youth took both horses across and tethered them to the front fence. Gladys came out with a worried expression on her face and said there was a cuppa on. They went inside and could see through the window to where Clem and Mr. Coles were talking. They couldn't hear the words but Mr. Coles's voice sounded quite loud and he was waving his hands. Clem stood in his usual relaxed way, his thumbs hooked into his coat pockets. The youth thought how perfectly the two men's postures summed them up.

"What d'you think will happen?" the youth asked Gladys.

"I dunno. But Clem won't put up with too much silly rot. He wouldn't take it from Izzard, so I don't s'pose he will from Coles either."

The youth sat and sipped his tea and a couple of minutes later he saw the blue ute go past the front window, with Dolly in the back. Clem came in and sat down to the big mug of tea Gladys set in front of him. He slowly stirred his usual three spoons of sugar into it.

"What'd he have to say, Clem?" Gladys asked.

"A few different things," Clem replied. "The main one I s'pose was that he reckons he can't have someone on the place who won't follow instructions."

"And?"

"He said I was sacked."

"And what did you say?"

"I said I quit."

"Good," said Gladys emphatically. But the youth was

watching her face just then and he saw a haggard look go across it.

"We'll be alright," Clem told her.

"Course we will."

"We got the house now, free and clear. That's the main thing. At least we'll never be without a roof over our heads again."

"That's for sure!" said Gladys firmly.

"He said we might as well go straightaway and he'll pay us the fortnight in lieu o' notice."

"Sooner the better," Gladys agreed. But again the haggard look went across her face.

The youth sat silently, wondering whether the sacking included him too.

The curreys left the next day, their few belongings piled into the back seat of their wheezing old Austin. The youth was outside the tractor shed when they drove along the road to where it went over the crest of the hill. The Austin stopped and Clem got out and began walking down. The youth went up to meet him.

"I thought ya might like to have these," Clem said. "I found 'em when I was gettin' me gear packed." He held out an old pair of spurs. "They're broken and you can't really wear 'em, but I thought ya might just want 'em anyhow."

The youth didn't know what to say. He took the old spurs and nodded his thanks.

They went up to the car so he could say goodbye to Gladys. She patted him on the hand and gave him a serious look.

"Listen," she said. "I just want to tell you somethin' before we go. The bush is alright for the ones who are born to it, or the ones who aren't too prone to broodin' and worryin' all the time. But it isn't the place for you. Specially not *here*. It won't do a boy like you an ounce o' good, bein' here. You need to be where there's *people*, and people your own age, so you can come out o' yourself a bit, not stuck in a tin shed on your own. Do you understand what I'm sayin'?"

"Um, I think so," the youth murmured.

"I'm talkin' to you the way your mother would, that's all. And I know Clem agrees with me."

"Yeah mate," said Clem earnestly. "Glad's bein' fair dinkum with ya."

"Thanks," the youth said, nodding to them both.

Clem reached across and they shook hands. Then he put the car into gear, and the youth stood back.

"You'll be welcome for a cuppa tea any time," Gladys said. "Ask at the store and they'll tell you where the house is. You can't miss it."

They drove off and were quickly out of sight below the crest. A minute later the car reappeared, much smaller in the distance, climbing the rough track that led to the front gate of the property.

MRS. COLES had come home but the youth hardly saw her. Her mother had come to stay, to help her cope. The old lady was about eighty and very talkative. She would come into the kitchen when the youth was sitting under "The Banks of the Burracoola" eating his meal. She would perch on a stool and talk about the daily news from the radio. The old lady loved the news and whenever she heard the fanfare of music that introduced the hourly bulletin she'd shout, "Turn it up! Turn it up! There's the news! Turn it up!"

The youth had no interest in current affairs, but the old lady didn't mind. She would talk to him about the state of the world. Her favourite idea was that something was always a "conundrum." It might be a particular person, or the government, or the international situation. "*That's* their conundrum," she'd say, after a long chatter about the ins and outs of some event or conflict. Or, "*There's* a conundrum for you!" she'd exclaim, wagging a finger. The youth hadn't been sure at first what the word conundrum meant, but he heard it so often from the old lady, and in so many connections, that he began to wonder how he'd ever got by without it.

The old lady was more interesting when she got away from the news and talked about the old days. She reckoned people had Gone Soft since her time: "They'll go to pieces nowadays, quick as a wink! Never did in *my* time! *We* always knew how to kick on!" And she didn't seem to sympathise much with her daughter's problems. One day the youth heard her shout to Mr. Coles: "You should put a rocket under that woman! Smarten her up! She'll never kick on at this rate!"

It had been awful having to leave the neat room in the shearers' quarters and come back to the dank tractor shed. The youth had thought of asking if he could keep on sleeping at the quarters. It was only a few minutes ride away, and it wouldn't stop him doing his chores or being on time for his meals. But Mr. Coles had been curt and remote with him since the Curreys left, and the youth couldn't get the courage up to mention it. He hadn't been sleeping properly because of being afraid of the rats. He had tried to seal up the crevices of the little room with wood and bits of hessian, but didn't feel confident that it was secure. He would've liked to have Dolly in the room with him at night, as protection, but she was kept on the chain most of the time now and the youth didn't dare interfere.

The darkness fell early in the evening. Once he'd had his meal at the house, and had been talked at by the old lady, there was nothing to do but sit in the shed and try to feel contemptuous of the rustlings and scurryings. He had not thought about Diestl the whole time he was with Clem and Gladys, but now he summoned him up a lot. He would spend time every evening slumped on the camp bed, his back against the wall, staring blankly in front of him, imagining the weight of the Schmeisser crooked in his right elbow. There was a scene where Diestl is holed up in the basement of a wrecked house. Enemy paratroopers have dropped all around and he must wait till they have gone away. In that scene Diestl too has to listen to the sounds of rats in the darkness, rats that have grown bold because of all the dead—or maybe even the living—bodies they've fed on lately.

As always, the Diestl mood would fragment after a while and he'd have to let it slip off. The sense of steely contempt would evaporate and he'd feel lost and helpless. That's when he needed to turn to the photos of Grace Kelly in his magazine. He'd look wistfully into her eyes and trace the shape of her lips or eyebrows with his finger. He'd whisper to her and imagine her whispering back. He'd get under the blankets and create a cocoon of warmth, and begin to kiss and cuddle his pillow and imagine Sweetheart responding. The youth didn't know what lovemaking was supposed to be like, exactly, but for him it meant feeling so safe in Sweetheart's arms that you could tell her everything you felt and yearned for, no matter how desperate or dirty it sounded, and she would understand.

If he was lucky, a spell in the Diestl mood and a session of cuddling with Sweetheart would leave him tired enough to go to sleep.

In the mornings he made the milking the last of his chores, then took the bucket of milk to the house and put it on the sink in the kitchen with a cloth over it. Then he'd sit down to the breakfast that was laid for him. As often as not the old lady would come in and talk at him about that day's news. She always got up very early and by breakfast time had heard at least a couple of the hourly bulletins.

After breakfast the youth went out to what had become his main work, chopping the serrated tussock out of the nearby paddocks. He wasn't sure whether he'd been put on this work because Mr. Coles understood how big a threat the tussock was or just as a way to keep him busy and out of sight. He'd wondered whether he might be put back to digging out under the shearing shed, but that topic was not mentioned again. Mr. Coles hardly spoke an unnecessary word to the youth now, except once or twice when the business with Clem was obviously rankling in his mind.

"Currey's a damn fool, you know. He had a good position here and he threw it away. Just threw it away! He's not a young man anymore, and he's getting a reputation in the district as a troublemaker. He won't find it easy to get another job. I think he'll rue the day he cut himself off with me."

The tussock-chopping was done with a long-handled hoe. You had to chop into the ground at the base of each clump of tussock tendrils, then lift the whole thing out of the ground. You could have the smaller tussocks out of the ground with a single quick chop, but bigger ones might take two or three chops around the base, then some levering before they came up. A big tussock could be as high as your thigh. The idea was to be methodical and have a strategy. You didn't just wander at random, chopping on a whim. You needed to work along a front, gradually whittling away, slowly pushing the line back to a fence and so having the paddock cleared, at least for the time being.

The tussock wasn't uniformly spread. In some places there were just a few here and there, like the first outriders of the horde. In other places they'd be beginning to group themselves enough to start dominating the ground. And in some areas, where they'd met no resistance and there'd been plenty of time to dig in, they were a dense mass completely covering the ground and not allowing a single blade of grass to survive.

You got into a sort of war mentality. Skirmishing with the outriders wasn't so bad. The heavier concentrations were harder work. You could chop all day before you saw much effect. That's when you got the sense of it being like a war. But it was when you gazed across the main body of the tussock hordes, saw them stretching away in a solid mass, felt them advancing on you with the silent intensity of all their straining and reaching, that you got a sort of watery sensation in your stomach. That's when you knew you didn't have the strength to prevail.

All this reminded the youth of something he'd once read about King Harold and the Anglo-Saxons in the year 1066 when enemies were coming at them from all sides. They'd had to march north to fight a great battle against the ferocious Vikings who'd landed there, and then straightaway march south again to face the invading Normans at Hastings. They'd won the great battle in the north, but lost the one in the south. It didn't matter how brave they were: they were just too worn out and the enemies were too many.

There was lots of time to think, out there in the paddocks all day long. The youth began to dwell on the story of King Harold and his people. Up till then he had always thought of loneliness and abandonment and courage and defeat in terms of an individual person. Like Diestl. But now he began to see that a whole people or tribe or army could be lonely and friendless in the world and be gradually going down in despair. One could be *part* of a larger thing and be going down *with* it. There'd be some consolation in that, thought the youth. You would have friends alongside you, sharing the ordeal, like in the shield-wall at Hastings.

He wished he could read more about 1066. He had no books with him, just his precious magazine with Sweetheart in it. He had to get some books to read. Or at least one book, a book about King Harold and his people going down so bravely. Reading about it, learning more of the story, would sustain him somehow. But the bare bulb in his room in the shed wasn't bright enough to read by, not properly. He had to squint just to read the captions to the pictures of Sweetheart. Maybe he could get a bed-lamp, as well as the book. That would set him up nicely. He had to get into Balinga. There'd be a bookshop there, and somewhere to buy a bed-lamp. But Balinga was a long drive away.

And besides, he had no money. He hadn't received any pay and was owed a few weeks by now. That wouldn't add up to very much, but it might be enough for what he needed to buy. He began to yearn for a trip to town and for some pay. He waited for a chance to raise it with Mr. Coles, waited for Mr. Coles to be in a better mood than his usual one. But time passed and the chance didn't present itself. So the youth went on day by day, chopping and hacking at the tussock, doing his feeding chores, then being in his room at night, either gazing blankly in the Diestl mood or sighing in the embraces of his blue-eyed darling until he felt spent enough to sleep. On Sundays he would saddle up the old mare and go for a long ride to the river and to the cliffs where the wedge-tailed eagles lived.

MRS. COLES began to be more visible round the place. The youth would see her hanging clothes on the line, or tending the plants at the front and side of the homestead. She had a sad, resigned look on her face, and would not meet the youth's eyes on the few occasions they came close enough for their glances to cross. The old lady would snap at her that she should be kicking on. But the old lady stayed friendly with the youth and would rattle away to him for five minutes at a time about the news and what a conundrum it all was. The youth only had to nod every so often, or shake his head, or mutter "Ah." The old lady told him he was a good conversationalist.

"Which is more than I can say about Misery Guts," she added, gesturing to somewhere in the house. "Won't kick on at all, that woman. I can't fathom a person like that. Can you? No, of course you can't!"

"It's a conundrum," the youth agreed.

One evening at the usual time he went to the bathroom inside the house to have his shower. He didn't do it every evening, just every second or third one. He always felt very uncomfortable about going into the private part of the house and kept it to the minimum. This time the bathroom door was ajar as he approached. He assumed the bathroom must be empty. He went straight in and found the old lady standing there with nothing on. She looked up at him in surprise. The youth was completely flustered for a few moments, then turned and went quickly out and pulled the door shut behind him. He went back to the shed and sat on his bed with his heart pounding. He half-expected Mr. Coles to come raging across at any moment to confront him. The old lady was probably telling him about it right now. How he'd pushed his way into the bathroom and stood there perving at her. And in a way he *had* perved. He'd been so surprised at seeing someone there that he'd looked straight at her body, at her breasts and the triangle of hair lower down. He thought it had only been for a couple of moments, but maybe he'd given the impression that he was really gawping. And the idea that he'd do that to such an old lady made it worse.

When it was time for him to go across and have his meal, he approached the back door hesitantly and went inside as quietly as he could. The meal was laid out as usual and he began to pick at it, feeling too anxious to want it properly. The house was quiet. Suddenly the old lady entered the kitchen and began to prattle on about the news as usual. It was about the Balkans this time. The youth didn't quite know what the Balkans were. He just kept his eyes on his plate and felt a growing relief that nothing seemed out of the ordinary. Maybe the old lady had forgotten what happened. Old people forget things easily. And yet her mind always seemed sharp as a tack. As she continued in full flow about the Balkans, Mr. Coles called from inside to ask where the envelopes were. She called back that they were on the desk where they were supposed to be. He replied that they weren't there. The old lady clicked her

tongue with impatience and began to go out of the kitchen. At
the door she paused and looked at the youth.

"Don't worry," she said with a wink. "It's our little secret."

A COUPLE of days later the youth got his chance to go to a shop,
though it was only the general store in Burrawah.

Mr. Coles had to pick up some things and the youth said he
needed a few odds and ends himself. "Better come along
then," said Mr. Coles. The youth summoned the courage to
mention that he didn't have any money and that he'd like to get
a bit of his pay to spend. Mr. Coles seemed surprised, then said
he wasn't sure whether there was anything owing to him. The
youth went red with embarrassment. Maybe he was demanding something he wasn't entitled to. And yet how could there
not be something owing to him after all this time? He screwed
up his courage again.

"Um, I just thought there *might* be something due."

"Well, there could be. I don't know. Mrs. Coles does the
books. I'll have to check with her. Remember, though, that you
got your coat and boots and hat as an advance on wages."

The youth had forgotten that. He flushed red again, feeling
that he'd put himself completely in the wrong. The thing was,
he didn't know what his weekly pay was supposed to be. No-
one had ever mentioned it and he'd never felt bold enough to
ask. Deep down he found it hard to believe that his services,
such as they were, could be worth anything.

Just before they left in the truck for the township, Mr. Coles
came from the house and handed the youth some money.
There were notes and some coins.

"That brings you till Thursday of last week," he said gruffly.
"Mrs. Coles has totted it all up."

The youth felt he'd created an unpleasant situation and
should apologise. But he didn't know what to say, so he kept
silent. Mr. Coles did not speak either on the drive into Burrawah,

except to yell at a steer that had escaped from someone's paddock and was standing on the road. "Get out of it, you beggar
of a blasted animal! Get the blazes out of it!"

Burrawah was a tiny place. There was just Dawson's general
store and a straggle of dwellings along a stretch of dirt road.
The general store was interesting, though. It was old-fashioned, with a wide verandah and rusted tin signs for brands of
tea and bleach and aspirin. There was a cockatoo on a stand by
the door. The bird was attached to the stand by a little chain
on its leg, like a convict, and looked very glum.

The inside of the store was dim and the youth had to let his
eyes adjust. But after a few weeks away from the world, it
seemed like Aladdin's Cave. There was a rack of magazines and
the youth scanned their covers eagerly. He was looking for anything about Sweetheart. At first he saw nothing, but then his
heart leapt. On the cover of *Home Ideas* was the headline: "A
Princess Looks Back: Does Grace Still Yearn for Hollywood?"
The youth picked the magazine up with shaking hands and
leafed through it. There was a three-page spread with photos of
her in various movie roles. What a wonderful find this was!
How right he'd been to ask to come to the store and to demand
some of his money! He felt upright and brave, like a knight who
has won his way to the fair lady by his undauntedness.

The store man was outside with Mr. Coles and the youth
could hear them talking about sheep-drench. There were no
books for sale and no bed-lamps. They would have to wait till
he could get to Balinga. He wanted to buy some food, something that would keep well and that he could have in reserve in
his room for those times when he didn't feel filled up by the
meals provided.

The storekeeper came inside with Mr. Coles and the youth
paid him for two large packets of biscuits, some toothpaste and
the magazine. He went outside with his purchases in a brown
paper bag and stood by the truck. He resisted the urge to peek

at the photos of Sweetheart again. Better to wait till he was back in his room. The sun was out and there was a cool wind blowing the clouds across the sky. He looked at the dwellings that lined the strip of dirt road in both directions. They were more like shacks than proper houses, all broken down and crumby. The Currey place couldn't be any of those. It must be somewhere further along, he figured, or a bit out of sight among trees. If he'd had a moment alone with the storekeeper he'd have asked about it, but hadn't wanted to with Mr. Coles there. The youth had been mulling over an idea for a couple of weeks. Burrawah was a fair way from Dunkeld if you were driving, because you had to go in the other direction first to reach the main gate of the property and get onto the public road. But if you were going across country on horseback it was hardly any distance at all. Maybe, he thought, he could saddle up old Gypsy one Sunday and ride over to the Currey place and drop in on them. He imagined himself arriving and casually hitching the mare to their front fence, then greeting them like a real Horseman who thinks nothing of riding rough country to say g'day to his friends.

Then he saw Clem. He'd appeared from one of the rundown shacks and was standing under a gnarled gum tree at the back. The youth was about to call out and wave, but something made him pause. Then Gladys came out of the shack and said something. Clem made a sharp gesture with his hand and Gladys made the same gesture to him and then turned impatiently away. At the shack door she turned and said something else, and again Clem made the abrupt gesture, and Gladys went in. They weren't in a happy mood, that was obvious. The youth thought Clem might turn his head at any moment and look across to the general store and see him standing there. But Clem was looking at the ground, like a man with the weight of the world on him. The youth stepped out of sight behind the truck, just in case.

The mental picture of the storybook cottage was gone, and the youth knew he wouldn't be riding over to say g'day.

He felt depressed after that, but he got by. He knew he had plenty on his side to keep him going. He had Sweetheart and he had Diestl. And as he waged his war against the tussock hordes out in the paddocks, he had the example of King Harold and the brave Anglo-Saxons always before him.

ONE EVENING the youth was going across to the house for his meal. He saw the light of a torch down near the bottom of the home paddock, near the pig enclosure. Mr. Coles was trying to pull up a length of heavy steel cable that had been lying half-buried in the grass for a long time. The youth had often noticed the length of cable and supposed it was from the days of the bulldozer. He could hear Mr. Coles grumbling at the brute of a thing to "Come up! Come up, blast you!" It was just like Mr. Coles, the youth reflected, to decide that some task had to be done right that minute and then to bluster away at it. The pigs were aroused and were grunting and oinking loudly.

He was sitting in the kitchen, eating, when Mr. Coles came bursting in.

"What the hell have you been doing to those pigs?" he yelled. "You've cut the beggars to pieces!"

The youth was too surprised and frightened to speak. He just sat with his mouth half-full and looked up blankly.

"I'm calling the police!" Mr. Coles continued. "Don't think I won't!"

The old lady came in and asked what on earth the matter was.

"He's mutilated those pigs!"

"What do you mean by 'mutilated' them?"

"He's cut them to pieces! I'm getting the police in!"

"You're not doing any such thing until we know what on earth has happened," the old lady said firmly. She turned to the youth. "Do you know what Mr. Coles is talking about?"

"No," he said, gulping the lump of food down.

"What!" snapped Mr. Coles. "You sit there and say that? Come with me!"

He took the youth by the sleeve of his jacket and pulled him from the chair and out of the kitchen. He flicked the torch on and began to march him down towards the pigs. The youth could hear the old lady calling to Mr. Coles not to go off the handle and to listen to what the boy had to say.

The pigs came grunting and snuffling to the fence and Mr. Coles shone his torch on them. The youth half-expected to see animals with legs and tails and ears lopped off and blood everywhere. But there was nothing visibly wrong.

"Look at that!" Mr. Coles barked, shining the torch onto the back of one of the pigs. The youth leant forward and looked. There was a pattern of little cuts across the skin of the back. He realised what they were. They were cuts made by the edge of the trowel when he whacked the pigs away from the trough to give himself a space to pour the mush. "Is that your doing, or isn't it?"

"Yes," the youth muttered.

"And you've done the same to all of them? All their backs are cut to pieces? Do you admit that fact?"

"Yes," the youth muttered.

"What did you do it with?"

"The trowel."

"And what the hell possessed you? Do you mutilate dumb animals for fun?"

The youth was wondering how he could have failed to notice the cuts before.

"I asked you a blasted question!" Mr. Coles yelled.

The youth was feeling so shaky that he could hardly keep upright on his legs. But the question offended him. Of course he didn't mutilate animals for fun! What did Mr. Coles take him for? There'd been a reason for whacking those pigs. It might have been the wrong thing to do—it was the wrong thing to do, he saw that now—but it wasn't fair to ask him if he mutilated animals for fun.

"I was just trying to keep them back from the trough," he said, in what he thought was a reasonable explanation.

"What!"

"When I was feeding them."

"What!"

"I didn't know the trowel was cutting them."

"You're a bloody maniac!" Mr. Coles shouted. "You're sacked! I want you off the place first thing in the morning! Be ready to leave at seven o'clock."

He walked away waving the torch and then called back: "I haven't decided yet whether I'll bring the police into it. I'm going to check all the other animals in the morning, to see if you've been harming them, then I'll decide. But if I decide not to call the police you can consider yourself bloody lucky!"

The youth stood there, still shaking, with the pigs grunting and snuffling horribly in the dark beside him.

He wasn't able to sleep that night and at first light he saw Mr. Coles going around looking at the horses and cows and dogs and chooks. At seven o'clock Mr. Coles was waiting beside the ute. The youth got in and sat with his bag across his knees. The old lady came to the back door and waved and called out: "Never mind! Never mind! We all make mistakes! You'll kick on!"

As they pulled away from the house, the youth saw one of the curtains move and Mrs. Coles's face there for a moment.

Mr. Coles stopped the ute in the main street of Balinga. He handed the youth an envelope.

"That's what you're owed," he said. "To the penny."

The youth got out and the ute drove off.

The youth returned to the city early next morning. He was tired and hungry and had almost no money left after the train fare. He took a bus to Bankington to see his mother and tell her he'd been sacked and didn't know what to do. He approached the Miami Guesthouse cautiously, not wanting to run into Mr. Stavros. After watching from across the street, he went into the lobby. Mrs. Stott was there.

"Well, hello," she said. "What brings you here?"

He replied he just needed to see his mother for a minute.

"She doesn't work here anymore," Mrs. Stott told him. "She left a week ago. Actually Mr. Stavros thought she'd be happier elsewhere. Didn't she let you know?"

Even in his confusion the youth registered that his mother had got the sack.

"Where did she go?" he asked.

"We've no idea, actually. She said she'd phone and let me know a forwarding address, but she hasn't so far."

He stood completely at a loss.

"Didn't you go to the bush to work?"

"Yes."

"And now you're back?"

"Yes."

"Well, if your mother gets in touch, I'll let her know you were here. Where are you staying?"

"I'm not sure yet."

"Well, phone me in a day or two and I'll let you know if she's called."

Mr. Stavros was getting out of his car in the front courtyard. The youth hurried through the back of the lobby and along the passage to the backyard and into the lane. He ran to the end and turned the corner. He imagined Mr. Stavros behind him, angry-faced.

When he was a couple of blocks away from the Miami he came to a park with a duck pond and some benches. He sat down to rest his shaking legs, glancing over his shoulder every few moments to reassure himself that he was in the clear. He looked at the water of the duck pond reflecting the clouds, at the grass, the trees, the paths, the rubbish bins, the bits of litter on the ground. Traffic passed.

It was all strangely distant and horribly close and real at the same time. The youth would have gone into the Diestl mood to make himself impervious to everything, but the Diestl mood was all used up for the moment. It was like an inner battery that needed time to recharge. He wished he could just go to sleep and not wake up until the battery was full again.

He counted his money. He had enough for a couple of meals. He thought he should maybe eat something now to keep himself going. He went across to a shop and bought a sausage roll with tomato sauce. As he came out of the shop a bus went past and he suddenly thought that he'd need bus fares, so had better be even more careful about what he spent. Then he wondered where he would need to go by bus and realised there was nowhere. He went back to the bench and ate the sausage roll and spilled sauce down the front of his shirt. Then he began to walk in the direction of the city centre.

The shop windows interested him as always and he mused to himself about a dozen and one things—an ornate lamp in an antique shop, a big photo display of a Bavarian beer festival at a travel agency, rockmelons piled up in a pyramid, ladies' fashions, kittens for sale. You could have a lovely time, walking for miles past shop windows, thinking your own thoughts. It was people who spoiled it, all the people walking in the opposite direction and giving you the Oncoming Look. The youth wished there were one-way footpaths, like one-way streets, with everyone going the same way and nobody having to look anyone else in the face.

He got to the downtown area and stood on a street corner for a long time unable to decide which direction to take. He thought he should probably go back to the main railway terminal. There was no reason to go there, except that the atmosphere was always tinged with human distress and your own distress didn't seem quite so pressing. He decided to walk in the opposite direction.

He wandered into the business area. There were big old-fashioned sandstone buildings with heavy timber doors and brass plates, and there were ultra-modern ones with glass fronts that let you see right into the lobbies. There were banks and insurance companies and government departments. They had an air of weight and importance. The youth wondered what went on inside them. The people in the street were the kind of people who worked in those places, confident-looking men in nice suits and well-groomed young women who left a whiff of perfume behind in the air when they walked past. There were posh cafes where those kinds of people sat having lunch. The youth stood outside one of the cafes—it was called a bistro—and watched some of them through the glass. At a corner table just inside the window sat an elegant blonde woman and a middle-aged man. The woman had a tiny bowl of lettuce in front of her and was picking at it with a fork, using the fork to make graceful motions in the air as she spoke. The youth had noticed her because she had a slight look of Grace Kelly. He watched them talking and wondered what it would be like to be one of those people. He tried to imagine himself going in and sitting down and ordering something. If he was invisible he would go in and stand next to the blonde woman and the man and listen to their conversation. He often thought about what he'd do if he was invisible. Sometimes he imagined the sex things he could do, like perving at girls in the shower, but mostly he thought how being invisible would mean you could learn about the world and the way things were. You could go unseen into these big important buildings, for instance, and learn how the world operates and the secrets of everything.

The youth realised the couple was staring at him through the glass. They looked annoyed. The man made a sharp gesture with his hand and said something. He said it with very clear lip movements, the way you would if speaking to a deaf person. It was "Get away!" The youth hurried off, feeling shaken. He thought he was watching them from the corner of his eye in a manner they wouldn't notice. It was shocking to find out that people were aware of you when you didn't think they were. It made you feel completely unsafe.

After a while he came to an intersection. On one corner was an imposing building with a row of columns along its front and the words STATE LIBRARY carved on it. The youth suddenly thought of King Harold and the Anglo-Saxons. The library would have lots of books about that. Here was the chance to get the whole story! He crossed the intersection and went up a grand flight of steps to the columns and then to a set of huge bronze doors that stood open.

There was a lobby with marble floors and a high elaborate ceiling and a wide staircase. The youth normally would have been intimidated by the grandness of it, but thinking of King Harold had given him courage. He went through the lobby into a reading room and stood amazed at the size of it. There were four levels of bookcases running right around the walls and the top three levels had balconies with quaint narrow stairs leading to them. There were about twenty long, heavy, polished tables where people sat reading or writing or just leaning back with their hands behind their heads. Big skylights in the roof made the light almost like daylight, except beautifully softened and quietened. And there was a strong aroma of the paper and ink and binding of so many books, and of so much old polished wood. He went to a chair at one of the emptiest of the big tables and sat down and looked around for a few minutes taking note of how people were behaving. Everyone was quiet and minding their own business. The only talking was an occasional low murmur from the people at the central counter. The youth began to relax. He left his bag on the chair and went to the nearest shelf and scanned the spines of the books. It was the Botany section. He went along the shelves, looking for History. He climbed one of the quaint sets of stairs and wandered along the balcony and looked out over the wide expanse of the room and breathed in the calm air and the good aroma.

He turned to the shelf behind him and saw a set of identical blue-covered books. They were the complete works of Charles Dickens. The youth had never read any Dickens, but like most people he knew about a few of the famous characters. There was Oliver Twist, for example, who asked for more. And there was Mr. Scrooge who hated Christmas and got visited by ghosts. He took one of the books out and opened it at random and read a bit:

I was so young and childish, and so little qualified—how could it be otherwise?—to undertake the whole charge of my own existence, that often, in going to Murdstone and Grinby's of a morning, I could not resist the stale pastries put out for sale at half price at the pastry cook's doors, and spent in that the money I should have kept for my dinner. Then I went without my dinner . . .

The youth leant more comfortably on the balcony rail and adjusted the pages to the light and read more.

. . . two pudding shops, between which I was divided, according to my finances. One was in a court close to St Martin's church—at the back of the church—which is now removed altogether. The pudding at that shop was made of currants, and was a rather special pudding; but it was dear, twopennyworth not being larger than a penny-worth of more ordinary pudding. A good shop for the lat-ter was in the Strand, somewhere in that part which has been re-built since. It was a stout pale pudding, heavy and flabby, and with great flat raisins in it, stuck in whole at wide distances apart . . .

He stayed on the balcony reading random passages from *David Copperfield* until his legs became tired from standing, and then he took the book back to his seat and read for anoth-er long while. He'd never been so held by any book before. It was so real, so true, so fully understandable. It was under-standable even when you didn't quite know the meaning of some things, like what the "Strand" was exactly. There was so much that was funny and cosy and quaint, and yet there was this awful bleakness all through it too. You could feel the cold of that world and the pinch of misery in its guts.

It began to get late in the afternoon and he felt very hungry. He left the book on the table and his bag on the chair and went out and bought a dry bread roll and a small carton of milk. He took these back to the front steps of the library. It was quite high there and you could see out over the city. There was a large park next to the library and another imposing building away on the far side of it. The air was turning cold and the youth shivered and finished off the last of the roll and milk and went back inside into Dickens's world, which was a strange far-off place and yet at the same time the actual world you were shivering in right now.

The daylight faded from the skylights high above. The electric light came on. The youth read some of the time and then to rest his eyes sat observing the people. There were enough of them to make the place seem occupied without being crowded. At eight forty-five a gentle voice came over a speaker announcing that it was fifteen minutes to closing time. The youth was one of the last to leave. A young woman librarian stood at the bronze doors to see people out. She wished the youth a good evening.

He stood on the library steps for a longish time, then began walking aimlessly. There was a long uphill street with many lights and flashing neon signs at the top of it. The youth went that way. As he got closer to the bright lights and neon he noticed women standing in doorways and at corners where dim side streets ran off. The youth kept his eyes averted and quickened his pace. He heard one or two of them murmur to him but he did not quite catch what they said. He felt horribly self-conscious. Just ahead of him a girl emerged from a doorway and drifted across the footpath. She was young and slim and wore a short skirt, black stockings and high-heeled shoes. The youth didn't dare look directly at her, but he saw she had blonde hair cut short like a boy's. She touched him on the arm as he drew level with her.

"Want a girl, love?" she said. For an instant they were looking straight at each other. The youth felt both stirred and stricken. The girl realised how young he was and stepped back. He strode on faster, then began to run, dodging around people. The momentary touch on his arm was still sending electric currents through him. He ran till he came to an intersection all garish with neon. He had to stop to wait for a break in the traffic and as he waited he tried to gather his thoughts. The women in the doorways must be prostitutes, and the girl who'd touched him had been offering to have sex. The youth didn't understand the exact details of having sex, but the thought of hugging and fondling that girl filled him with desperate feelings. Then he felt enraged that she'd interfered with him like that. He'd always minded his own business! Couldn't he walk along a public street in peace? It wasn't fair! He should have given her a look of such utter disdain that she'd have reeled back as from a blow from the butt of a Schmeisser. Diestl would have. The youth let himself go limp in the shoulders and his gaze grew blank and distant. He felt the rage fading away into cold contempt. He felt the familiar weight of the Schmeisser. It was all very simple, the youth reminded himself. If someone was a real threat you killed them. And you did it quickly and without it being personal. If it wasn't a serious threat you ignored it. The youth saw it clearly now. Like Diestl with that French girl from the farmhouse, the one who'd come to him wanting to be held because she was so lonely and scared. You just give them a blank look, then you limp on past them down your long road alone.

He walked on through the glow of the neon signs, past other women in other doorways. He came to darker, quieter streets and then the neon was far behind. He was in such a mechanical rhythm of walking that he didn't want to stop, even though he felt tired. Tiredness was good. It tranquillised you. He realised he was back in the business area of town and that it was practically deserted. He began to make mental notes of spots where it might be possible to sleep. There were dark laneways that might do. He had a worn old piece of blanket in his bag, and the bag itself could be used as a pillow. In Diestl's terms that was almost luxury. He let the Diestl mood slip off. It had served him well again, had got him through.

Passing a lane, he saw a building site a little way along it. There was a digging machine parked, and piles of debris, and what looked like a big wooden crate. He went along the lane.

It was dark there, away from the street-lights, and he had to let his eyes adjust so he could examine the crate. It was empty, and big enough for a person to lie down in. He wondered if he was tired enough to settle in the crate for the night. A torch suddenly shone on him and a gruff voice asked him what he was playing at. The youth shielded his eyes and tried to see past the glare of the torch. Two uniformed men came forward. They were security guards.

"What's your game?" one of them demanded.

"Nothing."

"What's in the bag?" the other asked.

"Nothing."

"Out doin' a bit of thievin', are you?" said the first.

"No."

There was a pause while they looked him up and down with the torch. He hadn't tried to run away and he didn't look like the sort of kid who wanted to be a tough guy.

"Piss off then," said one of the men. "And don't let us catch you skulkin' round here again. Understood?"

The youth said he understood. He walked back down the lane to the street and passed the security company car at the kerb. He remembered that he'd vaguely noticed a car like that pass him in the street before. They must've had their eye on him, and had seen him turn down the lane. That was really scary. It made you feel you weren't safe, not even alone in a deserted street at night.

Ahead, the youth saw the clock-tower of the main railway terminal. He went into the big hall of the country and inter-state trains. There were a few people sitting about on benches with their luggage beside them. One small kiosk was still open and an occasional announcement came over the loudspeaker. He went to a bench and sat down. It was just after eleven by the big clock.

The youth felt hungry. He counted his money and found he

could afford a sausage roll from the kiosk. He decided to wait. He noticed that there were two or three people lying on benches with bags or coats under their heads. He eased himself down full-length with his bag for a pillow. It was good to be lying down, but his mind was not at ease and he didn't feel like dozing.

He came alert to the sound of shouting. The police were removing a drunk up at the far end and the drunk was yelling and trying to resist. They got him out and the noise died away. The youth saw that the kiosk had closed. It was cold and he would have liked to use his piece of blanket but thought it might make him look too much like someone using the station as a place to sleep rather than just waiting for a connection. He then saw that the policemen had come back into the hall and were speaking to people on the benches and asking to see their tickets. The youth got up and hoisted his bag and walked away as casually as possible.

He found a phone box in the park across from the railway terminal. The park was dirty and stale, but it was dark amongst the gnarled old trees and he couldn't see anyone lurking about. The phone box's light was broken and so there was nothing to draw attention to it there in the shadows. The youth went in and swept the floor with his foot to make sure there was no broken glass, then sat down. He couldn't straighten his legs, and the shelf above his head made him keep his neck slightly bent, but he was by himself and out of sight and that was the main thing. He took his piece of blanket from his bag and draped it over himself. He became aware of a bad smell in the box. Like dogshit. He hoped he wasn't sitting in any of it, and that it wasn't getting on his piece of blanket. But he felt too tired and cold and cramped and depressed to care all that much.

He wasn't aware of sleeping but he must have dozed for long periods in between his twisting attempts to find a bearable way to sit. The dawn light was seeping into the park. He had a splitting headache and his whole body ached, especially his knees, neck and backside. He felt conspicuous with the light brightening, and there were increasing sounds of traffic. His mind was sluggish and he could not think where to go. He needed some food, and a drink of water. He decided to go back to the station. The daily bustle would be starting now and he could mingle with it. And there was a toilet there to use.

On the park benches nearby sat several derelicts. They were old-looking and had dirty overcoats on, and broken shoes with no socks. The youth glanced at them from the corner of his eye, then looked away in case he was giving offence. One of them got up and lurched towards him and began to speak in a harsh, gravelly voice. The youth was scared but forced himself to glance up as though he wasn't too bothered.

"Go on!" said the man. "Go on!" He was staring at the youth with raddled eyes.

"Sorry?" the youth said.

"Go on! Get out of it!" the man almost yelled. He loomed closer. "Go on, get out of it! Yer only young! Yer don't want this!" He waved his arm, taking in the whole park, or maybe the whole city. "Get the fuck out of it! Go and have a decent fuckin' life!"

The man swayed for a moment, then walked on unsteadily, his broken shoes scuffing the ground.

It took a couple of minutes before the youth could get his legs to work properly. He hobbled to the station toilet and splashed water on his face and drank a little out of his cupped hand. A man with his face all lathered was having a shave at the next basin. He boomed a cheery good morning and the youth muttered good morning back. The man wanted to have a conversation about how good it felt to be alive, but the loudness of his voice echoing in the tiled lavatory made the youth's head hurt. He felt so hungry he could hardly bear it. He went across to a kiosk and asked for a sausage roll. A young woman behind the counter snapped that he'd have to wait until they were ready to serve. He sat down on a bench and waited. A bit after six o'clock he went back to the kiosk and got a lukewarm sausage roll and ate it too quickly. He'd have liked to get a small carton of milk too, but he didn't dare spend the money.

The station gradually became busy. The only plan the youth could think of was to return to the library and spend the day there. It reopened at eight-thirty, he knew, for he had made a point of checking the notice outside the doors. He went out of the station and trailed through the streets and waited on the front steps until the bronze doors opened. He got *David Copperfield* off the shelf and went to his place at the big table and tried to read. But he couldn't focus on it. He leant forward with his head resting on his arms, but that didn't help. He was thinking about the dogshit smell in the phone box. He wondered whether he had that smell on him and was stinking the place out. He looked at people out of the corner of his eye to see if they were looking at him. They didn't seem to be, but then he wondered if they were deliberately *not* looking at him.

He left the library and went to the large park alongside. It was called Foundation Park. It had paths and trees and statues. The youth was looking for a spot to lie down. He found a nice patch of grass between a big spreading tree and a statue of Henry Lawson. He remembered how one time at school a teacher had recited a poem of Lawson's. It was called "Faces in the Street" and the youth had liked it. It was about someone studying the looks on the faces of people as they go past his window. One or two lines came back to him. The day was cool but sunny and the grass felt dry, so he put his piece of blanket down and lay on it and went straight to sleep.

He felt so hungry when he woke that he went immediately to a shop and spent the last of his money on a meat pie and a small carton of strawberry milk. The pie was a bit runny and the pastry wasn't very strong and it kept sagging in his fingers. Finally, half the pie fell on the ground. He drank the strawberry milk carefully so as not to waste a drop.

The youth did not know what to do. The imposing building on the opposite side of the park from the library turned out to be the State Art Gallery. He thought of seeing if it cost anything to go in, but wasn't sure he'd be allowed in anyway. He had never been in an art gallery and didn't know how they worked. Maybe only toffs were allowed in. Besides, there was the thing about the dogshit smell.

He made his way slowly back through the city to the railway terminal, going through the grubby park where the phone box was. He looked into the box and saw the smear of something running up one wall. He tried to think whether he would have touched that part during the night.

The youth sat in the crowded terminal. It was quite late in the day. Making contact with his mother was the key thing. That meant phoning Mrs. Stott to see if she had heard anything. But he didn't have the money for a call. He wondered whether he should walk to the Miami, but Bankington was a fair distance, and he didn't really feel up to it. Besides, he was scared of meeting Mr. Stavros. And it'd be for nothing anyhow. Why would his mother go out of her way to ring the Miami after she'd got the sack? And it wasn't as if she was aware of his situation. As far as she knew he was up in the bush having a great time.

The noise of the train announcements was giving him another headache, so he went out of the big hall and into the street. The evening peak hour was starting and there were lots of people coming to catch trains. The youth wondered whether he could ask someone for some money. Just enough to ring up. But he knew he couldn't do it. All those Oncoming Looks were too real. It wasn't like in the poem, where the faces in the street are passing a window behind which the watcher is snugly hidden.

The youth felt so much at a loss that he thought he might cry.

"It isn't that bad is it?" said a voice beside him. There was a nicely dressed man with a briefcase.

"Pardon?"

"From the look on your face, anyone would think you had-n't a friend in the world."

"No, just thinking about something," the youth said.

"Are you travelling?" the man asked, indicating the youth's bag and the terminal building.

"I've come down from the bush."

"Ah," the man said. He looked into the youth's face for a longish time.

The youth did not mind being looked at as much as he might have. There was something attractive about the man. He seemed very clean and fresh and there was a smell of after-shave. And there was something else that was giving the youth a very odd sensation. The man had cool blue eyes and gold-rimmed glasses. The youth had a photo of Grace Kelly gazing all cool and blue-eyed through gold-rimmed glasses just like these, giving him that very same look.

"So, do you have a place to stay?" the man asked softly.

"My mother's living here somewhere. I need to contact her."

"I see."

The man kept regarding the youth as though trying to decide something.

The youth gathered his nerve and blurted out: "Could you spare the price of a phone call please?"

The man smiled.

"Of course. But perhaps I could buy you a meal as well. There's a place just along here that's quite nice."

"No, I'm okay thanks."

"Are you sure?" the man said. "I have the time to spare, and you look as though you need some pampering . . . Yes, definitely some pampering, I'd say."

The youth felt a rush of grateful emotion. Some pampering would be awfully nice. Or a good hot meal anyhow.

"Just the phone money would be great," he murmured.

"Of course, if you're positive that's all you need," said the man. He fished a coin from his pocket and handed it over. His manner had become a bit more brisk. "Perhaps we'll bump into each other again," he said. "I hope we will. I often go past here."

He paused, as though giving the youth a moment to say something. Then he turned and went into the flow of people going by.

The youth felt panic. He almost ran after the man. He wanted his kindness back. He wanted to be gazed at again in that intense way, and to have more of that peculiar sensation of seeing the blue eyes through the gold-rimmed glasses. He thought for a moment he might faint. It occurred to him he might be coming down with something.

When he got through to Mrs. Stott he learnt that his mother had been in touch that afternoon and had left her address and phone number.

THE WOMAN was working as a housemaid at a hotel called the Viceroy's Arms, about ten minutes walk from the railway terminal. The youth found the place and went into the reception area. There was no-one around so he went back outside. He was leaning against the wall, lost in his thoughts, when the woman came along the footpath. She had to say his name twice—the second time quite sharply—before he realised she was there. She led the way to a cafe and ordered a pot of tea and a plate of chips. The youth explained about being sacked from Dunkeld and having no money and nowhere to stay. He told it in a halting way, trying to minimise how bad it sounded, but he knew it was confirming how stupid and useless he was. The part about him coming away from the job with almost no money, for instance. The woman seemed to think he'd let himself be diddled.

"Where's this gear, then, that took so much of the wages they owed you?"

"I had to leave it behind."

"Why?"

"It was a bit bulky to carry."

"So you left a coat and boots and hat that you'd paid through the nose for?"

"Yes."

"Because you didn't want the bother of carrying them?"

"It was really bulky," he said again, staring down at the table.

The woman's voice went harder. "*You've* been a pretty bulky item for *me* to lug around for the past fourteen years. But I made the effort, didn't I?"

They agreed that he had to smarten his ideas up.

For the time being, the woman decided, he'd have to stay secretly in her room in the staff area of the hotel. She had no money to give him for accommodation elsewhere, and it would have to be secret because the owner, Mrs. Kincaid, was a prize bitch who'd jump at any excuse to be nasty.

"She's already shitty about me having your brother here. If she sees you occasionally, we can say you're living somewhere else and just visiting."

They went back to the Viceroy's Arms and up to the woman's room where the boy was watching cartoons on TV. The room was small and dark and the window looked onto a brick wall and a network of pipes. The youth used his piece of blanket and a rug to make himself a makeshift bed on the floor in a corner. They decided that he shouldn't leave the room between eight in the evening and eight in the morning. He had a tin to pee in so he wouldn't need to go down the corridor to the Gents. And the rest of the time he shouldn't hang around the premises. If Mrs. Kincaid queried him in the corridors he was to say that he was on holiday from his job as a jackeroo, that he was staying at a friend's place nearby, that he just popped round mornings and evenings to see his mother and brother, and that he'd soon be going back to the bush.

At about eight-thirty each morning the woman started her cleaning work, the boy set off for school and the youth wandered into the city. Each day the woman gave him enough money to buy the paper with job ads in it, and to get a sandwich for lunch.

The first few days he bought the paper and looked at the columns under "J" for Junior Positions, but couldn't see anything that related to him in any way. He would look at, say, "Junior Shop Assistant," and know that it was pointless to try. Or he'd see "Junior Process Worker," and realise that he didn't have the faintest idea what that meant. So he stopped buying the paper. That gave him a bit extra lunch money.

He went to the State Library every day and finished reading *David Copperfield*. He found a book of Henry Lawson's poems and read "Faces in the Street." Then he discovered "The Ballad of the Drover":

> *Across the stony ridges,*
> *Across the rolling plain,*
> *Young Harry Dale, the drover,*
> *Comes riding home again.*
> *And well his stock-horse bears him,*
> *And light of heart is he,*
> *And stoutly his old pack-horse*
> *Is trotting by his knee.*

But then they come to a flooded river:

*Now Harry speaks to Rover,*
*The best dog on the plains,*
*And to his hardy horses,*
*And strokes their shaggy manes:*
*"We've breasted bigger rivers*
*When floods were at their height,*
*Nor shall this gutter stop us*
*From getting home to-night!"*

And so they plunge into the river, and Harry Dale gets dragged under, and Rover goes back to find him:

*The faithful dog a moment*
*Sits panting on the bank,*
*And then swims through the current*
*To where his master sank.*
*And round and round in circles*
*He fights with failing strength,*
*Till, borne down by the waters,*
*The old dog sinks at length.*

The youth couldn't think of that poem without wanting to cry. He thought it must be the best poem ever written. It was almost as tragic as King Harold and his people going down.

He had found a really good book about 1066 and read and reread the main parts of it. When the emotion got too much he would lean his elbows on the table and cover his face with his hands, pretending to rest his eyes. That meant he could let his face crumple up and the tears run down. And if he looked flushed and red-eyed afterwards, people would assume it was from the strain of so much reading. Sometimes he worried that people knew he was crying behind his hands, but mostly he was too full of his feelings to care. If he felt especially emotional he would go out into the park and pace up and down by the statue of Henry Lawson and sob the feelings out. He knew that Lawson understood everything. Harry Dale and King Harold were the same. They were the knights and warriors and horsemen who bear the brunt and face the odds. It was always the same story:

> *The thunder growls a warning,*
> *The ghastly lightnings gleam,*
> *As the drover turns his horses*
> *To swim the fatal stream . . .*

They were the heroes who defy the thunder and lightning, and whose faithful companions remain at their side through thick and thin. Diestl was one of them, except that he was alone. He didn't even have a faithful dog to swim back and drown with him out of devotion. The youth felt how sad that was.

He would be so drained that by the time he returned to the Viceroy's Arms in the evening he had no courage left for his own needs and was full of nervous dread of meeting Mrs. Kincaid. So far he had only glimpsed her through the window of the main bar area. His mother had told him that Mrs. Kincaid prowled the corridors looking for things to nitpick about, and that she could tell if so much as a pin was out of place.

The youth pictured Mrs. Kincaid as a gaunt figure in black, with piercing hate-filled eyes and probing fingers like a witch. In the room at night he'd listen for sounds outside the door, and would imagine a long hooked nose sniffing at it, and long claw-like hands rubbing across it, as though seeking a way in.

"HERE'S A job to apply for," the woman said flatly one evening, putting a copy of the classifieds down in front of them. "The one I've circled."

It was for a pageboy at the Majestic Cinema in the city.

"What does 'pageboy' mean?" the youth asked, a knot of anxiety forming in his stomach.

"General dogsbody, I suppose."

"How would I know what to do?"

"They'll tell you."

The youth looked as dubious as he felt.

"Cheer up," the woman said. "You might not get the job. But you *are* going to ring up and apply for it. How do I know this? Because I'm going to walk you to the phone in the morning, then stand and watch you make the call."

There was no way out.

A lavish musical was showing at the Majestic Cinema. It was called *Pacific Paradise*. The youth hadn't seen it but he knew some of the songs because they were often on the radio. The door of the manager's office was open and a burly man sat behind a desk. The youth fought the urge to turn and run. He showed himself in the doorway and was waved in. He stammered that he'd rung that morning, about the pageboy job.

"How old are you, again?" asked the manager.

The youth said fifteen. The woman had told him to say that because fifteen was the school-leaving age.

"The job is evenings only—from seven till eleven. That okay?"

The youth said it was. The manager told him how much he'd be paid and the youth said that was okay too.

"In the cleaner's room there's a couple of uniforms. See if they fit."

The cleaner's room was a sort of large cupboard with mops and brooms and buckets in it. Two navy-blue uniforms were hanging behind the door. The youth tried both of them on and found that the second one didn't fit too badly except for being a bit long in the sleeves and legs. He went back to the manager's office and the manager looked him up and down in the uniform.

"You'll do," he said. "Are you ready to start?"

The youth mumbled that, um, he had to get home because, um, his mother wasn't very well . . .

The manager looked irritated and told him to front up the next evening then, at a quarter to seven.

The youth spent the next twenty-four hours sick with dread. The woman gave him a pep talk. She said that he'd taken the bull by the horns and now he just needed to continue in the same spirit and do his best and show a bit of gumption. He didn't reply. He couldn't explain that he was afraid of the usherettes. Just going through the foyer to the manager's office had exposed him to the glances of three of them. He'd wanted to sink through the floor.

He turned up at the proper time the next evening and the head usherette explained his duties. Her name was Sharlene. She was middle-aged and had a hard face and a busy manner. The youth took in almost nothing of what she was telling him. He was thinking that he would make a dash for it. If he could get into the street he could disappear within a few seconds. There was a laneway through to the next block . . .

But somehow he found himself doing the first of his nightly duties, sweeping the front footpath with a straw broom. It wasn't so bad out there, away from the foyer where the usherettes were. The front was all lit up and there were big glossy photos and posters on display. The youth felt stirred by the glamour of it. When people went past they would look at the photos and posters and peer through into the red-carpeted foyer. You could tell they were impressed.

He tried to hold himself in a more dignified way and sweep with a certain pan-*at*-chee. At the same time, he had to appear to take all the excitement for granted and be quite relaxed. So he swept like a person who is connected to all the fame and glamour of the world but is unaffected by it.

That lasted only a few minutes before he had to go inside

and sweep the foyer and then the staircase that led to the Dress Circle. He kept his eyes on the carpet and tried desperately not to drop the broom or trip over his own feet. He could feel the eyes of the usherettes boring into him, but once or twice when he gave a furtive half-glance in their direction they were looking away. He was halfway up the Dress Circle stairs when one of the usherettes came down them. She was the nicest-looking one, the youth thought. He had heard another usherette call her Natalie. The youth kept his eyes on the carpet and stepped close to the wall to give her plenty of room to pass. He sensed her coming level with him, then saw her nice legs and high-heeled shoes beside him.

"You're doing a good job," she said.

He didn't dare look up.

"Do you think you'll enjoy being one of the gang?" she asked.

He nodded without looking up.

"You don't have to be shy with us," she said. "We won't eat you."

He forced himself to look up and saw she was smiling at him, then she continued down the stairs. For a few moments the youth felt a sense of lightness and ease. Then there came a burst of giggling. He saw Natalie and Sharlene with their heads together at the ticket box. He saw Sharlene look in his direction. He stared down at the carpet and tried to focus all his concentration on the movements of the broom. He told himself the giggles weren't about him. He knew that he was oversensitive and needed to fight against it. The giggles meant nothing. He told himself he was sure of that.

When the crowd began to arrive for the eight o'clock session the youth had to stand at the foot of the Dress Circle stairs with an armful of glossy programs. After interval he had to fetch a big wooden shutter from a storeroom and carry it to the foyer, place it on the front of the ticket box and click it securely into place. The shutter was heavy and the youth staggered beneath it and took a long while to get it into position. Natalie asked him if he was okay and he nodded yes, straining every muscle to appear as though it was nothing at all. After that he had to go around and empty all the ashtrays in the main foyer and the Dress Circle foyer. Along with the sweeping, those were his main duties. The rest of the time he was to be available if needed.

When he had nothing to do he went to the cleaner's room and sat on an upturned mop-bucket and felt the utter relief of being alone. There was always a game of cards going on in the manager's office, with different people there according to what time it was. Before the movie started the projectionists would be in there, then after the session began there'd be various usherettes and the ladies from the lolly counter. The manager hardly ever left the card game and seemed to let Sharlene run everything else. From his refuge in the cleaner's room the youth could hear the talk. He listened for any mention of himself. The third night he heard one of the usherettes go to the manager's office and say that a patron had chucked up. There was a collective groan.

"Where's that kid?" the manager asked. "What's his name?"

None of them could quite remember.

"Anyway," said the manager, "get the kid on to it."

"Have Nat get him on to it," Sharlene suggested.

"Why Nat?"

"'Cos I think she's won a heart there."

The youth had only a minute to register what he'd heard. Natalie came and found him and sent him in with a bucket and sponge to clean up the vomit. She lent him her torch so he could see what he was doing.

The fat man who'd vomited was still sitting there. He was only one seat from the aisle so the youth was able to reach the mess. But it was awkward, down on his knees, leaning in past the end seat, holding the torch with one hand and trying to sponge up the smelly gobbets with the other. The man tried to be helpful, moving his big feet from one side to the other. There was a tender love song on screen just then, and the youth thought he heard the man humming the tune. Then there was a moment of comedy and a scatter of laughter came from the parts of the audience furthest from the vomit area. The man gave a belly laugh.

"Enjoying yourself, are you?" said someone in an angry voice.

"Isn't it marvellous!" said someone else.

"You wouldn't credit some people," said another.

The youth was able to look up for an instant at the man's face lit by the screen. He felt sorry for him. It was so awful that the man could only pretend it wasn't happening, or at least that it was only a little mishap and hardly worth anyone taking notice of.

The youth had done all he could. He got to his feet to go. Two of the nearest people thanked him, and someone said, "You're a hero!" He knew this had been said partly to make the fat man feel bad, but it was partly sincere as well.

He went to Natalie to give her torch back. He felt he'd gained in stature. He'd coped with the situation. He'd been called a hero. And it was her torch that he'd used, her torch that she'd entrusted him with.

"It didn't touch any vomit, did it?" Natalie asked when he tried to hand it back. He could see how she was keeping at arm's length from him. He realised he had a smear of vomit down his sleeve.

"It's alright," she said, backing off and walking away. "I'll get another torch."

The youth went to the cleaner's room and got some steel wool and disinfectant and rubbed the sleeve of the jacket till the material began to fray.

That night he accidentally wore the tie of his uniform home and forgot to bring it back with him the following evening. He did the top button of his shirt up and hoped he looked presentable enough.

He was sweeping the footpath when he saw the manager looking out from the foyer. What was the manager doing downstairs? The youth figured he must've been told about the tie. Then Sharlene went across and said something. The youth was sure it was about him. The manager went back upstairs. The youth continued to sweep but felt weak and ill. He wished he could summon the nerve to go up to the manager and explain about taking the tie home by mistake.

Later, as he was carrying the big wooden shutter towards the ticket box, the manager walked past him. The youth began to feel shaky and the weight was suddenly too much. The shutter overbalanced and a corner of it banged against the wall. The manager stopped and came across and examined the place where it had hit. There didn't seem to be a mark there. "That was lucky," he said. He gave the youth a look and the youth was sure he was glaring at where the tie should be.

The following night the youth stood in a doorway across from the Majestic, trying to get a grip on himself. He knew he had to stop being so sensitive. It was getting ridiculous. He had to show a bit of gumption. But he felt unwell and had had the runs all day and finally had to hurry across the road to get to the toilet. After he used the toilet he went to the cleaner's room and put his uniform on. Then he needed to go to the loo again. After that he swept the front footpath and then the foyer, trying to keep well away from the usherettes. He was worried that he might smell from having the runs.

When the crowd began to arrive for the eight o'clock session he went to his place at the Dress Circle stairs and stood there with the programs. He hoped he could get through half an hour or so without needing the loo. As the patrons went past him he worried again that he might be giving off a pong, but told himself not to brood on the idea. He knew he brooded too much.

Patrons kept going past him up the stairs, but hardly anyone wanted a program. The youth got the sense that people were murmuring and whispering.

Natalie came down the stairs and went across to the ticket box. He saw her make a gesture of waving her hand in front of her face, like someone waving a bad smell away, and he saw the usherette in the ticket box grimace in reply. The youth told himself not to read meanings into everything. Sharlene appeared and Natalie said something to her and Sharlene looked over towards the stairs.

Then Sharlene came across the foyer and went past him without a glance. She stopped halfway up the stairs, as though she'd forgotten something, and came back past him again. Then she stopped once more, as though she'd remembered her reason to go upstairs, and turned and went past him a third time.

A party of patrons walked towards him. There were two couples and a young girl of about eleven. She was one of those plump girls who wear glasses and are always fussing about something. She wanted to get a program and fiddled in a purse for the coin while the two couples stood chatting. They fell silent and seemed to look at the youth in an odd embarrassed way. The youth told himself not to imagine things. The girl found her coin and got handed a program and the five of them moved up the stairs.

"God, doesn't he *stink*!" one of them said.

A minute later the manager came down. He told the youth he might be better suited to another line of work and reminded him that the position was casual, so there wasn't any notice period. He'd be paid for the five nights. The youth kept his eyes lowered as he left the building and there were no goodbyes.

For several days he didn't tell the woman he'd been sacked from the Majestic. She was always tired from the housemaid work and fed up with having Mrs. Kincaid on her back. If she became irritated with the youth she'd snap: "It's enough that I've got myself and your brother to keep, and a vicious bloody harpy to please, without having you being gormless!"

So he pretended he was still a pageboy. He would stay out till after eleven each night, wandering the streets after the State Library had closed, then go back and creep to the door of the room and knock softly to be let in. This interrupted the woman's hard-earned sleep and made her more irritated.

She was looking for another job through Mrs. Hardcastle's agency. She wanted to be someone's housekeeper, or companion to an invalid, to have a live-in job in a proper house where she could provide for the boy. Finally Mrs. Hardcastle found her a job as housekeeper–companion to an old lady in a country town in the north of the state. She gave Mrs. Kincaid her notice. "And I'd have given her the back of my hand as well," she said the next morning, "if she'd so much as looked sideways at me!"

She told the youth they needed to sit down and discuss his situation, now that they'd be leaving the Viceroy's Arms. He revealed that he was no longer a pageboy. The woman looked at him and shook her head.

"You know you've got your whole life to get through, don't you?" she said quietly.

The youth nodded.

"And do you understand that you don't get unlimited chances? You can make mistakes at your age and get away with it, but you need to start making a go of things sooner or later, and sooner is better. Am I talking to a brick wall?"

"No."

"I'm glad to hear it."

The woman phoned Mrs. Hardcastle to ask if she would give the youth another chance after his poor showing with Mr. Coles. Mrs. Hardcastle spoke of how her clients were like members of her own family. She spoke of the heartache she had to suffer because of being so often let down. She spoke of how her friends told her she was too soft a person to be in business but that she didn't know any other way. She would take the youth back onto her books. In fact she had an opening for him right then. Junior farmhand. Mr. Blackett. Wheat property. Was the youth interested?

"Yes he is, and he'll take it," the woman said flatly into the phone.

The youth tried to sound like someone who is determined to turn over a new leaf. He remarked that it was good of Mrs. Hardcastle to help him.

"Don't be stupid," the woman replied. "She's helping you because I'm forking out the fee. She'd have Jack the Ripper on the books as long as the fee was paid!"

THE YOUTH was collected from outside Munnunwal railway station by the whole Blackett family. They'd been shopping in town and came past on their way home. The youth had to squeeze into the back seat of the station wagon alongside the three kids. Mr. Blackett was a tall, thin man with sandy hair who tried to have a bit of conversation but gave up because of the noise the kids were making. Mrs. Blackett was freckle-faced and seemed pleasant but was also put off by the rowdiness.

The youth was being pressed against the door by the nearest kid, Greg, a boy of about twelve. Next to him was a toddler. Against the other door was the girl. She was about fifteen and the youth's thoughts had been focused on her from the first moment.

Greg was grizzling about not having been bought something he'd wanted.

"I never get anything!" he moaned.

"I net gen anyink!" screamed the toddler in turn.

"Don't start the baby off, please Greg," said Mrs. Blackett. "Let's all settle down."

"I net gen anyink!" the toddler screamed again.

"Shut up," said Greg.

"Please don't speak to people that way," said Mrs. Blackett.

"He's not people," Greg replied. "He's a drop-kick."

"Don't be horrible," said Mrs. Blackett. She handed a packet of jubes to the girl. "Here Meredith, share these around."

The girl opened the packet and held it across to the youth. He was reflecting on her name. He liked the lilt of it. He was afraid to look at her directly, but he'd got a quick first impression outside the station. She had leant out the window and given him a look up and down which made him horribly self-conscious, but which hadn't seemed unfriendly. She had a freckled face like her mother's and brown hair cut quite short.

The youth went to take a jube from the packet she held out, hoping she wouldn't notice his hand shaking. Greg grabbed the packet and some jubes went on the floor. The toddler tried to grab the packet too, screaming, "I net gen anyink!" Meredith snatched the packet back and a scuffle began, with Greg whining and the toddler shrieking.

Mr. Blackett slowed the car and drew to the side of the road.

"Who knows what I'm wondering at this moment?" he asked in a very serious voice. "Greg? Do you know what I'm wondering?"

"Yes Dad," said Greg.

"Will you tell us, please?"

"You're wondering what the Lord thinks of us."

"Exactly right," said Mr. Blackett.

"I net gen . . ." the toddler started to yell, but sensed there'd been a change of mood. Instead he grabbed at the packet again. Meredith pushed his hand away and inserted a big purple jube into his mouth.

"Yes," Mr. Blackett went on. "I'm wondering whether the Lord is shaking His head over us right now. Do you think He might be, Greg?"

"Yes Dad," said Greg.

"Do you think so, Meredith?"

Meredith was looking out the window.

"Meredith?"

"What?"

"Do you think the Lord is shaking His head?"

"I haven't the faintest," she replied. "Why don't you ask Him?"

The youth saw Mrs. Blackett shoot a frown at Meredith.

"I *will* ask the Lord, Meredith," Mr. Blackett said, "but unfortunately I already know the answer. I don't want the Lord to have to sorrow over the behaviour of this family, I really don't. And what about the fact that we have a new friend with us? Shouldn't we be making his introduction to this family a joy rather than a horror? Greg?"

"Yes Dad."

"How about us apologising to our new friend?"

The youth cringed.

"Greg?"

"Sorry," Greg murmured.

"Yeah, sorry," said Meredith, glancing across.

Even in the depths of his embarrassment, the youth felt it was nice of Meredith to have said that. She didn't have to. Only Greg was being pressed.

"There we are then," said Mrs. Blackett, sounding pleased and happy.

"Okay!" said Mr. Blackett, turning back to the wheel and starting off again. "Send those jubes round, O Merrie-daughter-of-mine, and don't forget dear old Dad!"

"I net gen anyink!" yelled the toddler.

It was wheat country, flat country. The youth leant against the door and watched the blaze of sunset at the horizon. He was still hoping what he'd been hoping ever since he got into the car: that he wasn't giving off a stink. He kept sniffing the air to see if he could detect anything, but you never can when it's yourself. He listened to every word of small talk, trying to tell from the tone of the voices whether they were gagging from his pong. He was trying so hard to keep himself clenched and contained that it was making it worse all the time. He told himself not to be over-sensitive, not to imagine things.

It was a relief when they arrived at the property and the youth was shown his quarters and left alone there. He was in a converted garage a stone's throw from the house. It was properly lined and clean and comfortable. There was a bed, a dressing-table and a wardrobe, but the one small bulb didn't light the room very well. That was a worry. The youth had his two special magazines, the ones with the photos of Sweetheart, and he wanted to be able to see them properly. If only he'd bought himself a bedside lamp, like he'd thought of doing when he was at Dunkeld.

To check the light he took out one of the magazines and looked at the cover. There she was, gazing out at him, but slightly dim. He began to feel furious, perhaps as a reaction to his misery in the car. Did they expect him to live in the pitch fucking dark, like a bat in a fucking cave? He began to swear under his breath. There was a knock at the door and the youth paused and then opened it.

"Everything alright?" Mr. Blackett asked.

"Yes," he replied.

"There's some food on," Mr. Blackett said.

The youth sat down with the family and Greg was asked to say grace. The toddler screamed "Me say gace!" over and over until he wearied of it. Mrs. Blackett told the youth it was only a rough-and-ready meal that night because of them having been to town, but to eat up because in their house it was "first in, best dressed." The youth was afraid Mr. Blackett had heard him swearing and felt very uncomfortable. Also the toddler was in a highchair right beside him, flicking bits of food. He felt a baked bean hit him on the neck and slide down inside his collar. The only good thing was that Meredith was busy making extra toast.

The talk at the table fizzled out and they ate in silence, except for the toddler. The youth was convinced now that Mr. Blackett had heard the swearing, that he was very disturbed by it and that his mood had dampened the others. Either that or the youth was stinking the place out. It was probably both. The silence got worse and the youth got more and more clenched, trying to close off the pong. He grew faint from the effort of staying in control and was afraid he'd fall off the chair.

Then some talk began. Greg mentioned school, and Meredith said how fed up she felt there. It seemed to be a well-worn topic. Mr. and Mrs. Blackett reminded Meredith about prospects and the importance of having some. Meredith groaned and rolled her eyes.

"Oh, not again, please."

"You don't want to be without prospects, do you?" asked Mr. Blackett.

"Okay then," Meredith snorted. "I'll have half-a-dozen in a brown paper bag, thank you. And a pound of sausages as well!"

"Punna sosses!" cried the toddler. "Punna sosses!"

They found this amusing and the mood lightened.

The youth was able to slip away from the table and escape outside.

NEXT MORNING there was a single place set for him in the kitchen. He sighed with relief.

"It's such chaos with us, breakfast time," said Mrs. Blackett. "I thought you might find it pleasanter to have yours in peace when we've finished."

While the youth ate his breakfast he could hear voices and bustle as Mrs. Blackett got Meredith and Greg into the car and drove off. She was taking them a couple of miles to a crossroads where the school bus would pick them up. From somewhere outside, the youth could hear Mr. Blackett talking to the toddler.

The youth finished his breakfast, rinsed the dishes at the sink and went outside. He looked at the flat land stretching all around. The sun was well up now and the last of the dew was drying in a slight wind.

Mr. Blackett and the toddler were nowhere in sight. Then Mr. Blackett appeared at the door of the big shed and called the youth over. The shed was full of tools and bits of machinery. Mr. Blackett had some kind of mechanism in pieces on the bench and was trying to do something with it with one hand while holding the toddler away from the bench with the other.

"Just fetch me that Phillips head screwdriver, will you," Mr. Blackett said. The youth didn't know what a Phillips head screwdriver was, but went to the shelf that Mr. Blackett pointed to and got the only screwdriver he could see there. He handed it across, and was told it was the wrong one. The youth went back to the shelf and looked again. He found another screwdriver and took it across. It was the wrong one again.

"Isn't the Phillips head there?" Mr. Blackett asked, puzzled. The youth started to mumble that he wasn't sure what a Phillips head was, but the toddler began to squirm and whine and Mr. Blackett got distracted. Then Mrs. Blackett arrived and took the toddler back to the house.

"Ah, peace at last," said Mr. Blackett. "Now we can get some work done."

The youth stood around, watching Mr. Blackett. He was asked to fetch this or that and mostly did not know what the item was, or what it looked like. He was asked to hold this or that in place while Mr. Blackett adjusted something or unscrewed something, and half the time he did not hold it properly or in the exact position. Everything Mr. Blackett was doing was a mystery. He did not grasp the process or the logic of any of it, and so could not understand which tool would be needed next, or which piece of metal would need to be held or adjusted. And the more he tried to concentrate the more confused and fragmented his thinking became. "Oh well, we all have to learn these things," Mr. Blackett said when the youth had confessed to not knowing what a ballpein hammer was. When Mrs. Blackett came in cheerfully at mid-morning with tea and scones on a tray, she asked how it was all going.

"Oh well, we'll get there eventually," Mr. Blackett replied. "With the Lord's help."

Mrs. Blackett's smile wavered when she registered her husband's tone of voice and she gave the youth a glance of reassurance, but the youth understood that he was already trying Mr. Blackett's patience.

That evening the youth sat at the family table with his eyes downcast and listened to the chatter. Meredith had had a bad day at school, she said, because another girl was spreading rumours about her. Meredith didn't say what the rumours were. The youth sat staring at his plate and wondering what kind of rumours could be attached to Meredith, and hoping she would say more about it. Mrs. Blackett told Meredith she should ignore the other girl's behaviour, or, better still, try to make friends with her. Meredith snorted at this. Then Mr.

Blackett gave a quote from the Bible about forgiveness, and Meredith snorted again. Mr. Blackett told her she was not to be unseemly at the Lord's table. The youth cast a quick glance at her face and saw that she was flushed and was biting her lip. Nothing more was said for a few moments, then Greg chimed in.

"She said you started it."

"What?"

"Carol Metcalf said you spread rumours about her first."

"She's a liar!"

"You are!"

The toddler began screaming. Mrs. Blackett stood up and tried to shush him, while Mr. Blackett was saying something to Greg about not tormenting his sister. The youth watched Meredith stalk out of the room and slam the door behind her. Mrs. Blackett got the toddler quietened and asked who wanted dessert.

A little later the youth went outside. The sky was cloudy, but there was a moon partly visible and a breeze blowing across the paddocks. He went past the woodheap to the door of his garage room. He saw a shadow move and made out Meredith standing a few paces further on, gazing out over the flat expanse. He went to go quickly into his room so as not to intrude on her, but she had turned and was looking at him, the moonlight on her face.

"Why did you come here?" she asked.

"Sorry?" he said.

"I wouldn't come here in a fit." She didn't sound hostile, just unhappy.

"I came for a job."

"You came from the city, didn't you?"

"Yes."

"I wish I could get to the city."

"What would you do there?"

"Be a hairdresser."

"Do you like hairdressing?"

"It's alright," said Meredith. "It's a living."

"Would you have to learn it?"

"Of course. You do an apprenticeship. My Aunt Patricia would take me on. She's got a salon in the city. She's told my parents that I can come down to her and learn hairdressing, and have a life in the city, but they keep saying I'm not ready to leave home yet."

"How old do you have to be to do hairdressing?"

"I'm fifteen. I could leave school now and start as soon as I like."

"I knew a girl who was a hairdresser," said the youth, feeling very daring. "Her name was Polly."

"Did you go out together?"

"Yeah. We sort of had a few dates and stuff."

Meredith did not reply and the youth began to wish he hadn't said anything about Polly. It was a bit too personal and also Meredith might be thinking he had made it up. The breeze strengthened and brought the sound of a creature bellowing from somewhere. The moon came out and lit everything up for a few moments. It embarrassed the youth to see Meredith so clearly and to have her see him. He began to mutter goodnight and to go into his room, but Meredith spoke.

"You could come to Con's, if you like."

"Sorry?"

"Con's place in town. It's a milk bar and cafe. There's a jukebox. I go there on Sunday morning while my family goes to church."

"Don't you go to church with them?"

"No."

"Why not?"

"I don't believe in it, that's all. We had a lot of big fights about it. Now my parents and I have an arrangement. I go to town with them on Sunday morning, but if I don't want to go to church I don't have to. So I mostly go to Con's."

"Ah," said the youth.

"You could come to Con's too, if you like."

"What happens there?" he asked.

"Nothing much. I play the jukebox a bit. Anyway, it's up to you."

"Thanks," he murmured.

"I'm going in," Meredith declared abruptly. "I'm getting cold." And without saying anything else, she went quickly past him and inside.

The youth stayed out there for a long time, gazing at the moon. He was thinking about what had just happened. He'd had a long private talk with a girl and she'd invited him some-where. He reflected on it from every angle he could imagine. Yes, that was what had happened. He'd been asked out by a girl! He was part of the great flow of life now. He could feel the vibrancy of it in his veins and in the air around him, in the earth and in the moon. He had this forever now, this fact of having stood in the moonlight talking to a lovely girl about life and everything, and it couldn't be taken away.

The longer the youth sat there, though, the colder and more remote the moon became and the emptier the night grew, and the glow of what had happened began to fade. He told himself what a paltry thing a brief bit of happiness is.

He went inside eventually and lay on the bed without undressing. He wondered how it would be if he gathered his things and left now, just walked away. Then he remembered that he had no money. He was trapped here at least until he got his first pay. He would stay quietly inside himself, he thought, and just go through the motions. He would not speak an unnecessary word or look anyone in the face. He would be beyond it all, like Diestl. Diestl! How could he have forgotten Diestl, even for an hour! It was Diestl who always got him through. The youth began to let go his grip on the quilt and to let his body sag on the bed. The bed was in a bombed-out house in a bombed-out village somewhere, and Diestl was just passing through and needed some shut-eye. The youth made the motion of settling the Schmeisser comfortably against his stomach where his hand could rest easily on it.

He began to picture the scene that often came to him: The Beautiful Girl Alone in the Village. This was not a scene from the movie, but one inspired by what the youth had learnt from Diestl's journey. The scene could vary in its details but was always the same basic situation. The girl has been hiding somewhere like a bombed-out cellar and comes to Diestl in her loneliness and fear. The two of them lie side by side for a few hours. Then Diestl gets up before dawn and leaves the village and the girl forever. The scene was painful and yet consoling. It said that there was no turning from the path that the Diestls of this world must walk. But it also said that now and then, when you least expect it, there might be a moment of sweetness and consolation. The price of that occasional sweet moment, though, was that you never try to prolong it or make more of it than it really is. If you try to prolong it, or enlarge on it, you are breaking the agreement you have with life—and life will punish you by not letting the odd sweet moment happen anymore. It was quite simple and fair, the youth thought.

MR. BLACKETT wanted to attend to an irrigation pump that was giving trouble. There was no school that day and Greg was home.

"Get the Clanger, son," said Mr. Blackett. Greg ran off to a shed and there was a sound of an engine starting and he drove out in an old stripped-down car. It had no roof or doors or windscreen and there were rust holes along the sides. Mr. Blackett slung a toolbox in the back and got in beside the boy. The youth squeezed in beside him. They sped off across the paddocks, the wind in their faces. The youth soon understood why they called the car the Clanger. Whenever the gears were changed, there was a loud metallic clang. But it didn't seem to have any bad effect on the way the car ran. Greg was a good driver, the youth thought, although he had to sit on the very edge of the seat to reach the pedals. They came to a big artificial ditch with a pipe running along it and some kind of pump half-submerged in water. They got out of the Clanger and Mr. Blackett began to take off his boots and socks. He rolled his trouser legs up.

"I'll come in with you, Dad," Greg said, starting to remove his shoes.

"That's alright, son," Mr. Blackett replied. "I've got my *paid* off-sider here." He gave the youth a look. After a moment, the youth realised he was supposed to go into the water. He took his shoes and socks off and rolled his trouser legs up too. Mr. Blackett got his toolbox out of the Clanger and waded across to the pump. The youth followed gingerly. The water was cold and there was a current that made it swirl around his knees. But it was the feel of the bottom that worried him. It was soft, squelchy mud. He wondered what creepy-crawlies might live in mud like that. Mr. Blackett asked the youth to hold the tool-box for him. It was heavy and the youth's arms began to ache with the strain of it almost at once. He tried bracing it against his thigh and that wasn't so bad except it meant that he had to stand twisted at an awkward angle.

"Dash it!" said Mr. Blackett. "I've left the multi-grips back in the shed."

"I'll get them, Dad," cried Greg. He had the Clanger started and was off in a moment. They watched the car going away. It hit a bump and they saw Greg bounce up out of the seat and then heard loud revving as he shoved his foot back on the pedal when he came down.

"That boy is what you call a real live-wire," said Mr. Blackett. "Don't you agree?"

"Yes," said the youth politely.

"It makes you wonder what work the Lord has in store for him." Mr. Blackett took a spanner from the box and began loosening a nut on the pump. "Do you ever wonder what work the Lord might have in store for *you*?" he asked.

The youth said nothing.

"I think the Lord would be concerned about you at the moment."

The weight of the toolbox and the twisted way the youth was standing were starting to become unbearable.

"Do you know why?" asked Mr. Blackett.

"Sorry?"

"Do you know why the Lord would be concerned about you?"

"No," said the youth. He wanted to adjust his stance, but was afraid of losing his footing in the mud.

"I'll tell you, shall I?"

"Alright," said the youth.

"Because you seem to be at a loss. You've seemed that way the whole time you've been with us."

The youth tried to reposition his feet carefully in the mud.

"Do you feel that yourself?" asked Mr. Blackett, who had stopped using the spanner and was examining him.

"I suppose so," said the youth.

"You suppose *what*?"

"What you just said."

"What *did* I just say?"

The youth felt insulted. Did this man think he was too stupid to know what was being said to him? Just because a person doesn't like to get into private issues, and tries not to respond when someone else starts getting personal, that doesn't mean they're too dumb to understand. He looked Mr. Blackett in the eye and spoke very clearly.

"You said that the Lord might be concerned about me

because I seemed to be at a loss, and that I've given that impression the whole time that I've been here."

Mr. Blackett seemed taken aback. He began using the spanner again and then they heard the Clanger returning. Meredith was at the wheel. She alighted and came to the edge of the water with a pair of multi-grips. She had on shorts and a T-shirt and her legs and feet were bare. She waded across to them and dropped the multi-grips into the open toolbox. The jolt of it nearly made the youth lose his grip. He just managed to regain hold of it before it could tip sideways and the tools spill out.

"My fault," said Meredith, quickly bending to help him.

Between them, they got the box back up to waist height. Meredith's hand was clamped over his underneath the box and her shoulder and bare arm were pressed against him.

"Whoa there," said Mr. Blackett. "That was a close one. Have you got it?"

"Yes," said the youth. "But I need to put it down for a sec."

He and Meredith waded side by side to the bank and put the toolbox down. The youth didn't know whether to be relieved at having the weight of it off his muscles at last, or bereft at Meredith taking her hand and arm away. She watched him rubbing his thigh.

"Did I make you sprain something?" she asked.

The youth shook his head.

"What happened to your brother?" Mr. Blackett asked Meredith.

"Mum needed him," she answered. There was something abrupt in her tone.

"Oh well, not to worry," said Mr. Blackett. "We can work you just as hard." He gave a hearty laugh as though trying to smooth away her abruptness. But Meredith didn't smile or bother to glance in his direction. Instead she continued to look at the youth.

"Sure you're okay?"

"Yes," he replied. "I'll just give the multi-grips to your dad."

He bent to the toolbox but Meredith pushed his hand aside, picked the multi-grips up, waded briskly in and across and handed them over, then turned and splashed her way back.

"Thanks," said Mr. Blackett, turning to the pump with a troubled expression and tinkering with it again.

"Come for a walk," Meredith said to the youth.

"Can't," he replied. "I'm supposed to be working."

She took him by the elbow and pulled him forward.

"We're going for a walk," she called to Mr. Blackett as they went away along the bank. The youth walked carefully because of his bare feet and being worried about creepy-crawlies on the ground.

"Oh, okay, sweetie," said Mr. Blackett.

There were some beautiful trees growing alongside the irrigation ditch. They were thin and tall and upright, but very green, and they rustled in the breeze and the light glinted off their leaves. Meredith said they were poplars that her grandparents had planted.

"Your whole family tradition is here then?"

"Yes."

"Does it feel nice, to know you belong so much in a place?"

"It does, sometimes."

"And yet you want to get away."

"I'm not asking for a voyage to the moon. Just to go to the city and be a hairdresser. I mean, I'd be coming back for holidays. It isn't such an extreme demand, is it?"

The youth shook his head.

"To hear my parents talk, you'd think I was asking to go and be a whore in the streets of Babylon!"

The youth was embarrassed by the word "whore." For a long time, he'd believed that a whore was a whale or a porpoise or something like that. He'd read a story about the old sailing days and one of the characters had said that something was "whiter than a whore's belly." The youth had got a picture in his mind of some kind of sea creature swimming beside the ship and turning over and showing a pale underside. But later he'd seen the word in other places and knew it didn't mean any sort of sea creature. He wanted to ask Meredith exactly what it did mean, but he could hardly speak for the constricted feeling in his throat. Meredith had got a pace ahead of him as they walked and he couldn't take his eyes off her bare legs and her bottom and her straight back and shoulders and the back of her neck. She had a lovely strong way of walking. The youth was having to hurry to keep up.

"That's enough," she said, halting so suddenly that he almost ran into her. "We can go back now."

"Can we stop for a minute?" he asked. "My feet are hurting."

"Let's sit up there," Meredith said, pointing to a rise with a giant tree-stump on it. The youth was fearful of the long grass they had to wade through, but Meredith strode ahead.

From the rise you looked down on a broad sweep of wheat-fields going away to low hills in the distance. Behind where they sat were the irrigation ditch and the line of poplars. The fresh breeze rippled the grass all around.

"How old are you?" Meredith asked.

"Fourteen," he replied. "Why?"

"Just wondered," she said. "Have you got any sisters?"

"No."

"I didn't think so. You haven't mixed with girls much, have you?"

"Not all that much."

"Except your hairdresser friend; Milly, was it?"

"Polly. It wasn't anything really."

"Do you mean you made her up and there wasn't any Polly?"

"No, there was a Polly."

"Okay, I believe you, even if you are a dud."

"A what?"

"A dud. Dad said to Mum that you're a dud and they'll probably have to let you go." She put her hand on his shoulder. "I probably shouldn't have told you that."

"It's alright."

"If it's any consolation, they think I'm a dud of a daughter. So we're duds together."

"I don't think you're a dud."

"I don't think you are either."

"I suppose I should get back. Your dad'll be getting angry."

"No, he won't. He's in his humble phase at the moment. That's when he's regarding me as a heavy burden put on him by the Lord and he thinks he should be long-suffering about it. I took you away so he won't go crook at you. Anyway, what does it matter? He reckons you're a dead loss in any case."

They stayed up on the rise watching the grass rippling and the clouds going across the sky. Meredith lay back on the stump with her hands under her head and closed her eyes. The youth did the same.

They were side by side like that when Mr. Blackett came up behind them, clearing his throat.

"Ah, there you are. I was starting to think you'd run off."

"No such luck," murmured Meredith without opening her eyes.

MR. BLACKETT was working a lot in the machine shed, fiddling with the dismantled irrigation pump and other things. The youth hovered around trying to look useful, but knowing he wasn't being any real help.

Mr. Blackett tried to get him to talk about Meredith and the youth responded as politely as he could without saying anything.

"You and Meredith get on pretty well."

"I suppose so."

"The two of you find a lot to talk about?"

"Not all that much."

"She confides in you, I dare say?"

"Not really."

"She's the apple of our eye, you know, that girl."

"Mmmm."

Then Mr. Blackett would look sort of mournful as though he was on the verge of saying something else but thought better of it. Ever since Meredith had told him about being a dud, the youth had been expecting the sack to come at any time.

"It's obvious that you have no interest in this work, and no aptitude for it," said Mr. Blackett after he had raised the subject of Meredith again and the youth had answered in the usual way. The youth assumed this was the sack about to happen. But Mr. Blackett went on.

"Well, not everyone is mechanically minded. What sort of work do you like? What were you mostly doing at the last place?"

The youth told him about chopping the tussock.

"Ah well, you could do much the same thing here. We don't have serrated tussock. The noxious weed in these parts is Paxton's Pea. If you like you can start cutting it tomorrow, going along the fence lines and other places where we can't plough it out. That would be a useful job. It does need seeing to."

NEXT MORNING the youth equipped himself with a hoe and went off along the fence line. He felt as though he'd been let out of prison. It was a cool and windy day, just what he liked best, and the knowledge that he'd be left to himself for hours was like a tonic.

Paxton's Pea was a prickly weed with small purple flowers. It grew in clusters of stalks that came up to waist height and the first dense patch of it was about half a mile from the homestead paddock. Paxton's Pea could give you a nasty scratch. You had to wield the hoe from slightly side on and try to chop under the base of the cluster without brushing your hands against the prickles. After a quarter of an hour the youth had the hang of it and there was a swathe of chopped green and purple on the ground. But the backs of his hands were scratched and bleeding. He didn't mind. "First blood," he said aloud. "First blood in the battle."

He felt more cheerful than at any time since he had come to the Blacketts'. It was so good knowing what your work was, knowing that you had a talent for it, and being left alone to do it at your own pace, thinking your own thoughts and being able to speak those thoughts out loud to yourself when you wanted to hear what they sounded like.

A lot of the thoughts were about Meredith. He imagined talking love talk with her. He didn't exactly know what love talk was, but he supposed it was like in movies when the two people tell each other things like, "I can't live without you" or "I'd die if you went away." The youth murmured these things to himself and they sounded about right.

These thoughts about Meredith led to other thoughts. Thinking about Meredith's unhappiness, the way she was trapped by circumstances, made him think of King Harold and his people trapped in their time and being so brave, almost winning through in spite of the odds and only going down in the end. That was the thing about Meredith, the youth realised. She was brave. You could sense that in the way she looked you in the eye without wavering, and in the strong way she walked, and the firm way she spoke. He imagined himself and Meredith as two of King Harold's people, a house-carl and a shield-maiden. They had survived Hastings and escaped to the forest. They would be outlaws in the greenwood and harry the Normans. They'd be dressed like Robin Hood, and have lots of snug hideaways, and sleep in each other's arms with the rustle of leaves around them. Other loyal people would join them, and they would love and defend each other to the very end. The youth thought again about the love talk. It didn't seem so appropriate now. It was a bit soppy.

No, they would not say things like that to each other, or perhaps would only say such things now and then. Mostly they would talk like fellow warriors, planning their raids or tending each other's slight wounds. They would cling together in desperate relief after every action. The danger of their lives would make every minute together sheer joy. But then he thought of Meredith really getting hurt, getting slashed with swords or hit with battle-axes, and it was too distressing. No, she wouldn't do that sort of fighting. She would be a brilliant archer and pick off Normans at a distance. And she would have deep knowledge of herbs and potions, and about the phases of the moon, and about ways of setting spies to find out the enemy's doings. That's the kind of warrior she would be—graceful and smart and able to avoid getting any hurt worse than a scratch. And there would be lots of times when there wouldn't be any action. They would have their life in their favourite forest glade, with fruit to eat and the music of lutes or harps and a twinkling campfire to sit at with their companions, laughing and cuddling and being happy together.

The youth cut Paxton's Pea every day. It left him exhausted by the evening, but it was a good exhaustion, especially the feeling of being daydreamed out, of having imagined his way through everything that had occurred to him. In the evening after the meal, he would go straight back to his garage room and turn the radio on to the hit parade and sit outside and watch the evening sky with its huge play of colours and cloud patterns. Most evenings Meredith came out and sat there too. They listened to the music and watched the sky and did not say anything much. A couple of times Greg tried to join them, but Meredith told him to get lost. The first time he tried to argue, but Meredith got more hostile and said she'd beat him to a pulp if he didn't piss off. Mrs. Blackett put her head out the door to ask Meredith if anything was the matter. Meredith called back sharply that nothing was the matter except that a person wasn't allowed to have a minute's peace around here. Mr. Blackett came out a bit later to go to the shed for something. He looked across at them and made a gesture as though to say, sorry to intrude, and he hurried back inside as soon as he came out of the shed.

"They think we're having a deep and meaningful talk," Meredith said. "So they're tiptoeing around to show me how understanding they are."

"We can have a deep and meaningful talk if you want to," said the youth.

"Christ no!" Meredith retorted.

"That's okay," said the youth. He'd been wondering whether to tell her of his vision of the two of them in the forest, dressed in green and harrying the Normans. He was relieved that she'd answered in such a definite way. It was a risky thing, telling your daydreams to someone, especially someone who was in them.

"I shouldn't do that," said Meredith after a moment.

"Do what?"

"Make the Lord's name a profanation."

"What's a profanation?"

"A swear word. I disagree with a lot of what my parents believe—well, *most* of it, actually—but I don't believe in insulting the Lord. *Their* Lord, I mean."

"No," he agreed. "It's probably best not to."

"But Christ!" she snorted. "The way they behave! The way they control me all the time! You see it, don't you?"

"Them controlling you?"

"Yes."

"Not all that much. But then I'm not sure what to look out for."

She was taken aback. "They do it in their own special way," she explained. "Or they get other people to do it. Like Pastor Eccles."

"Who's he?"

"The church pastor, in town. They used to get him to give me little talks for spiritual guidance. It was so awful. This little buck-toothed man, you wouldn't believe how buck-toothed he is. It's like being talked to by a big rabbit or beaver or something. He won't speak to me now."

"Why not?"

"He asked one day where I would seek succour when the Lord's face was turned from me. I said I'd ask Beelzebub. I shouldn't have said it, but I was really angry."

"No-one is religious in my family," said the youth.

"That's why you keep so calm. You aren't being hounded all the time about the state of your soul and whether you'll be ready to go before the Throne of Judgement at the drop of a hat."

The youth felt amazed by the bit about him being calm.

"Do I seem calm?"

"Yes, incredibly," said Meredith. "That's why you have a beneficial effect on me, I suppose."

The youth couldn't speak for a minute or two. He felt so full of amazement and gratitude. No-one had ever told him before that he was beneficial.

"How do I seem calm?" he asked after a while.

"Oh, I don't know, you just do," Meredith said. A song she liked had just come on the radio and she started singing along with it. It was called "Honey Bunny." The youth hadn't especially liked it before, but Meredith's liking it made it seem the finest song in the world. She looked across at him in the last of the sunset light.

"It's as though you're always thinking of something else, something really big and interesting, and so you're not bothered too much by what's happening around you. As my father said, 'One never has his full attention.'"

"He said that?"

"His exact quote. Except that it isn't completely right, is it?"

"Isn't it?"

"I don't think so, because I think I have your full attention sometimes."

The youth stared past her.

"Isn't that true?"

The youth said nothing.

"I know you like looking at me when you think I don't know."

The youth kept staring past her.

"You don't have to admit it if you don't want to," she said. "I know how much you keep your feelings to yourself. I don't mind you being keen on me. I mean, assuming you are. We're the wrong ages for each other, of course. You'd need to be older, but if we were the right ages we might have got together. I mean, if it turned out that way and neither of us was tangled up with someone else."

The youth said nothing. He was so full of feelings that he could hardly breathe. After a while Meredith got up to go inside. As she went past him she touched him lightly on the arm.

"It's alright," she said softly. "Don't get anxious about it."

"I'm famous for being calm," said the youth. "Haven't you heard?"

HAVING SOMEONE in your life made springtime happen. That was the phrase that came to mind. Meredith made springtime happen, the way Romeo and Juliet must have done for each other. Meredith had studied *Romeo and Juliet* at school and gave the youth an outline of it. She liked it because it showed the star-crossed lovers refusing to be controlled by their parents. The youth wanted to find out more about the idea of being "star-crossed." It had struck him deeply when Meredith remarked, "I think we're all star-crossed in some way." It made sense of a lot of things.

Each Sunday morning the Blacketts had asked him whether he'd like to go to town with them, but he hadn't taken up the offer. He was nervous about Meredith's invitation to Con's cafe. It was one thing to be with her on the property, but another thing in town. There might be other people at Con's— friends of hers, people she knew from school. Then again, Meredith had only mentioned Con's that one time and the youth wondered if she had changed her mind. It could all be horribly embarrassing, either way. He wished he could go to town by himself and quietly reconnoitre, the way Diestl would. The youth hadn't thought about Diestl for a while. The thing with Meredith had replaced Diestl for him, at least on the property.

The next Sunday he accepted the offer to go to town. It was very quiet in the car. The youth was on the far side of the back seat from Meredith, with Greg and the toddler between them. She stared out the window and did not speak. They got to town and slowed at a corner.

"Will this do you, sweetie?" Mr. Blackett asked Meredith. Meredith nodded yes and got out. The youth assumed she was going to spend the church time at Con's. He looked at her for a sign that he should come too, but there was none.

"Bye, darling," said Mrs. Blackett. "See you in a while."

Mr. Blackett was looking at the youth in the rear-view mirror, as if to see whether he intended to go with Meredith, but Meredith was already walking away. They drove along the street and came to a church with groups of people out the front. They parked and got out of the car. The youth didn't know what he was supposed to do. It must have shown on his face.

"Would you like to come and worship with us?" Mrs. Black-ett asked. "You'd be very welcome."

The youth mumbled that he felt like a stroll and would see them later. He walked quickly off in no particular direction. He looked back and saw them turning the corner to where the church was and greeting another family that was heading that way. He didn't know how long the church thing took and what time he should come back. He half-thought to return and ask them but didn't want to face them again just now.

The streets of the town were very quiet. The railway tracks ran past nearby. He reckoned the station was along to the right and he knew the main street was near the station. He began to notice things and think about them, the way he did. He came to some old stone buildings with narrow doors. He paused in front of one and looked at the details of the windowsills and the doorknobs, and the marks on the woodwork. He reflected on all the people who must have gone in and out over the hun-dred years or so that the building had been there. There was a folk song about this town. The youth had heard it sung. It told how a bushranger was shot on the outskirts. He had been on his way to visit his sweetheart, who was the shanty-keeper's daughter, but a jealous rival had tipped off the troopers and they laid an ambush. The song said the bushranger had stood his ground, returning fire, but had been riddled with a hun-dred bullets. There was more to the song but the bit about the hundred bullets had stayed in the youth's mind. He felt tears welling up. How sad everything was. As the tears ran down his face, he thought of all those across the ages who'd gone down under the weight of their enemies, but whose memory lived on. *In our tears*, thought the youth. *They live on in our tears.* It seemed a tremendous insight. Yes, the heroes live in the deep moments of our tears. He walked on, hardly seeing where he was going. He could have walked for hours, the way he often did when his heart was full.

There was a horse in a vacant lot and the youth stopped and the horse ambled over to him and he patted it across the fence. It was a pale creamy colour, with a long flowing mane. He could see into the depth of its eyes, and he felt that the horse understood what he was feeling. The Bushranger's horse might have been just like this one, or even King Harold's horse. There was something regal about it, and dignified. A horse that understood the gravity of things. The youth thought of the thousands of years that horses and people had been together. Maybe horses had a folklore of their own, and knew about events in the past, but from the horse's point of view. Maybe the horses' history was full of its own heroes—like Traveller. Traveller was Robert E. Lee's horse, and had carried him through the Civil War, with the South always outnumbered and outgunned yet returning blow for blow as it slowly went down. There was a photo of Lee mounted on Traveller in the final days, and the pity of it all is as much in the horse as the rider, the way the horse is standing, full of fortitude in spite of all being lost.

The youth gazed into the horse's eyes and they became more lustrous, as though there were tears in them. The horse heroes live in the tears just as the human ones do, thought the youth.

He heard his name being called. He thought at first that it was a voice inside him, but then he turned and saw a car at the kerb and Meredith looking at him from the passenger-side window. There was a young man at the wheel.

"Are you alright?" asked Meredith.

The youth nodded.

"Are you sure? You look upset."

"No," said the youth, wiping his eyes with his sleeve. "I got dust in my eyes and they're sore."

Meredith kept looking at him as though she didn't believe what he said and wanted to ask him more about it. But the young man in the car said something to hurry her.

"Listen," she said. "Could you do something for me? Would you tell my parents I've gone to Auntie Pat's place in the city, that I'll get in touch with them tomorrow, and that there's no need to worry. Can you tell them that?"

"Yes," said the youth. "If you want me to." He had stopped feeling emotional and the wetness on his face was drying. "But shouldn't you tell them yourself?"

"No," she replied. "I have to just go and then talk to them about it afterwards. It's the only way I'll be able to get out of here. I have to get away from everything here. I'll go mad otherwise."

"I'll tell them, then," said the youth.

"Thanks for everything," said Meredith.

"I didn't do anything."

"Yes you did. It made things a bit better, having you around lately." The young man in the car said something again. Meredith waved her hand to the youth and the car pulled away. She called back: "I'll probably see you when I come back for holidays."

Then they were gone around a corner.

"Well, what do you think of that?" the youth said, turning again to the horse. The horse looked gravely back at him.

CON'S CAFE was in the main street. It had a milk bar on one side with a cafe section with tables and chairs on the other. There was a jukebox. The youth looked at the list of songs it could play and saw that "Honey Bunny" was there. He would have liked to play it, but he didn't know how to, and anyway it was quiet in Con's and the youth didn't want to be the one who broke the stillness. He ordered a milkshake and sat at one of the tables and imagined being there with Meredith.

The youth got a knot in his stomach when he remembered he had to pass on Meredith's message. He wished he hadn't agreed to it. It was always like this, he thought to himself. You take on the idea of something, just as an idea, then you're stuck with it in the real world. He tried to rehearse exactly what to say. If he had it all prepared he might be able to just blurt it out in one go. Then he would have done what he'd agreed to do. After that, it wasn't his problem. He was just a messenger.

"We thought we'd find you here," Mr. Blackett said when he came in. "Ready to roll?"

The youth nodded.

"Where's Merry?" Mr. Blackett asked, glancing around.

"She went," mumbled the youth, making a gesture of departure with his hand. Mr. Blackett seemed to think he meant that she'd gone to the loo.

"No hurry," he said, and went across to the counter and bought a packet of jubes. "We'll see you outside."

Greg was hanging around the jukebox. When his father had gone, he searched his pockets for a coin to put in.

The youth went out and found Mrs. Blackett changing the toddler's nappy on the hood of the car and Mr. Blackett across the street talking to someone. Mrs. Blackett finished changing the nappy and put the toddler into the back seat. She smiled at the youth. There came a blare of music from inside. Greg had found his coin. The song wasn't "Honey Bunny" though. What a pity, thought the youth. Mrs. Blackett asked him if he'd keep an eye on the toddler while she went in to fetch Meredith.

"She's gone," said the youth. "She left a message for me to give you."

Mrs. Blackett's face twisted.

"Tell me," she said.

So the youth told her the message. She called out to Mr. Blackett and he came over the road. The youth repeated the message.

"I'll wring that girl's neck!" Mr. Blackett cried. "Lord help me!"

"No," said Mrs. Blackett, taking him by the arm. "It isn't so bad. She said she's going to Pat's. She'd have no reason to say that if she didn't mean it."

"But who is she with *now*?" he snapped. "That's the immediate issue."

"Oh Lord," groaned Mrs. Blackett.

Mr. Blackett told the youth to describe the young man and the car. He said how it was a red sedan with a big rubber spider stuck to the back window.

"That's Ken Cunningham!" cried Greg, who'd joined them. "He only got the spider the other day."

"Ken's alright," said Mrs. Blackett. "If she's with Ken, and she goes to Pat's place, then it isn't as serious as it could've been."

"I'm still going to wring her thoughtless neck!" said Mr. Blackett. "Did you know she was planning to do this?" he demanded of the youth.

The youth said he'd known nothing. He was beginning to feel offended by the ugly looks he was getting.

The man Mr. Blackett had been talking to came across and asked what was wrong, and they fobbed him off as best they could. Then the toddler began bawling. The Blacketts decided to go to Pastor Eccles's place. They could phone the city from there and alert Auntie Pat. And phone the Cunninghams. And get the pastor's advice about it all.

Pastor Eccles's place was an old weatherboard house next to the church. When they pulled up at the kerb Pastor Eccles was talking to a couple of people out the front. Even from a distance the youth could see that his buck-teeth made him look like a big rabbit or beaver or something, just as Meredith had said. The Blacketts went up and spoke to him and after a minute the youth heard him saying, "Yes, you must make your calls. That's the first thing." He ushered them into the house, together with the people he'd been with before. Then he turned back and introduced himself to the youth and asked him to repeat Meredith's message again. He listened carefully. Then he invited the youth in for a cup of tea or a soft drink, and to join them in prayer.

"Have you given your life to the Lord Jesus?" he asked in such a straightforward way that the youth was touched.

"Um, not really," he replied.

"What do you mean when you say 'not really'?"

"I mean I'm not religious."

"Ah well, neither am I, for that matter. Religion isn't the issue. The issue is Jesus. But look, I think I'd best go in."

The youth said he'd prefer to stay outside for a while because Mr. Blackett was angry with him, as though what had happened was his fault.

"I'll have a word with him," said the pastor. He put his hand on the youth's shoulder and looked into his eyes. "You seem a decent young chap to me. But even if you are deep-dyed in iniquity, the Lord loves you still. That is the rock upon which all stands."

He went inside and the youth stood with tears welling in his eyes. The way the pastor had spoken about the Lord loving him had been so simple and sincere, like someone pointing out that two and two make four. At first it seemed a bit comical, having this big rabbit or beaver talking to you, but you quickly forgot the buck-teeth and began to be grateful for the kindliness. And yet Meredith hadn't got on with him at all. How odd.

Greg was sent out with a mug of tea and a biscuit. He said they'd phoned Auntie Pat and she was to ring them back the minute Meredith showed up. It was about four hours' drive. The Cunninghams had confirmed that Ken had left to drive to the city that day. They were upset that the Blacketts were upset, but were sure Ken had taken Meredith in good faith, and would look after her. The Cunninghams were on their way over.

The youth wandered around the building. Through one of the windows he saw the Blacketts and the others kneeling with heads bowed in prayer. He went quickly past and then meandered along the street.

He came to an old stone church with a graveyard beside it. The youth went in through a rusty gate that was half off its hinges and walked aimlessly among the gravestones. The inscriptions were faded and hard to read but they all appeared to date from about a hundred years ago. He remembered the Bushranger in the song, riddled with a hundred bullets. The people buried here might've known that Bushranger, might've been the very people the song told of—the shanty-keeper's fair daughter, the jealous rival, the troopers who set the ambush and let loose the hail of deadly shots. The youth felt tears welling up again. He went and stood on tiptoe and peered through a window into the old church. It was empty and bare, the pews gone. He stared into the space that had heard so many hymns and prayers, so many marriage and funeral services, the space to which so many people must have brought their hopes and fears and disappointments.

The day was turning overcast and windy. The youth shivered and buttoned his jacket tighter. He moved to a sheltered corner of the wall. The stone still held some of the sun's warmth, so he set his back against it. After a while he sat down and put his arms across his knees and rested his head on them. It was cosy there, hearing the wind among the gravestones and round the church walls. He thought of Meredith. Then he thought of how Diestl would force a way into this musty old shell of a building and use it to get some shut-eye. And then he thought about the shanty-keeper's fair daughter lying low in the churchyard, and the jealous rival whose passion was long spent, and the troopers whose writ no longer ran. Then he thought about the Lord who loved even those deep-dyed in iniquity . . .

Greg found him there a long while later, half-asleep.

They'd had a call. Meredith was at Auntie Pat's and perfectly okay.


THE YOUTH sat at Pastor Eccles's kitchen table. The Blacketts had gone and the pastor was on the phone to the local motel arranging a room for him that night. The motel owners were members of his flock and there'd be no charge.

They often put people up gratis for one reason or another, the pastor said. In the morning he would drive the youth back to the Blacketts' property to collect his belongings and then deliver him to the railway station in time for the train to the city.

"I'm afraid Mr. Blackett is adamant that you be let go," the pastor had explained. "I discussed the matter with him to the extent I could. But in the end, of course, he is answerable to the Lord for the wellbeing of his own household, and that responsibility is heavy on him just now."

"It's alright," the youth said. "I wasn't a very good employee."

"You know you are welcome to use the phone if there's anyone you want to call. Parents? Family? Is there anyone it'd be helpful for you to speak to?"

"Not really," the youth replied.

Pastor Eccles looked at him sadly. He had to get ready for the evening church service now, he said, but they'd have a chance to talk in the morning.

The youth had a few minutes to browse through the bookshelves in the pastor's loungeroom. There were lots of books about archaeology and others on history. The youth's eye fell on a title: *Year of Decision*. It was about 1066. It was old and battered, but it looked very readable and had lots of illustrations. He was leafing through it eagerly when Pastor Eccles came in.

"You have an interest in that?"

The youth said he did.

"Keep it, then, with my compliments."

The youth could hardly believe his luck.

The motel was only a minute's drive. Pastor Eccles dropped the youth off, saying he'd be back around nine in the morning.

The youth had a snug night, propped up in bed reading *Year of Decision*, then sleeping soundly.

On the way out to the Blackett property Pastor Eccles told him how he'd studied to be an archaeologist. Fresh out of uni, he'd been offered the chance to go on a dig in Persia. A week before he was due to leave he found the Lord and resigned from the trip. He'd never regretted his uni studies though.

"What I learnt from archaeology was that life is about layers, layers of love, grief, trust, conflict, creation, experience. You need a good eye for surfaces, but the *spadework* tells the story."

They reached the Blacketts and the youth fetched his belongings from the garage room while Pastor Eccles went into the house. He came out and handed the youth an envelope and some wrapped sandwiches.

"The Blacketts aren't here," he said. "They left first thing this morning for the city. They're anxious to get firm arrangements in place for Meredith. I gather she'll be working in her auntie's hairdressing salon. The envelope is the money owing to you, and the sandwiches are to have on the train. The Blacketts wish you well and that the Lord will keep you."

On the way back to town Pastor Eccles wanted to hear of the youth's life and background. He had a way of asking questions, of probing from different angles, so that you ended up telling him what he wanted to know. The youth supposed that was the "spadework" learnt from archaeology. So he told about them escaping from Vladimir, and then a bit about Dunkeld and being adrift in the city. He knew it all sounded pretty negative. Of course he couldn't speak of the support Diestl gave him, or of how Grace Kelly made his life worth living.

When they got to the railway station they saw the train already pulling in. They had to hurry. Pastor Eccles handed the youth a piece of paper and said it was a note of introduction to something called the Alison Street Mission.

"Do call in there and say hello," he urged.

"I will," said the youth as he stepped into the train.

"May the Lord bless you," Pastor Eccles said, shaking his hand.

"Same to you," replied the youth.

As the train pulled away the youth thought again how much like a big rabbit or beaver he looked, standing there on the platform, waving.

## 6. The Pleasures of India

The Astro Private Hotel could be scary at night. Drunken men staggered and swore in the corridors and there were scuffles and yells. On the youth's second night there someone banged on his door in the wee small hours and bellowed, "Open up, ya fuckin' cunt! I'll punch ya fuckin' head in!" The youth leapt up and stood big-eyed in the dark, trying to make sense of it. Had he offended someone in some way? He thought it must be a mistake and that they had the wrong room. He called out, "This is room eleven," but his voice was faint with fear and anyhow the banging and bellowing drowned it out. He wondered how strongly built the door was. Then a voice called from another room for the man to shut the hell up and that people were trying to sleep. This increased the man's rage and he went along the corridor hammering on doors and shouting for the dirty fuckin' bastard to come out and say it to his face. The youth imagined that in each room there was someone standing in the dark like himself, hoping for this to stop. After a while the angry man went away, still bellowing threats. What frightened the youth most was that the man had sounded cold sober.

The youth might've left the Astro after that second night except that he'd paid a month's rent in advance and had very little money left. He'd paid the month because he'd been scared of being homeless in the street again. With a roof over his head he could focus on finding a job.

He was determined to smarten his ideas up. No more daydreaming. No more being a dud like Mr. Blackett had called him. He would be keen, and on the ball. The phrase "being on the ball" had struck him. Life was like a football game, he thought, and a football game is all about the ball—where it is, who has it, what's being done with it. If you are a football player you don't stop and daydream. You stay focused. The youth had never taken any notice of football, but now he believed it held a deep truth about life. He told himself he would start going to football matches to soak up the spirit of it. He'd go and watch Ronnie Robson, the greatest player of all time. There were always articles in the paper about Ronnie and the youth had taken to reading up on him.

Each morning he left the Astro and walked up the busy street to the big intersection called Telford Square. As he walked he would try to throw off the sense of the night's darkness and squalor and fear. He'd breathe deeply, and flex his limbs, and imagine his system taking in the day's pure energy. He'd imagine himself getting taller and tougher and incredibly fit, like a champion footballer who's ready to give a hundred and ten per cent and then some. He had heard a radio commentator say that about Ronnie Robson. "Ya can't bank on much in life," the commentator had declared, "but ya can bank on this: Ronnie Robson will give a hundred and ten per cent and then some!" And the co-commentator had agreed: "Ya never said a truer word, Bill! And by gee, ain't he tuned like a Swiss watch!" The youth tried to imagine how it felt to be Ronnie Robson, fit and focused and tuned like a Swiss watch.

So he would arrive at Telford Square and buy a paper at the newsstand on the corner, deepening his voice and making a point of calling the vendor "mate." He would slap the folded paper under his arm and stride away like a man with a hundred and ten per cent to give.

But it never lasted.

Devon Street, the main street that ran through Telford Square, was always full of traffic and people. There was always the Oncoming Look on the footpath. At first, while he still felt slightly tall and tough and tuned, he was able to keep up a confident return gaze and a half-grin of friendliness. But after a minute it got too hard and he would lower his eyes and hunch his shoulders. After another minute he'd feel so exhausted by the eyes and bodies and movements of other people that he needed to get out of the crowd.

He had found a coffee shop called Don & Di's along Devon Street. It was poky and not very clean, but the youth liked it because there were never many people in there and it had potted plants. The potted plants meant you could sit at one of the little tables and be half-hidden by some tall ferny thing, yet have a good view of the street through the window and enough light to read the job ads in the paper. The man behind the counter was always unshaven and there was always the same waitress wearing the same grubby apron. The youth figured they were Don and Di. Both had distant manners and ignored the customers when they weren't actually serving them, so the youth felt fairly relaxed. After the first few times Don and Di had got used to him and Di would silently bring him a coffee without anything being said. He would spread the paper on the little table and start circling ads in the "Juniors Wanted" columns. He would circle half-a-dozen or so, then sit looking out at the street, feeling how good it was to be safe and hidden behind the potted fern. But then after a while he would start to feel he'd probably stayed too long and that Don and Di must be getting fed up with him occupying a table and only buying the one coffee. Sometimes he'd order another coffee just to show he was a proper customer and not abusing their hospitality. That phrase kept running through his head: abusing their hospitality. He began to sense that when they ignored him it wasn't because they were indifferent but because they were seething with disgust. One morning this thought kept whirling in his mind until he felt sick with it. He felt he had to say something, to make his position plain to them, to address the hatred which he knew was festering.

As Di happened to pass his table he made a terrific effort and blurted: "Thanks for the hospitality!" He didn't want to seem to be looking directly at her so he kept staring through the front window at the street.

"Beg yours?" she said.

The youth had used up all his determination and could not bring himself to speak again. He kept staring ahead.

"Did you say something?" she asked. "Did you want another coffee?"

He tried to say, "Thanks for the hospitality," again before his throat went tight and he trailed off. Di thought he'd said thanks to another coffee and so brought him one. She went away and after a while he stopped shaking and got hold of himself.

The youth knew his thinking had gone peculiar for a while. He put it down to the way he'd tried to model himself on Ronnie Robson, the way he'd tried to be positive and optimistic and on good terms with the world. Diestl's example never led him astray like that. Diestl had always been good for him and had always kept him safe.

After that the youth put on the Diestl mood whenever he entered the coffee shop. He would imagine the place half-wrecked from bombing and would mentally kick aside bits of debris as he limped over to his table behind the fern, unslinging the Schmeisser as he sat down. He'd had a false start at Don & Di's. But now he was back on track. Now he could even look Don and Di in the face if he had to. Now he could give them the blank stare of a man at home with death and ruin and who just didn't care.

The youth never applied for any of the jobs he circled in the paper. He would leave the coffee shop intending to ring from the phone box on the corner of the square. He would stand near the phone box for a while and look down the list of circled jobs and try to decide which seemed least threatening. He didn't quite know how to judge the threateningness of a job ad. He trusted his intuition. He would go into the phone box and spread the paper and lay the coins out on top of the phone. He would dial the first digit or two of the number. But then it became too real. If he kept dialling he would have to talk to a real person and state what he was calling about and maybe arrange to go for an interview. And if he got a job he would have to keep going there. That was the worst thing. You could front up once, maybe, and get through the ordeal of it, and then escape. But a job meant going back time after time. Of course he wouldn't get the job anyway, even if he went for an interview, so why put himself through the ordeal? He would decide to leave the call until later. He needed to walk about. He could phone later with a clearer mind.

He developed a route that took him into a park in the city centre: past a pond, along the edge of some flower beds, through a tunnel of big overarching trees, past a World War I howitzer on its concrete base, round a statue of an explorer, and then to a big chessboard built into the ground with black and white squares of marble. By the time he'd walked this route, often more than once, he would tell himself that he'd lost his chance of job-hunting that day but would make a fresh start next morning.

Next morning would be a whole new ball-game. Next morning would be the first morning of the rest of his life.

AFTER THREE weeks his money was nearly gone. Not that he needed much—just enough for a coffee at Don & Di's, and a paper, then a cheese roll for lunch and an evening meal of baked beans on toast at a cheap cafe he'd found on the far side of Telford Square.

His only other regular expense was for exchanging magazines at a second-hand bookshop he'd discovered in the same area. For a very small sum you could get a bundle of *Women's Weeklys* and *Woman's Days*. And for an even smaller sum you could take them back and exchange them for a fresh lot. The youth went through a bundle of magazines every few evenings.

He loved the whole world of them—cookery, fashion news, gardening, home decorating, the doings of the Royal Family. He thought of these magazines as his direct line to knowledge he'd never have otherwise. He read the advice columns and felt he was getting to the heart of human intimacy. He read the beauty tips. He read the household hints. He was always alert for pictures of women who had a touch of Grace Kelly's look. Now and then he found pictures of Sweetheart herself. He carefully cut them out and stuck them in an exercise book. He called this the White Book because it had a white cover. Sometimes he cut out pictures of women who didn't resemble Sweetheart all that much but still had an appealing quality. These interested him because he felt he was being broadened, being helped to see the wonderful variety of the world. The shape of an eyebrow, the curve of a throat, an expression in the eyes—these could be enchanting even if they weren't just like Sweetheart's. But hers was the ultimate beauty. Nothing would ever change that.

He'd bought himself a bedside lamp at an op-shop. It was a bit chipped, and the on–off switch was loose, but it worked fine and had cost almost nothing. So now he had a really good light to see and read by. It made all the difference. The evenings with the magazines were his best times, even though he had to keep an ear cocked for trouble in the corridor. He had a procedure for when he needed to use the toilet. It involved listening at the door, opening it a crack, looking out and scanning the passageway, locking his door behind him, then gliding quickly and quietly along to the loo. The toilets and showers and washbasins were in a big dank room that echoed every sound. Now and then other men came in while he was there but they minded their own business. The youth would glide back to his room with door key in hand for a rapid re-entry.

One night as he went to return to his room there was a woman standing in the corridor. She was swaying a bit from side to side. The youth half-thought to turn and retreat to the loo till the passageway was clear, but kept going.

As he went to pass her he got a whiff of alcohol. The woman turned to him as he was side-on to her, so that they were facing each other close up. He dropped his glance and saw how low-cut her dress was at the front. She put her hand on his arm and stopped him for a moment. He got the scent of her tousled hair and warm body mixed with the alcohol. She breathed some words. He did not catch what they were, but they sounded nice, like an invitation. He moved on and went into his room. He put his ear to the door and heard the woman come along the passage and stop and gently knock. His heart beat wildly. There was another gentle knock. He heard her murmur something and then she moved away from his door and was gone. The youth lay down on his bed, stirred and flushed. It had felt so good to be right up close to her like that, with her hand on his arm and her red lipsticked mouth so near. He hadn't realised how the smell of a woman's tousled hair and warm body could flood through you and leave you weak in the knees. He got out the White Book and looked at his photos of Grace Kelly. *She* would give you those feelings if you got right up close to her, but even more powerfully because she was so much lovelier than any other woman. The photos of her suddenly had a more physical meaning. Her beauty was embodied for him in a new way. He spent most of that night cuddling his pillow and whispering love talk. Mostly it was Sweetheart, but now and then it became the woman in the corridor, and that felt almost as delicious.

AT THE Astro you were supposed to keep your rent paid at least a week in advance. The youth was now less than a paid-up week ahead and he was afraid the manager would challenge him about it. The manager was a tall, pale man who spoke very quietly in a foreign accent. He had blotchy skin and looked ill. He sat all day long in the little office inside the front door and never appeared to do anything other than sit with his hands clasped in front of him. He was always there when the youth came or went, and if he was facing the corridor he would give a passive stare and a nod of the head so slight it was hardly a movement at all. If he was facing away from the corridor and you entered or left very quietly he appeared not to be aware of you. But one day the youth noticed there was a framed photo on the wall which reflected the office doorway, so even when the man was facing away he still saw you go past.

The youth thought of him as the Pale Watcher.

Entering or leaving the Astro was now an ordeal, because of the rent. Every so often at other times, too, the youth would remember that he was nearly penniless and would be homeless any day now. It sent a pang of misery through him, but he did not know what to do about it and so tried to let the thought pass.

He was lying on his bed one evening. He felt slightly unwell. He had been at the library and then spent a long time in the park in a strong wind. He'd enjoyed the bracingness of it, but it had chilled him, and then there'd been some rain as he meandered home and he'd got wet as well. So he was stretched out, thinking he'd rest with his eyes closed for a quarter of an hour and then browse through his magazines till he felt properly sleepy. There came a jingle of keys and his door opened and the Pale Watcher walked in and closed the door behind him. He put the bunch of keys in his pocket and stood looking down at the youth. He smiled, or at least the youth assumed it was a smile. It might have been a grimace of pain. The man

said something softly in his foreign accent, but the youth did
not catch it. Was he asking for rent? The man saw the pile of
*Women's Weeklys* and *Woman's Days* on the bedside table. He
flicked through some pages of the top one and said something.
Again the youth didn't catch it, but he did not want to seem
too impolite so he nodded as though he'd understood. The
man sat down on the side of the bed. The youth was very
embarrassed by the closeness and looked up at the ceiling. The
man was looking him in the face and the youth stared up more
fixedly. The man stretched himself out on the edge of the bed
and the youth could feel his breath on the side of his face. This
was even more embarrassing, so the youth tried to keep
focused on a smudge on the ceiling. He felt the man's hand on
the outside of his thigh. It lay heavy there for a few moments,
then moved slowly to the inside thigh. It started to rub there,
back and forth. The rubbing didn't feel unpleasant, but the
man's breath had a slightly sickly odour and the youth wanted
to get up and away from it. He was trapped, though, against
the wall. The man began whispering words. They might have
been words in his own language. They had a sing-song rhythm,
like a lullaby. The man's mouth came close to the youth's ear
and the hand came up and rested on his crotch. The youth
could only think of the sickly breath going into his ear. He
wondered whether it would offend the man very much if he
scrambled up and off the bed. He could say he'd suddenly
remembered he had an urgent appointment. The hand was trying to undo the zip of the fly. The youth made a slight turn of
his body towards the wall, as though just casually adjusting his
position. The movement took the fly zip from the man's fingers. After a moment the fingers moved to the zip again and
again the youth turned his body another slight degree. The
man stopped whispering the words and took his hand away.
He sighed and the youth felt the little rush of air against his
face. The man swung his legs off the bed and stood up,

smoothing his clothes and his hair. He gave the youth the smile or grimace or whatever it was, then left the room as swiftly as he'd entered.

The youth was glad to be free of the sickly breath, and of the embarrassment of the closeness, but he was worried that he'd offended the man. And there was something else—a small, sharp sense of loss. He wasn't quite sure what he felt, but he knew it wasn't a hundred per cent relief. What had just happened had been exciting as well as embarrassing. There'd been that half-scary flushed feeling you got when you thought of the Pleasures of India.

*The Pleasures of India* was a phrase which had popped into his head one day and which evoked for him the power and mystery of the erotic. It prompted a mental picture of himself in some sultry foreign place that smells of jasmine and sandalwood. It is dusk. The street is sinuous and there are many narrow doorways. There are windows red with the glow of lamps behind crimson curtains. Enticements of spice and wine fill the air. There is a tinkle of wind-chimes and faint hypnotic music on Eastern instruments. The thrill and sweetness of life are so close. Intoxicating sex is all around. But you are still out in the street. You don't know which particular doors to approach, what kind of knock to give, what password to use. You need someone to impart these things, but since you'll probably never have anyone you will probably always be out in the street, always outside looking in. Yet just knowing that those intoxications exist in the world is a kind of consolation. If they exist, there is perhaps a chance that you *might* get to experience them somehow. It might happen by dumb luck, or somebody's sheer generosity, or an unlooked-for smile of Fate. And the person who might bring you to it—guide you to the door, tell you the password—need not be the most likely one. You wouldn't know who it would be until it happened. There was the *Magic of Possibility*. That was the other phrase that came to him. The Pleasures of India came through the Magic of Possibility. The Pale Watcher had seemed the wrong person, but that didn't mean he couldn't be the bearer of the Possibility. The woman in the corridor that other night had seemed much more the right person, but the Possibility wasn't carried through. It had to be carried completely through and handed to you in a way that you couldn't refuse. If that woman had had a key and had entered like the Pale Watcher did, if *she'd* got on the bed with him and put her hand on his crotch . . . Or if the Pale Watcher had persisted . . .

The thing about the Pleasures of India, and the thoughts of Possibility, was that afterwards they left you feeling sad and empty. You paid dearly for those moments of flushed excitement. But then again, he'd understood that. That was the bitter wisdom Diestl stood for and had drummed into him. Hope for nothing and you won't be disappointed. Expect nothing but the long road and your limping shadow for company. Otherwise you're bringing the misery on yourself and you deserve every bit of it.

TWO MORNINGS later the youth went to pass the office on his way out. There was another man there with the Pale Watcher, someone stocky and tough-looking. When he noticed the youth he barked a question in a foreign language. The Pale Watcher nodded in reply.

"What you do?" demanded the stocky man.

"Sorry?" said the youth, stopping.

"Why you no pay?"

"Pardon?"

"Must pay rent! I am Owner! You owe money for room!"

"Um, I'm a bit short," the youth said.

"Must pay!"

"I can't, at the moment," said the youth. He was thinking that he could offer to get his things and leave at once.

The stocky man had come out of the office and was face to face with him against the wall of the corridor. The man looked him up and down as though he hadn't really seen him properly until now. He seemed to soften a bit, although his voice was still an aggressive bark.

"Where your father?"

"I haven't got a father."

"Where your mother?"

"Up in the bush."

"What bush?"

"The country. A country town. Up north."

"Your mother pay. You give telephone number, I talk to her, tell her you owe rent."

"I don't know her number," said the youth. "We've been out of touch." He was feeling very intimidated now, backed up against the wall, and he felt his chin trembling with distress. He knew if he had to say any more he would not be able to keep his voice steady.

"You pay rent tomorrow!" the man said. He looked at his watch and turned back into the office and began to bark at the Pale Watcher in their foreign language. He glanced back at the youth still standing against the wall.

"I have no time now, but I speak to you tomorrow. Not to pay rent is stealing! You steal from me, I call police. You understand?"

He waved the youth away and went back to barking at the Pale Watcher. The youth supposed it was a bawling-out for letting people get in arrears.

Back in his room the youth tried to think what to do. Maybe he could pack his things and slip away. But the thought of being homeless was like an icicle in his heart. This room, shabby as it was, seemed especially cosy now. But it wasn't just a question of a roof over his head. He was so broke that he could hardly buy a bread roll or a carton of milk to exist on.

He recalled what the Owner had said about contacting his mother. He decided to search his bag for the scrap of paper with the phone number on it, the number of the old lady the woman was working for up north. He took his bag from the wardrobe and began to rummage in it. He pulled out a woman's brassiere and a leather wallet. He sat on the bed and looked at these two items. He'd never seen them before. He was completely puzzled. He held the bra up by its shoulder strap and examined it. It was a bit frayed and not very clean. He took up the wallet and opened it. There were only a couple of crumpled bits of paper. One was a garage receipt for a car tune-up. The other was a doctor's appointment slip in the name of Tony Lee and dated months ago.

The youth felt that awful sweaty, swirling sensation that came when he was unsure about the reality of what was happening. Had he got the bra and wallet from somewhere and forgotten about it? Had he stolen them? He tried to remember himself stealing them. He could imagine himself doing it, but was he remembering it? He didn't think so.

He suddenly understood the items had been planted on him. His heart beat hard with the shock of the thought. Someone's wallet and a woman's bra: together they showed him up as a thief and a perve. How long had they been there? Couldn't be more than a few days, he figured. He thought of the way the Pale Watcher had come into his room so casually, key in hand. But why would the Pale Watcher want to plant stuff on him?

The youth racked his brains. After a while he felt the need to lie down and try to let the sweaty, swirling sensation fade. As soon as he'd stretched out, though, he got a mental picture of the door opening and the Pale Watcher looming in. He got up and slid the little security bolt, then lay back down. The wallet and the bra were on the bed. They felt very dangerous, like time bombs ticking beside him.

He went out early next morning. He wanted to take all his belongings with him, but was afraid they'd stop him if his bag was too full. He imagined the Owner grabbing him and barking right into his face again. He imagined the man searching his bag and finding the bra and wallet and calling the police. He was scared of the Owner and pictured himself trying to run away but going weak in the legs and not being able to move. Part of the reason the stocky man frightened him was that his manner was a lot like Vladimir's.

The youth intended to take the bra and wallet out with him and get rid of them in a rubbish bin. He put most of his belongings in the bag as well. He left behind a woolly jumper that was too bulky, and some magazines that he knew he could live without if he had to. The bag looked a bit full, but not absolutely bulging. He left his room and went quietly along the corridor. Another tenant was at the office door. The man was speaking quite loudly and breaking off every few moments with a hacking smoker's cough. Now and then came a faint murmur of the Pale Watcher's voice. The Owner didn't seem to be there. The youth darted past the other tenant and into the street and half-ran to Telford Square and joined the stream of people along Devon Street. After a minute or two of brisk walking he felt he was free and clear and slowed down. He came to the park. He sat on a bench and set the bag beside him. He thought what a nuisance it was going to be to be burdened with it all day long.

He'd not brought his bedside lamp with him. It had clean slipped his mind. How stupid! He loved that lamp, chipped and shabby though it was. He loved the little circle of light it made. He thought of the cosy times he'd had with his magazines in that circle of light, and the times of deep emotion too, reading and rereading the wonderful key chapters of *Year of Decision.*

He was hungry. He'd not eaten since the middle of the previous day. He searched his pockets for money and found he had enough for a bread roll and a carton of milk. He went to a shop and bought a buttered roll, then returned to the park. He had decided to keep his last coin for some milk later on. He ate the roll carefully so as not to waste any crumbs, then washed it down with gulps of water from a tap.

Across the street was the State Museum. It was a big stone building in an old-fashioned style that he liked. He had passed it many times, had looked in through the glass doors, and had read the sign that told what the hours were and that admission was free. He had never gone in because he had the State Library to go to and thought he'd keep the museum up his sleeve. Now he crossed from the park and went up the front steps and peered in through the glass doors. It was just past nine o'clock. He went in very cautiously, the way he did with any place that was unfamiliar, ready to retreat if anything seemed untoward. He had on his look of vague boredom. He always wore that expression in a new place so that if he was told to get out he could pretend he hadn't been interested anyway.

There was an information desk with postcards and souvenirs for sale, but no-one was attending it. A woman's voice was coming out of an open office door. The youth went through one of several archways which led off the entrance hall and found himself in a long two-storey gallery full of glass cases with stuffed animals in them.

There was a musty smell that he liked, the smell of an old building that had got shabby, with chips in the plaster and paint peeling off the walls here and there. It was also probably the smell of stuffed animals that had been there a long time. The youth stared into the yellow eyes of a stuffed lion. Its mouth was drawn back in a snarl. He wondered how long ago the lion had been alive. Fifty? A hundred years ago? He felt the poignancy of time and of life. This lion had been alive under the sun of a day gone forever. That phrase went round and round in his mind: *The sun of a day gone forever.* He stayed staring at the lion for a long time, then moved on to other creatures in other cabinets. There was an antelope with long spiral horns, a group of three chimpanzees lolling on a tree branch, a crocodile in a long narrow case, and a rhinoceros standing braced with its head down and its long sharp horn poised to make an upward hooking motion at an enemy. The gallery was so crammed with glass cabinets that the youth had to turn sideways to squeeze between them. There was a chair in a corner and when he felt like taking the weight off his feet he sat down and gazed around at the exhibits and the shabby walls and the little balcony that ran around the upper level. Nobody else came into the gallery while he was there and it was beautifully quiet. The hours drifted by.

On the walls were some painted scenes of African landscapes. They looked like they'd been there a long time and were a bit faded. The youth stared at these, gazing into the distance of the flat veldt, or up at the white peak of Kilimanjaro, or into a depth of jungle. All the while he was thinking about the sun of a day gone forever and some of the time he wasn't entirely in his body, or even in his own mind. It was as though he had entered into the lives of those animals under that sun of Africa long ago. He was in the heat and rush and desperation of those lives, and also in their stillness and alertness and self-control. He kept coming back to the stuffed lion and staring into the yellow eyes. At certain moments he felt he might swoon and faint if he wasn't careful. It was like the feeling you get once in a while when you gaze at the starry night sky and for an instant comprehend it—except this was a flash of the fiery sun and the pounding blood of the beasts of the earth.

It was mid-afternoon. The youth had wandered into a courtyard of the museum. There was a kiosk that sold sandwiches and drink, with a middle-aged lady behind the counter. There were no customers just then and the lady was reading a newspaper spread in front of her. The youth was drained of all emotion. He felt hollow and hungry and wanted to lie down. He thought of leaving the museum and going back across the road to the park and stretching out on the grass. He tried to decide whether to buy a carton of milk from the kiosk with the last of his money.

The courtyard was separated from the street by a high iron-railing fence. There was a pushbike outside on the footpath, leant against the railings. It was a very good bike by the look of it. The youth idly wondered whose it was and why it was there. It'll get pinched if its owner doesn't watch out, he thought.

He bought the smallest carton of milk the kiosk had and drank it quickly. Well, that's it, he told himself: now I'll be going hungry. For a moment he felt like bursting into tears but then decided he was too tired to care. He thought again about going over to the park for a lie-down. He wondered if he would soon be like those ragged men he saw scavenging in the park bins.

The thought of the bins reminded him of the bra and wallet he still had in his bag. He had to get rid of them. He could slip them into a bin as he passed. He could do it with one swift motion and without even slowing his walk. That way it would not catch anyone's eye. He could put the items into a paper bag first. But he didn't have a paper bag and didn't know how to get one. The problem began to seem enormous. He thought how many paper bags he'd used and thrown away in his life. If only he'd known how crucial a paper bag would be one day. He imagined himself going up to the lady in the kiosk and asking for a paper bag and her telling him to piss off. Or what if she demanded what he wanted it for? He tried to think of a reason he could give for needing a paper bag, but nothing came to him. And what if the lady guessed his real purpose? She'd have him thrown out of the museum and he'd never be allowed back in again. And the museum would send a message to the State Library, and he wouldn't be allowed in there either. He'd have nowhere to go in the whole huge city. He felt like crying again.

The youth left the courtyard and went out through the building to the street. Instead of crossing to the park he turned right and went around the corner and towards the pushbike leaning against the railing. He had decided to steal it if he could. As he walked towards it he saw there was a small side door to the museum. That was why the bike was there. Its owner had gone in that door. Drawing level with the doorway, the youth tried to glimpse inside but could only see the street reflected in the glass. Another couple of paces and he was at the railings, next to the bike. He paused and pretended to be adjusting the shoulder strap of his bag. As he did so he looked through the railings at the kiosk. The kiosk lady was now leaning with her back to the counter, holding the newspaper up in front of her. The youth glanced down at the bike. It was not chained to the railing. He took hold of the handlebars and began walking the bike away. After a few paces, when he saw that it wheeled freely, he swung onto the seat and began to pedal. The footpath ran quite steeply downhill and the bike got up speed while he was trying to get the feel and balance of it. His bag began to slip round to his side and he took his left hand off the handlebar to adjust it. This made the bike wobble. He tried to steady it but brushed against a wall, putting him more off balance. He saw he was approaching an intersection and tried to brake with the pedals, but found there was no foot-brake. He fumbled for the handbrake and squeezed it and the bike began to slow a little, but not enough. He tried to slow some more by dragging his feet on the ground. He hit the metal pole of the traffic lights at the intersection. The bike at last skewed to a stop.

For a few moments he didn't feel any pain. He was too concerned with whether someone might be chasing him. He looked behind. There was no-one. People in the cars at the lights were looking at him. A girl leant from the passenger side of one of them and asked if he was okay. The youth nodded yes. He lifted the bike and began to walk it away along the footpath. He found he could not hold the handlebars proper-ly with his right hand and that his right arm and shoulder were full of dull pain. He walked for three blocks, the pain getting worse all the time. When he felt safe enough to stop he leant the bike against a bus-stop seat and sat down and tried to mas-sage his shoulder, but that only made it hurt more. For half an hour he sat quite still and tried to think himself away from the pain. He still felt afraid that any moment he'd hear a yell of accusation and feel himself grabbed.

He got up and tried to keep walking briskly but his arm and shoulder were stiffening and there were such throbs of pain in them that he could hardly hold the bike upright or guide it properly. He shuffled along with painful slowness, the bike veering crookedly all over the footpath. At one point he let it overbalance and fall, and as he made a grab for it he lost his own balance and went sprawling. He was on his uninjured side, but the jar of the fall sent such pain through his hurt arm and shoulder that he groaned aloud. A young chap was walking past and asked him if he was alright and began to help him up. Just then a police paddy-wagon approached and the youth thought he was gone for sure. But the paddy-wagon cruised by and there was just the nice young chap being friendly and helpful.

"Haven't quite got the hang of it yet, eh?" he said, indicat-ing the bike.

"No," replied the youth, forcing himself to smile. "I haven't had it long."

HE HAD THOUGHT, at the moment he'd decided to steal the bike, that he could sell it and get money. Now he had to think how. In one of the streets that ran off Telford Square there were three pawnshops close together. The youth had often stopped to look in their windows and had seen pushbikes there. He thought of the signs: SECOND-HAND GOODS BOUGHT AND SOLD AND MONEY LENT. He might be able to sell the bike at one of those places. Or maybe he could pawn it. He didn't know what pawning involved, exactly, but he could play it by ear.

It took a long time to walk the bike to Telford Square and he was very tired and sore by the time he reached the pawnshops. He would have bought a cool drink if he'd had the money. He approached the front of one of the pawnshops, then lost his nerve and went on past. The second one was a bit further on. He got to it but again did not feel braced enough to stop and enter. The third pawnshop was across the street, but he could not face the ordeal of crossing through the traffic, so he turned and wheeled the bike back past the other two again. Then he turned and passed them a third time. This was ridiculous, he told himself. He was just making himself conspicuous. The pawnshop people would be seeing him through their front windows and thinking he was acting suspiciously. He had to brace himself and then do it.

He went straight to the nearest of the pawnshops and leant the bike carefully against the front window. There was a sign above the door saying: ready money, with a badly painted picture of a big hand holding a wad of notes. The youth went in. There were two men sitting on kitchen chairs amidst the second-hand goods. They were talking about football. One was saying that Ronnie Robson was overrated, and the other was replying that, on his day, and pound for pound, Ronnie was still the best player in the world.

"Nah, mate," said the first, shaking his head.

"I'm sayin' *on his day*, mate, *on his day*!"

"Ah well, yeah, *on his day*," the other conceded.

"And *pound for pound*," said the first one. "That's what I'm saying: *pound for pound*!"

"Ah well, yeah, *pound for pound*."

The youth was standing near the counter, looking around at the merchandise.

"And what can I do *you* for?" asked the man who believed Ronnie Robson was still the greatest on his day and pound for pound.

The youth was taken by surprise.

"Um, I've got a bike . . ." he began to say.

"Let's have a squint then," the man said.

The youth went out and got the bike and manhandled it awkwardly through the door, his arm and shoulder throbbing from the exertion. The man came over and put his hand on the seat of the bike and ran his eyes over the wheels and frame and chain. He flicked the gears and squeezed the hand-brake. Then he lifted the bike slightly off the ground and let it drop down. It made a solid clunk of a sound.

"Yeah, I'll give you somethin' on it," said the man. "How much were you lookin' for?"

"I'm not quite sure . . ."

"I'll go three quid. How's that?"

"Good."

The man went behind the counter and began filling in a form.

"Got some ID there?" he asked, putting his hand out.

The youth shook his head.

"I need *somethin'*," the man said. "Anythin' with a name on it will do." He had stopped filling in the form.

The youth had a sinking feeling. Then he remembered the wallet.

"Just a sec," he said. "My wallet's in my bag."

He rummaged in the bag and found the wallet and removed it carefully so as not to accidentally pull anything else out with it—like a bra, maybe. The man saw how he was having trouble with his arm and shoulder.

"Got a crook arm, mate?"

The youth said he had.

"Playin' footy, was it?"

The youth said it was.

He fished in the wallet and took out the doctor's appointment note for Tony Lee and handed it over. The man wrote Tony Lee's name and address down on his form. Then he asked for the youth's signature. The youth wrote "Tony Lee" as carefully as he could, but with his sore arm it was hard not to have it scrawling all over the paper.

"You'd play for, what, Under 16s?" the man asked.

"Yeah," said the youth.

The man tore the top copy off the pad and handed it over with the money.

As the youth turned to go the other man spoke.

"Ask *him* what he reckons. Go on. He plays footy."

"Alright," said the man at the counter. "Listen. He reckons Ronnie Robson's overrated, whereas I reckon that, on his day and pound for pound, Ronnie's still the best there is. What's your angle on it?"

The youth was starting to feel a bit more at ease, because of the bike thing having gone so well. He tried to look like someone who ponders long and deeply on football matters.

"Well," he said, "the thing about Ronnie Robson is that he'll give you a hundred and ten per cent and then some."

"Yeah, that's right," said the man at the counter, pleased.

"And he's tuned like a Swiss watch," the youth added.

As he turned and went out he heard the two men starting to discuss what he'd said, as though it was quite profound.

He only began to shake when he'd got well away. Then he felt pleased at how well he'd done. Forcing himself to stop shilly-shallying and just barge in and do it had been the key. It had been a lesson. Fortune favours the bold, he reflected.

The youth went back to Telford Square. As he passed the

newsstand he noticed a photo of Ronnie Robson on the front of the paper. He bought a copy and went to Don & Di's coffee shop and ordered a hamburger with all the trimmings, and a milkshake, and read the item about Ronnie having signed a new contract for his football club for a record amount. That must have been why the two men at the pawnshop were discussing whether Ronnie was still as great as ever. "It isn't about money," a club spokesman was quoted as saying. "It's about letting Ronnie know he's appreciated." How wise a thing to say, the youth thought. He reflected again that there was much wisdom in football. It was about "finding your values." That was a phrase of Ronnie's. The youth had read it in one of his magazines, in an article about sports heroes who do good work for charities. There'd been a photo of Ronnie visiting an institution for boys who'd got in trouble with the law. The picture showed a crowd of them gathered round Ronnie and him holding up a football, and underneath was a caption: "*Finding your values is the key,*" *footy star tells delinquent*s. The article said that Ronnie had been in trouble himself when he was fifteen. He'd come from a broken home in a little coalmining town and had stolen a car for a joy-ride and been put on a good-behaviour bond. "*I found my values in football,*" he told the boys, "*and I know each of you young blokes can find your values in some field of endeavour.*"

The youth felt the tears welling. He wanted to find his values, he really did. He gazed at the photo of Ronnie and Ronnie seemed to return his gaze and to understand what he was feeling.

Di brought the hamburger with all the trimmings. The youth wiped his eyes and took up the knife and fork and found he could not work his hurt arm well enough. So he picked the hamburger up with his good hand and tried to eat it that way. But it was so stuffed with trimmings that bits of meat and onion and tomato and blobs of sauce fell onto the plate and onto the table and into his lap. He felt embarrassed and left the hamburger and sipped the milkshake instead. He had started to think he'd go back to the Astro and pay a week's rent. But the pawnshop money had only just been enough for that. Now, because of the hamburger and the milkshake, he'd left himself short. Why didn't he stop to think before lashing out like this? It had been the sheer relief of it going so easily at the pawnshop. That was it. He'd been too relieved to think straight, but now he realised how little he'd really got for the bike. It hardly met his needs. He would be homeless anyway, for all his trouble.

Two policemen came in and stood at the counter talking to Don. One of them turned his head towards the youth and gave him a long look. Then they went out. The youth sat for a long time trying to get calm. Di came over and asked him if he wanted anything else and saw the mess he'd made with his hamburger. The youth glanced again at the front of the paper and there was a sneer in Ronnie's expression that he hadn't noticed before.

It was late afternoon and he wanted to lie down someplace quiet and doze and forget himself for a while. He went along the street towards the Astro and approached the doorway cautiously. An angry voice came from inside. It was the Owner's and he was arguing with a tenant in the hallway, the same tenant who'd been there that morning, the one with the smoker's cough. The Owner kept shoving his face aggressively at the tenant's face, then backing away when the tenant hacked out a cough. That's how it looked, anyway. The youth only got a brief sight of them in the hallway before the Owner noticed him outside and started shouting, "Hey! Hey!" and waving him in. The youth stayed where he was. The Owner started to push his way past the tenant towards the youth, but the tenant wasn't finished arguing and wouldn't let him by. They began to scuffle, the Owner barking out words in his foreign language and the tenant hacking and coughing as they grappled.

The youth walked on quickly, his heart banging. He kept looking behind him. He saw the Owner emerge into the street and he started to run. When he looked back again the Owner and the tenant were grappling on the footpath and the Pale Watcher was there too, making gestures of distress with his hands but keeping well out of the fight.

When he'd got several blocks away the youth stopped to catch his breath and let the throb in his arm and shoulder subside. He saw a park and went to a seat and sat down. He stayed there until night came on. He had no thought of where to go or what to do. He was thinking of those few things back in the room at the Astro: his woolly jumper and some magazines in the wardrobe, and most of all his bedside lamp. He thought of the times, back in the room, when he'd leant a picture of Sweetheart against the base of the lamp, and alongside it his copy of *Year of Decision*, and so had made a little shrine in the circle of light, a shrine to Beauty and Love and Bravery and Death.

The youth was in the empty business district. He had got into Diestl's limping stride and went round and round the same few blocks for a couple of hours as the wind made desolate noises in the canyons of the streets.

At one point he saw a van stopped ahead of him under a streetlight. Its doors were open and three people were on the footpath, leaning over, talking to somebody hunched in a doorway. The van had ALISON STREET MISSION painted on its side, and an image of Jesus holding his hand out in succour. The youth had seen that van around the city a couple of times before, and had remembered the piece of paper Pastor Eccles had handed him. One day he would make contact, like he'd promised, but it would have to wait till he felt more resilient. You needed resilience to go and present yourself to a bunch of people. You had to be in a cheerful frame of mind. But if you were feeling cheerful and resilient you wouldn't bother, for you'd be content with your own company, your own thoughts. There was a contradiction. He found this idea of inherent contradiction interesting and walked for another hour on the strength of it. But then he was chilled, and his teeth were chattering, so he left the business district and wandered to the seedy end of town, thinking to get a cup of tea.

He took a short-cut down a lane. Halfway along he found an old sofa that someone had put out as rubbish. It was in a corner that was out of the wind and quite dark. When the youth's eyes had adjusted to the dimness he examined the sofa carefully. The arm at one end was ripped almost completely off and the stuffing was spilling out, but the rest of it looked fine. He knelt down and smelt it and noticed a scent of perfume. He thumped it a couple of times and watched and listened for movement. He was worried about cockroaches, or even rats. There was nothing. He was pretty sure the sofa hadn't been there long enough to be infested. He sat down on it and leant back and looked at the sky, which was clear and starry, despite the wind. He stretched lengthwise, his head resting on the sofa's good arm and his feet at the broken end. He felt cold, even out of the wind, but the softness of the sofa made up for it. It was easy on his sore shoulder and he was able to turn a little when he needed to vary his position. After a while he got his towel from his bag and spread it over himself like a blanket.

He woke in panic at some stage, feeling something touch him. He was afraid it was a rat and gave a cry of fear and disgust. It was a big ginger cat. The cat did not run away but stayed and stared at him, then leapt onto the sofa and snuggled against his legs. The youth was glad. He and the cat slept. When he woke again the cat was gone and first light was over the city.

He left the lane and went to the railway terminal and splashed water on his face at a basin in the toilet. He had a vague sort of chilled feeling. He also felt tired and had a headache, but he felt that way most times so it wasn't anything special. He wanted something hot to eat, and a big cup of tea. He remembered that he had the bike money in his pocket and for the time being needn't go hungry. He was still in one piece, and as soon as he found a cheap cafe he'd be having hot food and drink. He was managing fine. Diestl would be proud of him!

The youth slept on the sofa in the lane for three nights. The ginger cat kept him company for part of the time. There was no rain and he had no trouble.

Once a couple came along after midnight, arguing and swearing at each other. They stopped and kissed and fondled for a couple of minutes. Then they resumed their argument and walked on. The youth felt he was learning about life. He hadn't known that people could argue and have the hots for each other at the same time. Another night a derelict meandered by, muttering to himself. And a police paddy-wagon nosed along the lane and past him. He was frightened for the moment, but after the coppers had gone he felt reassured that he must be hard to see in the dark corner, shielded by the sofa's high back.

During the day he went to the State Library. He was there when the doors opened and he stayed till closing time. He took breaks to go and buy himself a bread roll or to stretch his legs in the adjacent park, near the statue of Henry Lawson. He was not bored. He did begin to wonder about the way he smelt, though. A couple of times people sat near him, then seemed to find reasons to move further away. He didn't care all that much because a lot of the time he was feeling quite out of himself, as though he didn't have a body anymore but was only a mind floating in a peculiar dimension.

The thought that he smelt bad only really bothered him one time. A beautiful girl with long blonde hair sat near him. He figured she was a uni student. She put a pile of weighty-looking books on the table in front of her, as though she was settling in for a long study session, but then she gathered the whole pile up and moved to the other side of the reading room.

Everyone in the place knew what had happened. They were whispering to each other about it. It filled him with cold rage. He kept his head very still and pretended to be reading his book but moved his eyes cautiously around. He caught sight of people making little signals to one another with their hands, or by moving their heads or mouths or elbows in particular ways. He felt anguish at the injustice of what they were thinking. He hadn't been fantasising about that girl. He didn't need to. He had Grace Kelly in his life. He wanted to get the White Book out of his bag and show them just how many pictures of Sweetheart he had. That'd wipe the smirks off their faces!

He wondered whether he was imagining some of this. Were they really signalling to each other? But he knew there were some things he had not imagined. There really had been a girl and she really had got up and moved away from him. Then the out-of-body feeling came back strongly and he wasn't totally certain about the girl anymore.

He stood up and left the reading room, putting on the Diestl mood to help him cope with the feeling that all eyes were on him. He went into the park and walked about. He thought about Diestl. There was a side to Diestl he had not paid enough attention to. He mostly thought of Diestl as the great symbol of detachment, of solitary survival, of being impervious to everything in the world. That was all true, but there was a whole other thing too. Diestl did not wander the earth randomly. He had a destination and a purpose: to get to the spot where he would make his stand, strike his blow, make the enemy pay. Diestl was like a walking time bomb. He kept himself apart and safe, not because his well-being mattered in itself but because he needed to get that bomb to where it would do most damage.

The youth stopped walking about and stood staring at the city skyline. He was picturing that skyline crashing down in flame and smoke. Diestl was beside him and spoke in an ice-cold voice: "That's it. You've seen the point at last."

THE APOLLO Cafe was down a side street near the railway terminal. It was dank and poky and every surface had a sticky unclean feel. But the youth liked it because the food was very cheap, and because there were piles of old magazines to look at. He had come there the previous three evenings to have baked beans on toast and a pot of tea and leaf through copies of *Equestrian World*. For some reason there were lots of copies of that magazine and the youth enjoyed searching for photos of young blonde women in boots and jodhpurs and riding coats. They reminded him of Sweetheart, and the thought of her in jodhpurs was very exciting.

He had ordered a pot of tea with the last of his money and wanted to linger over it as long as possible. The old sofa had been cleared from the lane and he had to find another place to spend the night. But he felt very headachy and had hot-and-cold sensations. The longer he could delay going into the streets the better. That was another good thing about the Apollo: you could hang about for a long time on one pot of tea without any-one minding. The regulars hung about a lot. They were mostly old blokes with grubby clothes and stubbly faces who had a smell of stale grog round them. They tended to eat their food carefully, as though their teeth were bad, and as though they knew they had to get a certain amount eaten for their own good, even if they didn't really fancy it. Some were quiet and kept to themselves, others talked a lot and joked with each other and with Mike behind the counter. Mike was a very large man with a hulking way of hunching his shoulders up, as if he were a wrestler preparing to grab you in a headlock, but he spoke politely and you felt safe in his cafe. Mike called the regulars by their names and some of them called him Mikey. There was one old chap called Deak who always referred to Mike as "Mine Host." Deak was gaunt, with white hair, and a bit shaky on his feet, but he had a grand manner and spoke like an actor recit-ing Shakespeare, using his hands to make elaborate gestures.

"Tell me, Mine Host," he would say, "how is the rat-meat this evening? Is it up to this establishment's celebrated stan-dards of succulence?"

"*You* tell *us*, Deak," Mike would reply. "You're the one who just had the stew."

Then someone might chip in with a comment about peculiar eating habits, and that might remind someone else of a yarn about tough times in the outback or whatever.

The youth listened to all the talk, but seldom looked up from the magazine in front of him. He could relax to some extent because he had developed a way of thinking himself into a kind of invisibility, the way an animal does when it stays very still and quiet and relies on that to keep from being noticed, even though it is in plain sight.

Now someone mentioned the bush, and Deak said: "I surmise that our young friend here might be a traveller from the hinterland. Am I right?"

The youth raised his eyes and found Deak and Mike and another two blokes looking at him steadily. It was a shock to find himself suddenly the focus of attention.

"Down from the country for a while, are you?" Mike asked.

"Um, yeah," the youth replied, looking back down at the magazine.

They didn't press him any further, though they must have been wondering about him since that first night he'd come in. It wasn't a place you saw a kid very often. He also realised how down-and-out he must look.

After a pause the conversation went on to other matters and the youth started getting ready to go. One of the old blokes was saying that Pastor Pete had given him a new jacket and that he felt like a new man in it. He had the jacket on and was running the zip up and down to show how good it was. It was brand new, he kept saying, not second-hand, and Pastor Pete had saved it especially for him.

Deak remarked that Pastor Pete was a scholar and a gentleman, and that the jacket suited the new owner's colouring: it was a sickly colour. The man replied that Deak should kindly pull his head in. Mike remarked that that was the best idea they'd heard all night. Deak made a sort of bow, like an actor acknowledging his audience. Then the talk went on to other things and the youth got up and laid his last few coins on the counter and left.

He stood outside for a minute. He'd hurt his sore shoulder when he'd picked his bag up too quickly. The pain was enough to make him wince. He walked to the next corner, and glanced up at the clock-tower of the railway terminus. It was only nine. The thought of the night ahead was too much to bear. He cursed himself for not having made better use of the past few days. He should've pinched another bike and pawned it. Except that he couldn't have gone to the same pawnshop as before. It would have to be a different pawn-shop, and each time after that a different one again. He wondered how many pawnshops there were, and whether it was always as easy as he'd found it. Probably not. Most pawnbro-kers were probably more suspicious, and would argue, and demand more identification. That man had been so taken up with Ronnie Robson's merits that he hadn't had his mind on the job. It being so easy that time had been a fluke, and pinch-ing bikes wasn't a real means of surviving. The youth's last bit of hope fled.

A police paddy-wagon was approaching, so the youth began to walk briskly. He knew he should appear to be going some-where, that it was loiterers the cops were scanning for. He came to a broad lane with a sign that said Alison Street. He turned down the lane and went along it till he saw that it came to a dead end. Just before the end, on the right, was an old warehouse. It had upper storey doors at the front and above the doors the sturdy beam that the ropes used to work from. ALISON STREET MISSION was painted in white letters and there was an image of Jesus holding out his hand, the same image the youth had seen on the side of the van those couple of times. A light was on above the old timber entrance door, but it was firmly closed and there didn't seem to be any sign of life inside.

The youth sat on the opposite kerb, vaguely trying to think where to go and what to do.

There was a flash of headlights as a vehicle turned into the lane. The youth jumped up, afraid it was the paddy-wagon. The vehicle came on quickly and pulled up in front of the warehouse. He was still a bit blinded by the glare of the head-lights and could not tell whether it was the coppers or not. He thought of running.

"Hello there," came a woman's pleasant voice.

The youth's eyes were adjusting and he saw a heavy-set young man getting out of the passenger side of the van. The woman who'd spoken was getting out of the driver's side.

"I'm sorry the place was closed," she said. "We didn't expect to be gone longer than half an hour. Just give us a minute to get organised and I'll put the kettle on. Do you fancy a hot drink?"

"Okay," the youth replied.

She led the way inside and the young man came behind car-rying a big cardboard box from the back of the van.

"Thanks, Rodney," she said. "I'll help you with the others in a moment."

"Can I help?" the youth asked.

"Oh, that'd be so kind of you," she replied.

So the youth helped Rodney bring several more cardboard boxes inside. Rodney was about twenty, the youth reckoned, and had a slack-lipped expression and a slightly shambling walk. If he and the youth got a bit in each other's way with the boxes, Rodney would lurch aside, keeping his eyes lowered.

"That's marvellous," the woman said when all the boxes were inside. "Thank you so much, Rodney. I can't think what we'd do without you."

She smiled at Rodney and he looked down at the floor bash-fully.

"And thank *you* so much," she said to the youth, beaming a smile. "Let's introduce ourselves. I'm Debbie Lambert."

The youth said his name.

"Pleased to meet you," Debbie Lambert said. Then she seemed struck by a thought. "Why does that name ring a bell?"

"I don't know," the youth replied.

"Well, it'll come to me, if it's meant to," Debbie Lambert said. "I'll plonk the kettle on. I could do with some tea, and I know Rodney never knocks back a lemon cordial. What do you fancy?"

The youth said tea would be fine.

Debbie Lambert led the way to a large kitchen at the back of the building. The youth took a seat at a big table and watched her set out mugs while an urn heated up. He had a chance to look at her now. She was in her early thirties, he thought. She had a pretty face and curly reddish hair. She wore a red tartan skirt and brown jumper and brown shoes. A pair of glasses hung by a cord around her neck and rested on the curve of her breasts.

Rodney was gazing at her from the other side of the table. You could tell he adored the ground she walked on.

When she had made two teas and a lemon cordial, she brought them to the table, then handed Rodney a packet of chocolate biscuits and asked him to open them. She said it as though it was *such* a piece of luck that someone as capable as Rodney was there for that particular task. A phone rang somewhere in the building and she smiled an apology and excused herself and went to answer it.

Rodney opened the biscuits with infinite care, his big hands picking at the sealed paper and his tongue lolling out of his mouth in concentration. When he'd got the packet open he pushed it delicately into the centre of the table with his finger. It was plain he wanted her to see it and be impressed, so the youth resisted his urge to grab a biscuit straightaway. An empty space in the row would spoil the effect. He sipped his tea instead. Rodney kept looking to see if she was coming back, his breathing heavy. Then he reached for the glass of cordial and lifted it with both hands. He took a mouthful but it went down the wrong way, or maybe up his nose, and he began to snuffle and gag and the rest of the cordial spilt into his lap. The snuffling, gagging noises were like the sounds Mr. Coles's pigs made. The youth felt alarmed. Then Debbie Lambert hurried back in and patted Rodney on the back and said soothing words to him. He started to recover and to breathe evenly again. Debbie Lambert leant over him and put her arm around his shoulders, making the soothing sounds close to his ear. Rodney seemed overcome with emotion.

Just then a group of people walked into the room.

There was a tall, good-looking man, then three shabby old blokes, one of whom was the chap from the Apollo Cafe with the new jacket, and a girl of maybe ten. The tall man looked at Debbie Lambert comforting Rodney and seemed to frown for an instant before he spoke: "So, what's happening? Any worries?"

Debbie Lambert gave Rodney a last pat and explained that he'd been distressed but was alright now. The tall man frowned again, but then shrugged it off. He asked one of the old blokes to do the honours with some tea or coffee, and then he turned to the youth.

"And how are you?" he asked.

Debbie Lambert introduced them, saying how helpful the youth had been earlier, carrying the boxes.

"That's the ticket," said Pastor Pete. "We'll have a chat later, if you like, and see whether we can return the favour and be of help to *you*."

The tea and coffee were poured and Rodney was given a fresh glass of cordial. The chocolate biscuits disappeared rapidly. The Lamberts talked mission business with the three old blokes, who were regular helpers it turned out.

The little girl had made herself a cocoa and sat at the table reading a book called *The Water Babies*. There was no doubt she was the Lamberts' daughter. You could see both of them in her face and colouring. She seemed a very composed child. When she saw Rodney trying to wipe the spilt cordial from his lap, she fetched a cloth and helped him, gravely explaining that you should dab, not wipe, otherwise you made the stain worse. Then she went quietly back to her book. The youth figured her composure was due to her knowing she was loved and looked after, and yet was accustomed to coping without fuss, like now, in a kitchen full of strange or needy people. He felt a sharp pang of envy. He wished he could be her brother and have the Lamberts for parents. A sense of longing welled up in him and there were tears in his eyes.

He became aware that Debbie Lambert was speaking to him.

"You're the boy Alan Eccles mentioned to us! I knew it would come to me. I'm sorry it didn't click straightaway. You do know Alan Eccles, don't you?"

"Pastor Eccles, yes."

"We have a letter for you, forwarded from the Blacketts' property. Alan said you'd promised to call in and say hello to us, so they forwarded it here. I'll just get it from the office."

She went away to fetch it.

"So, you're down from the bush?" said Pastor Pete.

"Sort of," the youth replied.

"And how are things with you right now?" he asked in a lower voice. "A bit grim, eh, by the look of it?"

The youth nodded, embarrassed.

"Broke, Baffled and Bereft. We all know how it can be in this world. Our Lord certainly knew what it was like, and if He had to go through it, none of us should think any worse of ourselves for having to."

The youth could not speak. The little girl had lowered her book and was looking across at him. So was Rodney.

"The first thing we can offer you is a chance to get freshened up. We have shower facilities here, which you'll no doubt be glad of when you've finished your tea."

So he did stink. He felt himself flushing hot and red. How polite they were not to have let on. He'd been ponging the place out all this time and Debbie Lambert had gone on being sweet and considerate.

She came back into the room and handed the youth his letter. "There we are. Safely delivered!" she said brightly.

The youth stuffed the letter into his shirt pocket and mumbled that he had Pastor Eccles's note of introduction somewhere. He opened his bag and began rummaging in it. He heard Pastor Pete say that the note wasn't all that important now that they'd got to know each other anyway, but the youth was thankful to have an excuse to keep his face lowered. He knew the note was crumpled somewhere at the bottom of the bag. He pulled a couple of bits of clothing up roughly and saw something white emerge and realised too late what it was.

The brassiere flew through the air and landed on the floor. It was perfectly spread out with the two cups and the shoulder straps in position. There was no mistaking what it was.

The youth stared at it. Everyone in the room stared at it. The youth heard Pastor Pete murmur, "Ah." Then Rodney began to bellow. He was pointing to the bra and making a noise like a bullock in distress, over and over.

The youth grabbed his bag and went to the door and through it. He thought he heard Debbie Lambert call, "Don't go!" but he wasn't sure with Rodney's noise filling the air. He couldn't work the latch of the front door of the building, but then it clicked and he was outside. He heard a last bellow from Rodney as the heavy door swung shut. He ran to the end of Alison Street and turned the corner and kept running for two blocks, then turned into a lane and then into a smaller lane that led off it. He stopped and listened. There was no sound of any-one behind him.

The moon had come out from behind clouds. The youth looked around and saw that the lane went on, so it wasn't a dead end that he could be trapped in. He put his bag on the ground and sat on it with his back against an iron fence. He stared at the moon while he regained his breath. He pictured the brassiere in the middle of the floor, with all eyes fixed on it, and Rodney pointing and bellowing like a beast. Maybe they were all still there, frozen in that moment.

He began to giggle. It *was* funny, no doubt about it. The giggle grew more intense and turned into a kind of sobbing and he knew he had to get hold of himself. Diestl had come up beside him and was speaking in that burnt-out voice of his: "Good. You can laugh. You understand that it doesn't matter. All that matters is the ending, when all the accounts are paid."

AT FIRST light he left the lane. He was so stiff from lying on the ground that he could hardly drag himself along, and his sore arm and shoulder were throbbing. He went to the railway ter-minal and sat down and read the letter he'd been given.

It was from his mother. She said it was the second letter she'd sent him care of the Blacketts. The first one had come back marked "Not Known." She'd tried to phone Mrs. Hard-castle to confirm the correct address but Mrs. Hardcastle's agency had closed down. She'd then phoned the postmaster at Munnunwal and been told that there were Blacketts all over the district and that the best bet was to try the ones near Bells Creek. The letter had reached the property the day after he'd left. The woman said she was anxious to hear from him and gave the number of the old lady she was looking after in the northern town. She said he could reverse the charges.

He phoned at nine o'clock from a booth at the terminal. A rude old voice answered.

"Will you accept the charges, Madam?" the trunk-line operator asked.

"Who the devil's phoning?" the old voice demanded.

"I don't know, Madam."

"You could try *asking* them, or are you a *complete* fool?"

"Will you accept the charges, Madam?"

"Don't be stupid. Why should I? Ask them what their business is!"

"You could find that out yourself, Madam, just by saying you'll accept the charges."

"What if I don't *want* to know their business, Miss Impertinence?"

"The caller sounds like a juvenile," the operator said patiently, as though making a last effort to get the call through.

"Juvenile? I don't know any juvenile! Let me speak to your supervisor!"

The youth heard his mother's voice come onto the line and say that the charges were accepted, and the old lady shouting, "Get the supervisor! Get the supervisor!" in the background.

He explained that he was back in the city and didn't have any money. The woman said she would wire some to the GPO. He should get it within a couple of hours.

"You're alright though, basically?" she asked.

"Yeah, basically," he replied.

After the phone call he went to the park to wait for the cash to be wired through. He wandered the paths by the flower beds and drank lots of water from a bubbler to keep himself from feeling hungry. He thought about the question: *Are you basically alright?* Is anyone ever basically alright, he wondered. Superficially alright, yes. Lots of people are superficially alright. He was superficially okay himself some of the time. But *basically* was a whole other thing. Diestl had taught him that. And King Harold. And the Bushranger shot with a hundred bullets. The youth knew that being alright wasn't the point.

The point was whether you made a fight of it, whether you hit back, whether you made your enemies bleed a bit before you went down under the hopeless odds.

He was stopped in the park by two policemen. They looked him up and down and asked him what he was doing and how old he was. He tried to look them in the eyes and not let his voice go too trembly. He said he was sixteen and was down from the bush and was due to go back that day. He was afraid they might ask to see a train ticket, or some money. He'd heard it was in the vagrancy law that the cops could ask to see some money, and if you didn't have a certain amount on you— enough for a night's accommodation—they could run you in. The two cops looked him up and down a final time, and one of them muttered that a bit of soap and water wouldn't go amiss, and they went on their way.

The youth hurried out of the park. He felt too exposed there now. He went into some narrow side streets and hung about for an hour or so. He felt shaken and humiliated, but gradually overcame it by thinking of Diestl being stopped by those cops on a lonely road somewhere. He could visualise every detail of them sprawled in a ditch with bullets in their heads.

# 8. PEONS

The youth was sitting on a stool made of a block of wood, in a circle of about a dozen men, staring into the flames of a campfire. Other men moved about further off, and the fire cast their long reeling shadows onto the sides of huts and caravans.

He had replied to an ad in the paper: "Cotton Chippers Wanted at Weegun." He'd phoned the number given, deepening his voice to make himself sound older, and his details had been taken. He'd been told to report at an address in Weegun by three o'clock the following Sunday. It was already Friday then, so he went and bought his train ticket straightaway. He had just enough money left to cover it. Weegun was a country town about four hours journey northwest.

The train arrived on the afternoon of the Sunday and the youth found the address in the dusty main street. It was a shopfront with a sign that said "Continental Cotton Corp." A group of glum-looking men stood outside. The youth approached the fringe of the group and listened to the talk. They'd not been allowed to sign on for the chipping work.

"They're not givin' any poor bastard a start," one of them was saying, a man with a red, bulbous nose.

"Friggin' Yanks," someone else snarled.

The youth's heart sank. There'd been some mix-up and there wasn't any job here after all. He was flat broke and had no idea what he would do now.

"We heard they was takin' blokes on, so we come," said Big

Nose. "Jeez, a bloke's gotta believe what he hears, don't he? I mean, where'd we be if we can't believe what we frigginwell hear?"

"I s'pose we'd be standin' here like gigs," said his mate. "Just like we're doin'."

A woman in a white American cowboy hat came to the door of the shop and asked the men not to block the entrance. They meekly moved back. The woman saw the youth among them and raised her eyebrows to him in a silent question: "Yes?"

He said he had phoned about the cotton-chipping and been told to report here.

The woman beckoned him inside. She had a name-tag that said "Rita." The shop was bare except for a small table with some papers on it. Rita asked him his name and ran her finger down a list. She found the name there. She looked him up and down and asked him how old he was. He said sixteen. She looked dubious for a moment, then put a tick beside his name and had him put his signature beside the tick. Almost all the names on the list had been ticked and signed. She told him that a truck would be outside at five-fifteen if he needed a ride to the property. The youth went out.

The group of men was crossing the road towards a pub on the next corner, so the youth tagged along behind.

"Won't give a workin' man a start," Big Nose was complaining. "But they'll take on a half-arsed kid. *He* ain't got a family to support."

"Well, neither have you," replied his pal.

"No, but I might have, for all them friggin' Yanks know!"

"Yeah, and I might be the Queen o' flamin' Sheba. So what?"

"Jeez yer an argumentative bastard!" Big Nose sighed.

"Comes from spendin' too much friggin' time round you!"

The men turned into the door of the pub and the youth walked on past. It was quiet in the street. A stray dog came

limping along and stopped just out of range of the youth, its
tail low. It looked thin and neglected. He would have liked to
give it some food. He felt in his pocket and found an old pep-
permint lolly which he unwrapped and threw to the ground.
The dog sniffed at it, then turned and loped away. The youth
wished he'd kept the lolly for himself. He was hungry. He had
just enough money to buy a packet of Perkins Plain Assorted
biscuits if he could find a shop open. He'd got into the habit
lately of living on biscuits, and Perkins Plain Assorted were his
favourite. Biscuits were so convenient and they tasted good.
And if you had a cup of tea to dunk them in, it was a feast. He
found a corner shop and bought a packet, then wandered back
to the railway station and sat on the platform, savouring the
biscuits and gazing at the expanse of sky.

The youth recalled from his reading that Henry Lawson had
been broke and hungry at Weegun. He'd sold a poem to the
local newspaper for two shillings and that'd kept him going.
The platform was the original one from the 1890s or there-
abouts, and the youth got so vivid a sense of Lawson there, of
a kind of time-warp, that it made him feel peculiar.

Just before five o'clock he meandered back to the shopfront.
Some of the same men were back there, hoping to get a start if
the people on Rita's list hadn't all shown up.

At five-fifteen a big flatbed truck roared up and stopped
and tooted its horn. A bunch of men had come out of the pub
and were having a last drink on the footpath. They came over
with their bags and began to climb onto the truck. The youth
got on too. Other men came from inside the pub and got on,
chucking their baggage into the centre with the rest, until there
was hardly any room left. One of the last to get on was a wiry
sharp-faced man with a gammy leg. It took him two or three
goes to heave himself up next to the youth.

"One time a bloke would've jumped up here like a wallaby,"
he said. "But that was back when a man had two good legs."

The truck moved off abruptly and everyone grabbed for something to hold on to. For the ten minutes of the journey the youth was so busy trying to keep from being jolted off the truck that he saw almost nothing. There was just an impression of flat fields with endless neat rows of green. Then the truck turned through an elaborate white-painted gateway. On an arch above it was a logo of the letter "C" intertwined three times to stand for Continental Cotton Corp. They were at the chippers' camp.

Now he was staring into the campfire. He'd had a meal of shepherd's pie and been allocated a bed in one of the huts. It was nice at the campfire, with the buzz of talk all around. There were bursts of laughter and shouts of greeting from elsewhere in the camp as people sorted themselves out. Some of the chippers were regulars, travelling workers who followed the fruit-picking round the country and had added cotton-chipping to their circuit. The dozen or so caravans mostly belonged to them.

The youth was very tired, and made his way to the hut. There were two beds in the little room. Someone's suitcase lay on one of them. Sheets and blankets weren't provided, but the youth had one small thin blanket of his own, and a big towel, and these would do. He lay down and drifted into sleep. At some point he became conscious of someone clanking into the room and muttering and coughing. The next thing he knew the light of morning was in the window.

HIS ROOM-MATE was the bloke with the gammy leg. But the leg wasn't just gammy, it was artificial. It was lying beside the man's bed, its straps and clips all loose. The youth went out and splashed water on his face from a tap. The sun was beginning to blaze up from below the horizon and the youth went back to the room to get a cheap cloth hat he had in his bag. He'd need it to shield his eyes from the glare. He burnt easily too, because of his colouring, and he knew he must be careful to keep covered all day.

The man was sitting on the edge of the bed pissing noisily into a tin. The youth averted his eyes and fumbled in his bag for the hat.

"You'll have to pardon me," said the man. "A bloke ain't got two good legs to walk outside to the pisshouse."

"That's alright," the youth replied, going out quickly with his hat.

A breakfast of scrambled eggs with tomato and bacon was served across a counter at the cook-shed. There was plenty of toast to go with it, and big mugs of tea.

At a quarter to eight there was a loud toot like a factory whistle and people began assembling at the edge of the camp. The flatbed truck was there. It had a metal rack attached at the back, full of long-handled hoes. A short man stood on the tray of the truck. He wore jeans, a check shirt, high-heeled cowboy boots and a white cowboy hat like Rita's. He put his hands on his hips and began speaking to the assembled men with a slight American accent. He said his name was Denny and that he was the ramrod.

"*Ramrod*?" muttered one of the men.

"Fuckin' *Hat-rack* would be more like it," muttered another.

There was a ripple of amusement. The hat did look very large in comparison with the figure underneath it.

Denny paused for a split second, then went on: "Some of you guys are old hands from previous years and you pretty much know the score, so I'll be lookin' to you to bring the new fellas up to speed. Rule Number One is that Alcohol and Non-Employees are strictly barred from Company property. So don't bring booze into the camp, and don't bring floozies either."

The youth wasn't sure what "floozies" were.

"The other Number One Rule," Denny went on, "is that

Jerk-offs and Wise-guys get no second chances. The Company's interested in one thing only: an Efficient Operation. Okay, let's go!"

About half the assembled men climbed onto the truck, the youth among them. The driver called to the remainder that they'd be the second load. The truck set off.

The property was like a showplace. There was hardly a blade of grass out of alignment. The fences were all white-painted and perfectly straight and even, and the dirt roads neatly edged and graded. Deep concrete ditches ran along the sides of the fields, with pipes and pumps, all white-painted and new-looking. In the distance, across the perfect flatness of the fields, you could see what looked like a depot of enormous-wheeled machines. Above it all was the sky, utterly blue and clear, stretching from horizon to horizon.

They got off the truck and picked hoes out of the rack and stood looking at the green rows of plants. The truck left to return to the camp and Denny drove up in an open jeep. He explained, for those who were new to it, what the work was all about.

At this stage of their growth, cotton plants were in danger of being choked out by weeds, so the rows had to be kept free of them. Since there wasn't any machine precise enough to remove the weeds without damaging the crop, the job had to be done by human chippers with hoes. You had to move slow-ly along each row and chip out any weed you saw, and "weed" meant anything other than the cotton plants. If the weed was right up against the stem of the cotton plant, it was best to bend down and pull it out by hand rather than risk harming the plant with the blade of the hoe.

"That's the other Rule Number One," Denny said. "Don't damage the product!"

He got back into his jeep and sped off.

The youth's confidence rose. This was just his kind of work.

It was like chopping serrated tussock or Paxton's Pea, except gentler and easier.

There were thirty of them and they were told to spread along the first thirty rows and get ready to start. A soft-spoken Greek named Panos was the foreman. He had a list of names and marked you off as present and working. He also had a whistle. At eight o'clock sharp he gave a blow on it and the chipping began.

The youth had the hang of it before he'd gone a dozen steps along the row. The hoe felt balanced and familiar in his hands and the chipping action came easily. But the work could be hard on the back. You had to keep bending slightly awkwardly to work the hoe from side on, as the weeds couldn't be seen from directly above the cotton plant. He decided to develop a more upright, straight-on stance. If anyone could find a better method, it was him. Using a hoe was the one thing he knew he had a gift for.

It was getting quite hot, although now and then a sigh of breeze came and ruffled the leaves a little. There was a powerful smell of earth. The youth had never seen such rich soil.

The one-legged man was a couple of rows along and he kept up a constant grizzle.

"Time was I'd've shot along here like a flamin' two year old," he'd say to no-one in particular. "But that was when a man had two good legs."

The youth thought how hard it must be to work the artificial leg in the soft soil, and how awkward to have to bend with it every few moments. When the man bent right down he would let out a loud groan of "Ahhhhh!" and you would hear a metallic click, as though a locking device was clicking in and out. Sometimes the man would have trouble raising himself from the bent position and would do the groan again: "Ahhhhh!" It sounded like a noise Long John Silver would make: "Ahhhhhh! Avast ye lubbers!" The youth thought of the man as Long John, and imagined him with a cutlass and a parrot on his shoulder.

A few rows away on the other side were two young chaps about twenty. They talked to each other in hoity-toity voices. They kept saying the word *sar-tra*. The youth could not follow enough of their conversation to figure out what *sar-tra* was.

Denny kept a watch on everything. He would walk along a row where the chipper had been, checking how good a job was being done. Sometimes he'd call the chipper back and show him where he'd missed some weeds or had damaged a cotton plant with the hoe or had trodden down the soil too much. Then he would cross a few rows and walk back along another chipper's line and check that out. He came along the youth's row once, but didn't say anything. Then he crossed to Long John and asked him how he was managing. Long John suddenly seemed invigorated. He declared that he was goin' like steam, and that he'd done more hard yakka in his time than he'd had hot dinners, and that young fellas nowadays didn't know they were born. But as soon as Denny was out of earshot he resumed his grizzling: "One time a man wouldn't've put up with a pissant like that, but that was back when a bloke had two good legs!"

Denny was constantly coming and going. He'd do some checking of the rows, then speed off in his jeep, then reappear twenty minutes later. Other times he'd sit in the jeep using a pair of binoculars. Sometimes he'd be standing up in the jeep, one hand on the windshield, the other holding the binoculars up to his eyes.

"Hey, look at that," someone said when they first noticed. "He thinks he's fuckin' Rommel!"

"Nah," said someone else. "It'd have to be Patton. He always wants to be a Yank!"

"He oughta watch out, standin' up there like that," another chimed in. "If the wind got under that fuckin' hat he'd take off!"

The truck came with the morning tea and Panos blew his whistle for a ten-minute break. The youth sat in the shade of the truck, with his back against one of the wheels. He sipped his tea and looked across the endless rows and listened to the buzz of talk. The two young chaps were going on with their discussion about *sar-tra* and he guessed that *sar-tra* was a person. They spoke softly in posh voices and it was hard to catch all they said, especially with other talk going on. They mentioned "tutorials" and "the campus" and a "Professor" Somebody and the youth guessed they were uni students. He looked at them admiringly from the corner of his eye. How clever they must be, he thought.

When the tea-break was over the truck driver pulled away with a lot of revving and a couple of wheel-spins in the dirt. Denny was nearby and yelled at him to take it easy. The driver stuck his head out and grinned and said something that nobody quite caught. The truck sped off. When it returned to pick the chippers up at lunchtime it approached fast and pulled up with a skid. Denny was a fair distance away, next to his jeep, but the youth noticed that he put his hands on his hips and stared in the truck's direction. They had their lunch-break back at camp. When they went to climb back onto the truck afterwards there was a different driver. Denny had sacked the other one.

"What did he sack him for?" asked someone.

"For bein' a lair," another replied.

"Somebody oughta front up to the bastard!" declared Long John. "Sackin' a bloke! One time I'd've had a go at him, no worries!"

"It ain't right," said someone else. "Sackin' a bloke just because he reckons he's a lair. Who's he to say anyone's a lair?"

"He's the ramrod."

"He's the fuckin' Hat-rack!"

"He's General Patton with pearl-handled friggin' revolvers."

"And besides, that bloke *was* a fuckin' lair."

"Yeah, there is that."

The new driver went very sedately.

THERE WAS what they called an ablutions block at the camp and it had an endless supply of hot water. The nozzles of the showers were broad and shiny and when you stood in the stream of water your whole body was enveloped in it. The showers were always crowded after knock-off and there was lots of talk and laughter and horseplay.

Later on, after the evening meal, the campfire would be lit. Two of the men had guitars and another a mouth-organ and they would play together. One of the guitarists liked folk music, the other was into rock'n'roll, while the mouth-organist only ever wanted to play "Swannee River."

The folk music chap was the best musician, so he generally played and sang what he liked and the other two tried to follow along. There was a song called "Deportee" that he sang a lot. He said it was by someone named Woody Guthrie. The youth loved that song from the first moment. The tune gripped his heart and he thought the words were the most beautiful poetry he'd ever heard. He wasn't sure what it was about at first, but gradually understood that it told of Mexican workers coming illegally into America to pick fruit, and then being deported back over the Rio Grande:

> My father's own father
> He waded that river.
> They took all the money
> He made in his life.
> My brothers and sisters
> Came working the fruit trees,
> And they rode on the trucks
> Till they took down and died.

Then there were some words in Spanish, and a part about being chased:

*Six hundred miles*
*To that Mexican border*
*They chase us like outlaws*
*Like rustlers, like thieves.*

Next there was the part about a lot of people dying:

*We died 'neath your trees*
*And we died in your bushes.*
*Both sides of that river*
*We died just the same.*

Then came the part that made it clear why the song had such a feeling of pain and disaster. It was about a plane crash, a plane full of those Mexican fruit-pickers being deported:

*The sky plane caught fire*
*Over Los Gatos Canyon.*
*Like a fireball of lightning*
*It shook all our hills.*
*Who are all those friends*
*All scattered like dry leaves?*
*The radio says*
*"They are just deportees."*

The youth could not stay seated by the fire after hearing that song. He had to walk far off into the dark by himself, to think about the deportees going down in flames at Los Gatos, and the Anglo-Saxons going down under the arrows, and Harry Dale the Drover drowning in the flood, and the Bushranger riddled with a hundred bullets. The refrain of the song was

"Goodbye Rosalita," and in that name was all the beauty and sorrow of the world. It made you see vivid red roses, and then the roses darkened with tragedy . . . Goodbye Rosalita, Goodbye Rosalita.

After a long time out in the dark, seeing the campfire flickering in the distance and the men leaving it one by one to go to bed, the youth would feel cried-out enough to be tired. He'd go to his hut and lie on the bed and try to keep his thoughts on dark Spanish roses until he could drift away in sleep, but it was hard to block out the sounds that Long John made, specially when he sat up mumbling and coughing and reached for his tin to piss in.

THE TWO uni students were usually working the nearby rows and the youth could listen to their conversations. It was only ever bits of conversation, but he began to piece the bits together. Their names were Simon and Patrick. They looked a lot like each other, except that Simon had black hair always neatly combed, while Patrick had an unruly mop of red hair. They talked a fair bit about *sar-tra*, and also about *nee-cha*, and sometimes about *hi-digger* and *shoppin-hower*. None of it meant anything to the youth but it sounded wonderfully intelligent and interesting and made Simon and Patrick seem like beings from another dimension. They also talked about films, though not just ordinary films. They liked "art-house films," whatever that meant.

"Let's face it," said Simon. "Beyond art-house, there's nothing remotely watchable."

"Absolutely," Patrick agreed. "Hollywood's a wasteland."

Then he heard them mention a film he'd seen. The youth had gone into a cinema near Telford Square one time, in the afternoon, not knowing anything about the movie but feeling overwrought and wanting to be in a cool dark place for a while. The film had impressed him because it had been so strange and foreign—Swedish, it was, with people talking very intensely to each other and shots of snow on the ground—and yet he'd been able to follow it, more or less. He felt like calling out to Simon and Patrick that he'd seen that film and that it just went to show that outside art-house there's nothing remotely watchable and that Hollywood is a wasteland. He imagined being friends with them and having interesting conversations. He could discuss 1066. Being uni students they'd know all about that for sure. He'd ask them where they thought it had all gone wrong for the Anglo-Saxons. Were the tactics too negative at Hastings? Had the effort of Stamford Bridge been too much? Yes, he should definitely have a talk to them about it. They'd probably be glad of a chance to compare notes.

He reflected on how he could get into conversation with them. He needed to have a topic ready for when the chance came. He spent hours trying to formulate something just right, something he could memorise. A question would be best. "Excuse me, I've just been trying to recall. Of King Harold's brothers, was it Gyrth or Leofwine who was with him at Hastings?" And they would reply: "Oh, both of them actually, and of course it was the other brother, Tostig, who'd turned traitor and joined the enemy side at Stamford Bridge."

Yes, a question about the brothers would do nicely. It felt good to have it up his sleeve.

At the moment, though, he was trying to think what "peons" were. Simon and Patrick were talking about "peons." They were very amused with the word and were looking across at other chippers and giggling between themselves. It sounded like a really good joke. The youth wished he knew the gist of it. He kept a grin on his face in case they looked across at him, so they'd know he was on their level and understood how funny it was.

Then they burst into loud laughter. Simon had said something about ruling the peons with a big hat. Patrick replied that the Yanks were working on a new super-hat that would control the world.

The mirth stopped suddenly. Denny was coming along behind them, checking their work, his big white hat bobbing. He did not say anything to them. He stepped across several rows and went back to where Long John was lagging a longish way behind the broad line of chippers. He stopped and spoke to him and then the youth heard Long John's voice rising and falling. "Goin' like steam!" he said. And, "These young blokes today don't know they're born!" And then there was low mumbling that sounded like excuses being made. Denny stood with his hands on his hips, listening to the apologetic mutter, then he said something in a soft voice and walked back to his jeep and drove off. Long John watched him go, then called to the chippers nearby, "One time a man woulda told that mongrel where to stick his fuckin' job!"

But when the truck came at lunchtime, the youth saw that Long John could barely drag himself to it. His face was very red and his breathing harsh. The false leg didn't seem to be bending when it should and he had to keep stopping to bang at the knee-joint with his hand. When he got to the side of the truck he could not hoist himself up and the second time he tried he fell backwards and sprawled on top of some cotton plants at the end of the row. Panos and another couple of blokes helped him.

"Jeez, mate," said one of them, "let's get movin' before the Hat-rack notices them busted plants and wants to dock yer friggin' pay!"

"Yes," said Panos, in his soft Greek voice, looking around at all the men. "Best we go. We have seen no damage of Product, okay?"

There was a chorus of responses.

"Seen nothin', mate."

"I was lookin' the other way, meself."

"Glare o' that friggin' sun blinds a man!"

"I wouldn't know a busted cotton plant if I fell over it."

"What, are there cotton plants round here?"

They helped Long John onto the truck, a couple of the men lifting him by the armpits from above.

"Once upon a time . . . a bloke woulda hopped up here like . . . like a flamin' sparra," he said, "but that was when . . ." It was coming out slower and more slurred than usual and it trailed off without finishing.

Long John did not return to the fields after lunch. He was having a lie-down, Panos said. The work was too much for a man with a false leg. Simon murmured to Patrick that that might be a false premise, and Patrick replied that a false leg was nothing compared to a false premise. The men were discussing how Long John had lost his leg in the first place. Someone said he'd lost it in the Korean War. The youth was asked what he knew, being the room-mate. The youth was embarrassed. He didn't like the room-mate thing being mentioned in front of Simon and Patrick. They might think it meant that Long John was a friend of his or something. He felt like making it clear to everyone on the truck that he'd hardly spoken three words to the man, and that he kept out of the room as much as possible because of him pissing in the tin and stuff. But he just shrugged and kept his eyes lowered.

Someone said they'd heard Long John had lost the leg in a train accident.

"He accidentally left it in a train," muttered Patrick.

"Along with his umbrella," Simon shot back.

"And his premise," Patrick answered.

The youth wasn't sure what "premise" meant, but he could tell it was a really clever joke and he chuckled, to show them he was still on their level.

When they returned to the camp they heard that Long John

had had a bad turn and that Denny had driven him into town, to the base hospital.

"Poor old bastard's feet never touched the ground," said one of the cook's helpers who'd seen him taken away. "As soon as they realised how bad he was they had him off company property like a shot. These Yank companies are always scared of gettin' sued."

"How did he look?" someone asked.

"Turnin' blue in the face."

"Did he say anythin'?"

"Nah, he looked unconscious."

Later someone said that Denny was in the shit with the Yank bosses for letting Long John have a job at all. A man with a bung leg, and a bit long in the tooth as well.

"Must've felt sorry for him."

"What, Shadrack? That'd be the day!"

"It's the Yanks who are the bastards."

"Shadrack's a Yank himself."

"No he ain't. He was born and bred at Mulangumby. He's no more of a Yank than you are. Mind you, his *hat's* from fuckin' Tombstone, Arizona!"

"And the hat does all the thinkin'."

"That's right. They didn't give Shadrack the hat to wear. They hired *him* for the *hat*, because it needed a set o' legs to walk around on."

"Anyone ever seen Shadrack without the hat?"

"Yeah, once, when the wind blew it off."

"What happened?"

"He started runnin' round in circles like a chook with a missin' head!"

"Like a big chook, eh?"

"Yeah, an enormous chook."

"Did someone put the hat back on him?"

"Yeah, after a while."

"Why after a while?"

"We needed the eggs."

THE YOUTH had the room to himself after that. It was nice to have privacy again. He could get the White Book out of his bag and look at pictures of Sweetheart before he went to sleep. And when he woke he could have another session with her. It was so good to lie there in the first fresh light, gazing at her face. She was as sweet and natural and trustworthy as the morning. Nothing could change that. It went without saying.

Different photos in the White Book drew him at different times. For a while it'd been the one he called "The Lonely Princess," an unposed shot of her at the opera. She is standing at the foot of a grand staircase with a program in her hand. Her hair is up and she's wearing a gown that shows the whole contour of her neck and shoulders. She is with a group of people—men in fancy suits and other women in ball-gowns—but they have all turned momentarily aside, so that she seems alone and ignored in their midst. How could those people be looking away, even for an instant? That picture called forth all the youth's tenderness. Even in the midst of the fame and glamour, she could be alone and unappreciated. Poor darling.

The picture he dwelt on now was the one he sometimes called "The Sword Maiden" and sometimes "The Highwayman." She is having a fencing lesson and is dressed like a man, like the most beautiful slim graceful man you could imagine. Her hair this time is fastened back. She is wearing high shiny boots and has a ruff of lace at her throat. She has just removed her mesh face-guard and is holding it down beside her with one hand while with the other she flourishes her rapier in a gesture of salute. The photo is being taken over the shoulder of the fencing teacher and she is looking and smiling directly at him, which means that she is looking almost directly at you also. As ever, she's cool and poised and lovely. But there is something else. It is apparent that even in her blonde coolness she is flushed and excited. She is scared of the sharpness of the blades, even with the safety tips on, and of the desperate quickness of the swordplay—but her fright has brought her fully alive. You almost feel the hum of it in her body. He had no experience of such things, but he knew that at the moment of that photo she was in a mood to make love. That was why he found the picture so thrilling.

Yes, she was all the beauty and thrillingness of the world, nothing would ever change that. Except that now that wasn't the whole story. Now there was another aspect.

The youth had seldom dreamt, or if he had he rarely remembered it. Now he was having a particularly vivid dream—or nightmare—that stayed with him. It took place in an amusement park. Sweetheart is operating the ticket booth of the Tunnel of Love. The youth is the customer and buys a ticket, not because he wants to take the ride, but to have an excuse to approach her and speak to her and have a moment of her attention. She seems to read his mind, and she tells him it is a serious offence to buy a Tunnel of Love ticket under false pretences. She will have to report him, she says. He reluctantly gets into one of the boats, which takes him into the tunnel. It is pretty and soothing at first, with the glimmer of fairy lights and the lapping of the water. Then the air becomes hot and oppressive and there's the reek of harsh perfume. The boat keeps turning up new tunnels until the youth fears he is hopelessly lost. The boat stops and he cannot make it go again. There is hardly any light. He knows that the water around him is dangerously hot and deep and he dares not leave the boat. Her voice comes from nearby:

"You're in a jam now, aren't you," she says.

He replies that he is.

"Would you like me to help you?"

He replies that he would.

"Tell me how much you want my help."

He replies that he wants it very much.

"Not good enough!" she snaps.

The youth begins to see a little better in the dark and makes out a cave or grotto near him.

A giant web extends out of it and is strung across the tunnel, and he sees that the prow of the boat is caught. He peers into the grotto and can almost make out a huge spider as big as a person. He realises that Sweetheart's voice came from the grotto. She is right where the spider is! He must warn her, save her. He senses that the spider is raising its huge fangs to strike. There comes a foul reek which he knows is the spider's breath as its mouth gapes for its prey. The youth tries to cry a warning but he cannot utter a sound. He tries to paddle the boat with his hands but the water is scalding hot. Then someone is coming up the tunnel behind him, wading knee-deep through the water. How can that be? The youth is mystified. He peers again into the grotto and makes out Sweetheart's face. She is very pale and anxious-looking and is trying to call him closer. Her face is right where the spider is. The fangs must be poised just inches away . . . Then he sees the person who has waded up to him. It is Diestl. The youth tries to tell Diestl that Sweetheart is there with the spider and in terrible danger.

"She isn't *with* it!" Diestl growls back. He grabs the youth by the arm and pulls him from the boat. The youth finds the water isn't hot at all and is only shallow. He and Diestl wade back along the tunnel until they see a chink of light in the roof. They climb up to it and break open a hole big enough to squirm through. They sit on the roof of the Tunnel of Love and look out over the amusement park. The youth is trying to fathom what Diestl meant by saying Sweetheart wasn't with the spider. He turns to ask him, but Diestl has vanished. The youth climbs down to the ground and thinks to return to the ticket booth, but an instinct warns him that if he does the whole horror will be repeated, that he will have no power to avoid it. Then he understands something. Only the top half of Sweetheart is visible in the ticket booth. The bottom half, unseen below the counter, has *spider's* feet. He hurries away from the amusement park, shrivelled with the horror of that knowledge.

There was something else. It was the truly haunting part, the part that made him wake up heartbroken. Even as the youth hurries from the amusement park, he knows that Sweetheart can be saved only if someone is brave enough to confront what she is. It's like the fairytale of Beauty and the Beast. If he returned to the booth with an axe and smashed it open to reveal the spider's feet, there would be a fearsome, inhuman shriek, then the spider's feet would scuttle away into the deeps of the tunnel and Sweetheart would be her sweet self again. But the youth is too afraid to venture back.

He wants to ask Diestl to return with him, but he knows that Diestl has no interest in saving Sweetheart, none at all, and that it comes down to an intolerable choice: he can have Diestl or Sweetheart in his life, but not both.

The youth understood that the dream wasn't Sweetheart's fault and that it shouldn't influence his feelings about her. And it didn't, really. It was merely that there was an extra dimension to those feelings now, a dark area at the back of them. You didn't need to take much notice of the other dimension, or of the dark, except of course when the dream was actually happening, or during that first minute or two after you'd woken and before the vividness faded.

You could speed that fading by getting the White Book out straightaway and gazing at "The Lonely Princess" or "The Sword Maiden." Almost at once the dream or nightmare would seem quite far off and almost unconnected to you. If you were lucky you could go the whole day without a single thought or image of it coming to mind.

Yes, the mornings were okay, mostly, now that he had his private space. He could cope with the Tunnel of Love thing. What he could maybe not cope with was the Terror Waking thing, but it had only happened once. He'd woken in a panicked gesture of trying to shield his head with his arm because Long John had stumbled across and swung a tomahawk at him. Except it wasn't Long John on a gammy pin, but an inhuman scuttling thing that hissed in a voice like Long John's but higher pitched: *One time we would've split your head open before you saw it coming, but that was when a girl still had two good legs!*

It was so nice to get out to the cotton rows and feel the sun and earth and air, to feel the solid weight of the hoe in your hands, and the action of your body as you worked. The youth had always lived most fully in his mind, but there were times now when he just wanted to exist in his physical self, like a tree or a bush, like a cotton plant having its leaves ruffled in the sunny, earth-smelling breeze, and not ever having to think.

THEY WERE paid at the end of their first week. Rita came with a tray of brown envelopes and sat in front of the cook-shed with her white hat pushed back and gave each chipper his pay as he came up and signed for it. Rita looked after all the clerical matters of the camp and she and Denny both lived in Company quarters elsewhere. They were said to be on together. They did seem very suited. Someone reckoned that if they mated they'd have a baby hat.

There was some unpleasantness because one bloke claimed he'd been underpaid. He was getting stroppy with Rita when Denny came up and took him aside. Denny explained that you only got paid for the time you spent out on the rows with a hoe in your hand, and that the bloke had been absent the whole of Wednesday morning. The bloke replied that he'd had a toothache somethin' terrible and had gone to Weegun to look for a dentist. Who was Denny to say a man couldn't get a crook tooth seen to? Denny explained in a patient voice that, funnily enough, the Company employed cotton-chippers to chip cotton, not to go to the dentist.

The bloke began to bluster some more. Denny told him to please get his gear and leave the Company's property. The bloke yelled that Denny couldn't sack him just like that. Denny replied that he just had. The bloke was a lot bigger than Denny and seemed for a moment to want to fight. Denny didn't do anything other than take his hands out of his jeans pockets, but there was something in the way he did it. The bloke walked away swearing and a minute later was in his car, churning up dust as he headed for the front gate.

A lot of the men went into Weegun on the Saturday afternoon, to go to the pub. The youth could've got a lift with someone if he'd wanted to. There was a picture theatre in the town and he thought of going to see what was on at the matinee. But he was feeling unwell. His arm and shoulder had seemed at first to have recovered from the hurt they'd got when he was pinching the bike, but the first few days of cotton-chipping had brought back the throbbing ache. He had tried to ease the strain by varying his method, using different actions and postures, even hoeing left-handed at times, but none of that had helped. He was sore all over, really, from using muscles he didn't know he had, and felt headachy too. He lay on his bed till mid-afternoon, then decided to go for a walk.

He left the camp and headed towards the big machinery depot that he could see in the distance. After a few minutes of walking he felt less unwell. There were wisps of white cloud in the sky, very high up, and a gentle breeze came over the fields. The land stretched away in the green-and-brown pattern that was everywhere and that he was accustomed to now, the green of cotton leaves and the brown of the soil. He walked with his head back, letting the sense of the sky fill him. Then he walked with his head down and focused on the smallest pebbles or puffs of dust or the tiniest leaves of the cotton plants. Then he walked with his eyes closed, concentrating on the sound of his own steps on the dirt road, or trying to catch the faint whisper of the breeze coming along the rows and through the leaves. It was like being the only person in that whole enormous land-scape and having every sense filled. Every sense except taste. He wanted to taste the landscape as well as see and hear and feel it. He bent and poked his finger into the soft rich soil beside the stem of a cotton plant and then touched his tongue with it. It wasn't a bad taste, apart from a hint of chemicals.

The machinery depot had high wire fences around it, and signs warning that the wire was electrified, and that you shouldn't touch it, and that Continental Cotton bore no liabil-ity if you did. The vehicles inside were like machines from some bigger-scale world. The youth assumed they were cotton harvesters. The tyres were taller than a man, and the control cabins were far up in the air. He walked slowly round the perimeter looking at the machines from various angles. Their size gave you a watery sensation in the stomach, as though there'd be nothing you could do to escape if they suddenly sprang to life and came after you.

A brick structure stood outside the compound and gave off a faint hum. Maybe it held the generator that sent the charge into the fence, the youth thought. It had no sign warning not to touch, so he gingerly put a fingertip on the brickwork. Nothing happened. He sat down with his back against it and opened the copy of *Family Realm* he'd brought with him. It had a piece in it that he liked, about sewing, with pictures of embroidered blouses that made him think of Russian peasant costumes.

He began to daydream about a summer afternoon on the Russian steppes, of being alone in that vast solitude. What would be over the horizon, he wondered, if this really was Rus-sia? He imagined birch forests, and churches with onion-shaped domes of gold, and beautiful intense girls with names like Natasha. There was the fabled city of Samarkand. Or was that more in China? He had a vague notion of caravans of camels going to Samarkand. Did they have camels in Russia? Surely it was too cold for them there. How patchy his knowledge was. It was all bits and pieces, not a seamless cloth. That was the thing, to have a seamless cloth of understanding. That's what going to uni gave you, he supposed. It was what Simon and Patrick had. He felt bad that he had no deep knowledge about anything in particular, except maybe about 1066, having reread *Year of Decision* so many times. He told himself to read more books, to take stock of life and the world. He made a mental note: Take Stock.

Sitting upright against the brickwork made his arm and shoulder ache again and he was drawn to a bush a short way off beside the wire fence. It had dense foliage and made a pleasant patch of shade and the grass there was too short to hide snakes. He lay down in the shade and closed his eyes and listened to the leaves rustling. The magazine lay open beside him. He would rest his eyes for five minutes, then go back to those blouse designs with their Russian look. And while he rested his eyes he would think about a beautiful Natasha . . .

A voice was speaking to him. At first he thought he was dreaming it, but he realised his eyes were open and he was staring into the green of the bush. He went to sit up and scratched the side of his face on a prickle.

"Hi there. You okay?" A white utility was beside him, and a man was leaning out of the driver's side. "You seem to have drawn some blood," the man said, pointing.

The youth felt his face.

"I'm alright," he told the man.

The man was looking him up and down without being too impolite about it. "Do you know you're on private land here?" he asked.

The youth replied that he was from the chippers' camp and had come for a walk to see the giant machines.

"Ah, I see. Well, we don't normally encourage folks to mosey round the Company's property too much," he said, not sounding angry or hostile, but just a bit wary.

"Sorry," the youth said, getting to his feet and brushing himself off.

"It's not that we mean to be inhospitable."

"No, I understand."

"There's a dandy little first-aid kit here," the man said, opening his glove-box. "Let's see if we have anything for that scratch of yours." He handed the youth a sealed packet. "That's an antiseptic pad, I think."

"Thanks," the youth said and went to put it in his pocket.

"You tear the end off."

The youth tore the end off and found a wet pad. He dabbed at the scratch. It stung.

"It smarts a little, I guess?"

"Yeah."

"Well, that probably means it's doin' some kinda good."

"Yes, thanks for that."

"I'm goin' your way—past the camp, I mean—if you'd like a ride."

The youth felt awkward and would have answered that he was okay and didn't mind the walk, but he thought maybe this was the man's polite way of telling him to get straight back to where he belonged. He picked up his magazine and got into the vehicle. It had the logo of the three intertwined "C"s on the doors and was very shiny and new, and inside there was a pleasant smell.

There was something impressive about the man too. He was distinguished-looking, with greying hair and bushy eyebrows. He wasn't just a security guard or something. He must be one of the big bosses. You could sense that he was *rich*. You could tell it by all sorts of things—the way his fingernails were so clean and pink, the heavy gold wrist-watch, the fine material of his blue shirt, the grey cloth of his trousers, the gleaming brown boots. The youth pressed himself against the door so as not to contaminate the man's space. He felt like a dirty peon, a deportee.

"So how do you like our little operation here?" the man asked.

"It's good."

*My father's own father*
*He waded that river . . .*

"You're a country boy, I guess?"
"No, not really."

*They chase us like outlaws,*
*Like rustlers, like thieves . . .*

"Well, the weather's holding out for us."
"Yes, it's been nice."

*We died 'neath your trees,*
*And we died in your bushes . . .*

"You find the work okay?"
"Yes, I don't mind it."

*The sky plane caught fire*
*Over Los Gatos Canyon.*
*Like a fireball of lightning*
*It shook all our hills . . .*

The youth felt like crying for the broken bodies in the canyon, and for the broken bodies on the hill at Hastings, and for all the others everywhere. He suddenly thought of Long John sprawled in the dust of the road that day beside the truck, unable to haul himself up. There was something about being in this spotless vehicle with this nice man that made you feel tight in the throat and on the verge of sobbing out loud.

*Who are all these friends*
*All scattered like dry leaves?*

The ute slowed.

"I'll set you down here, if that's okay."

"Thanks," said the youth, his voice muffled.

The man turned and looked at him and spoke softly.

"Are they treatin' you right, son, down there at that camp?"

"Yes," the youth replied. He had tears running down his cheeks from thinking about all the people scattered like dry leaves.

"You sure about that?"

He nodded yes.

"You can always talk to Denny Russell, you know. He's a real good guy. If anyone was beatin' up on you, or any kinda thing like that . . . And there's Rita, too, and she's a real under-standin' lady. If you feel like havin' a talk with either of 'em, you tell 'em I advised you to. Okay?"

"Thanks," said the youth, wiping his cheek with his hand.

The man's deep voice grew even softer.

"We've all been where you are, son, every one of us, especially round your age. But it gets better. It might not seem that way from where you're standin' right now, but it does."

"Thanks."

The man put out his hand.

"You take care now, son."

They shook hands and the youth hopped out and watched the ute pull away.

The man gave a wave and there was a flash of sun on a gold ring.

## 9. The Kiss

The youth trudged the remaining distance back to camp and lay on his bed. The aching soreness had come back and he dozed fitfully until he heard shouting and laughing. It was the men returning from the pub in Weegun. He stayed dozing on his bed for most of the Sunday as well.

On Monday he was hoeing his row when Denny came up to him and asked, "How're you findin' things?"

This was the first time Denny had spoken directly to him and the youth wondered if he had found fault with his work.

"Going alright, I think," he answered.

Denny pushed his big hat back on his head and put his thumbs in the waistband of his jeans, as though to show he was relaxed and not in any hurry to go.

"You made friends with Gus on Saturdee, I hear."

"Who's that?"

"Gus Gordler. The big boss."

"I didn't actually get his name."

"He said he came across you at the machinery depot."

"Ah, yes. Is that out of bounds?"

"Sort of."

"Sorry."

"Well, Gus wasn't concerned about that. He just asked me to make sure you're okay, that you aren't havin' any problems in the camp or with the other blokes."

"I'm fine."

"I told Gus you're a very good worker, which you are. And

that you're not a smart-arse." He glared across to where Simon and Patrick were. "Unlike some."

"He seemed like a nice bloke."

"Gus? Yeah. He is," Denny replied, turning back slowly. "Got no tabs on himself. Always has me and Rita to his barbecues. Likes a barbecue, Gus does."

Denny gazed around at the chippers and adjusted his hat and the youth expected him to move on. But he lingered.

"He was a bit dubious when he first saw you lyin' there beside the electric fence. Didn't know if it was a dead body or what. He said it suddenly brought a few things back to him. Gus was in the Company's operations in South America, and over there they've got Marxist guerrillas, sabotage, the lot. Over there there'd be Company men with tommy-guns guardin' those machines. Anyway, when he drove across to check on you he didn't know what to expect. Then he found a young fella asleep with a cookery book open beside him."

The youth half-thought to correct him that it was sewing, not cookery, but he didn't want to interrupt. This was too interesting.

Denny was scuffing at the soil with the toe of his brown cowboy boot, deep in reflection. "They killed his wife, you know," he said softly.

"Pardon?"

"The Marxist guerrillas. Gus and his wife were in the wrong place at the wrong time and there was a bloodbath. His wife and five others were shot dead in front of his eyes."

"Jesus," said the youth.

"That's why Gus was posted over here. To give him a quiet life for a while, and a chance to adjust."

"They must really hate the Yanks, then, over there."

"They hate 'em everywhere," snapped Denny. "Here too, even. I get sick of hearin' these no-hopers mouthin' off against the Yanks. I'm on the Yanks' side a hundred per cent. The

Yanks are about makin' things happen, producin' things, bein' efficient—and about makin' somethin' of *yourself* as well. Most people are *bums*, lazy bums who'd rather grizzle for fifty years instead of gettin' somethin' goin'! I grew up among grizzlin' bums, and I've had it all me life! It's either grizzlin' bums or pukin' little *smart-arses* who think the world's only there for them to have a fuckin' giggle at! People hate the Yanks because the Yanks show 'em up as the total fuckin' *losers* they are!"

His voice had got loud and there was no mistaking how angry he was. Simon and Patrick were bent over their hoes, working intently. The youth felt scared too.

"Anyway," Denny said, forcing himself to calm down, "I told Gus I'd have a friendly word with you. Like I said, you do good work and you've got a good attitude. I wouldn't mind havin' a few more like you. Keep it up."

He walked back along the row to where his jeep was, then got in and drove off.

A couple of the blokes on the other side called across to the youth, to ask him what had got up Shadrack's arse. The youth shrugged and called back that he had no idea.

He thought about what it must be like, having to be the ramrod to blokes who think you're a jumped-up little prick and a Yank toady, and some of whom would punch you black-and-blue if they thought they could, and who you in turn despise. He saw Denny differently now. The abrupt little man was trying to serve an idea much larger than himself, was trying to wage a noble fight against the endless no-hopers' grizzle of futility that would cover the whole world if it wasn't held off. The things that got him laughed at behind his back—the big hat, the jeep, the binoculars—were part of the fight. They were the warrior's equipment. Of course blokes would laugh at those things. That's what bums do, Denny would say—they laugh at what is noble and dedicated. And yet it was a bit harsh to call people bums and smart-arses, just like that, as though those words conveyed everything about them.

It all cuts too many ways, the youth thought, to be that simple.

It was like Gus Gordler's wife, and those others, being gunned down. There were sorrows on both sides, and it wasn't just the poor deportees who were scattered like dry leaves.

> Both sides of that river
> We died just the same.

The youth's arm and shoulder got worse with every day on the cotton rows. And the more he tried to spare them, the more strain it put on other muscles. His back was always aching now. He found it difficult to sit upright for any length of time and did not stay late at the campfire. He would go to the room and stretch out on the bed in the least uncomfortable position and hear the sound of the talk and laughter from outside. The glow of the fire came through the window and made flickery patterns on the ceiling. The youth reflected that this was how it'd been for Long John when he lay there, staring up, the stump of his leg raw from the day's chafing, the false leg unstrapped on the floor, the piss-tin under the bed.

It was good, though, to be able to lie back in the flickering dimness and listen to Keith, the folk singer. Being in the room, away from the others, you could let your tears flow free if the songs brought them out.

Keith was a fixture at the fire. He always had his guitar with him, and at some point, when the talk and banter had died down and blokes were starting to stare quietly into the flames, someone would say, "Bugger this! Give us a song, Keith." And each night Keith went through five minutes of stage fright before he got properly started. He would pick clumsily at the guitar strings and mutter that the tuning wasn't right, or he'd break off after the first few words of the song, saying that he had a sore throat and probably wouldn't sound too good. The chap with the mouth-organ would offer to play "Swannee River" to break the ice. So Keith would strum along with the mouth-organ and start vaguely singing the words and by the time "Swannee River" was finished he'd be into his flow. The mouth-organ chap's playing was pretty bad, really, but no-one minded as long as it got Keith going. When Keith was in his stride he'd do the songs like a real pro. They were mostly about poor farmers being evicted, or factory workers being sacked or underpaid, or hobos being beaten up by the railroad cops, or coalminers getting killed in faulty shafts. As Keith got going you'd sense the emotion rising in him and his voice would get stronger and his strumming more emphatic. The youth thought the songs were true and sad and stirring, but he also saw why Denny might call them the glorified grizzles of bums and losers. The suffering was laid on a bit too thick. Even "Deportee" was like that, the youth realised. But Keith sang a few songs that had a tougher tone. They told of striking work- ers getting guns and shooting back at the police, or of bank robbers who always made a point of destroying the mortgage papers in the vaults and so became folk heroes. Yeah, that's more like it, the youth thought.

After a while Keith would leave off the plight of the work- ers and begin to lighten up. He'd sing songs like "She'll Be Comin' Round the Mountain," songs that everyone knew and could sing along with.

Not everyone gathered round the fire in the evenings. The camp had sorted itself into various groups and circles. The car- avan people were a whole separate tribe.

The biggest, flashest caravan belonged to Alf, the camp cook. Alf travelled the country all year long, cooking for shear- ers, fruit-pickers and cotton-chippers, and when there weren't seasonal workers about he'd hold over in some town for a few weeks as a pub cook. He was a bald-headed bloke who never smiled or made conversation but had a set of stock responses he'd give to various remarks. If someone asked what was in the stew, Alf would say, "Dingo baits! Just for you!" Or if someone wondered what was for dessert, he'd snap, "What the cat dragged in!" But his favourite retort was the Like-it-or-lump-it one, as in:

"What's for breakfast, Alf?"

"Like-it-or-lump-it pie!"

Or: "What time will lunch be, Alf?"

"Like-it-or-lump-it time!"

Or:

"Where'd you learn to cook, Alf?"

"Like-it-or-lump-it college!"

Alf was known as a bit of a comedian, but the youth thought he was very depressed and just wanted to be left alone to do his work. It was hard being a camp cook. You were always on duty and had to do three meals a day for maybe dozens of people, plus morning and afternoon teas, and you had to do it with whatever stoves and fridges and facilities the place had. And the cooking had to be good and varied enough to keep people reasonably happy. No-one feels more friendless than a camp cook that everyone's disgruntled with.

One of Alf's offsiders had to leave for the weekend because of a family matter and Denny asked the youth if he'd like to make a little extra money by filling in as Alf's dishwasher. It was hard work, manhandling the pots and pans in the sink, especially with a sore shoulder and arm, but the youth got by.

Alf generally hunted people away from the cook-shed, but the stint as dishwasher gave the youth the right to hang around. You could make yourself a cup of coffee, or have a taste of the apple crumble, or sample a scone, or just enjoy the cosiness of the kitchen. It was interesting to watch Alf work. His face would be tight with concentration as he poked and fiddled with six different pots and pans on the stove, and with other things in the oven. At the same time he'd be rolling out dough, or slicing up fruit, or mixing jelly or custard. Whenever he had a free moment he'd go out to the back step, fling his arms wide, throw his head back and make groaning noises. They were stretching exercises, but it looked as though he were appealing to heaven for help. Then he'd shrug and come back inside to concentrate again for a while.

Alf wasn't snappish all the time. When it was just himself and his offsiders he didn't mind having a brief chat. Cooks and their helpers shared a code of mysteries, and even a fill-in dishwasher had a tiny share of the specialness of that. It was people outside the code—the flippant, the ignorant, the unappreciative—that Alf couldn't abide. The youth asked him how he'd gotten started as a cook. Alf asked the youth about his family and why he wasn't with them.

Camp cooks were very well paid and Alf's caravan was a beauty. It looked like a gigantic silver bullet, and he had a big-finned Pontiac car to pull it. As soon as he'd cooked his last crumb and morsel for the day, he'd go into his caravan, pull the curtains down all the way around, and not be seen or heard till morning. The youth learnt from Kurt, the dishwasher he'd filled in for, that Alf spent every night getting stupefied on vodka. He drank vodka, Kurt said, because it didn't leave a smell on you next day. Every morning he'd look hollow-eyed and shaky, but by the time he'd got breakfast rolling he'd be okay and snapping that the only thing on the menu was Like-it-or-lump-it.

The other caravans weren't nearly as flash, but they looked very cosy and comfortable in the evenings when they had their lights on and you saw the blokes sitting inside them, making themselves cups of tea from electric jugs or lounging on bunks with their hands behind their heads and cigarette smoke curling lazily up.

How the youth wished he had a caravan, with his own electric jug, his own bunk, his own tidy cupboards, and spaces for his magazines. How self-contained he'd be. He could sit on the step in the evening. That seemed one of the best things about a caravan. You could sit on the step and enjoy the fresh air and chat with passers-by, and maybe invite them in for a cuppa if you felt like company. On the other hand you could just go back inside and close the door and draw the curtains and be safe in your space with your own belongings.

He lay on his bed in the evenings trying to ease the ache in his arm and shoulder. He realised he was lucky to have the room to himself, and that it was the next best thing to having a caravan. He could turn the light off if he felt like resting his eyes or dozing, or just wanted to listen to Keith singing the songs of the downtrodden, or he could switch it on if he wanted to look at the White Book or reread parts of *Year of Decision*. If he felt like it he could lift himself on his good elbow and look through the small window above his bed. He could see the campfire with the men around it and the lighted caravans further over—and Simon and Patrick there.

Simon and Patrick had made friends with a bloke named Errol who owned the nicest of the caravans, aside from Alf's. They spent their evenings in Errol's van with a radio playing hit-parade songs. The radio got louder each night until it started to drown Keith out when he sang. Blokes would yell out to Errol to turn it down and he would adjust it a bit, but it would soon creep up louder again. Whenever anyone called to Errol about the radio Simon and Patrick would make impatient eye-rolling faces through the window, or to each other. It wasn't very fair to Keith, the youth felt. Quite bad manners, really. But then he supposed Simon and Patrick and Errol had a right to do what they wanted, just as much as Keith or anyone else did. The youth didn't know whose side he should be on. If it hadn't been for Keith he would never have heard "Deportee" or known who Woody Guthrie was. Keith had opened up a whole new world for him. But Simon and Patrick were a new world too, and in some ways an even more interesting one. He wondered what it was like to have a relationship like theirs, to be such close friends that you can talk and giggle endlessly between yourselves, to be so in tune that you can finish one another's sentences. He wondered what it was like to be at uni together and understand *sar-tra* and *nee-cha* and *hi-digger*, and to automatically know what "peons" were and how to turn the idea of "peons" into jokes and wisecracks.

And there was something else, too, something the youth couldn't get entirely clear to himself. Watching Simon and Patrick, he'd notice how one of them might tousle the other one's hair, or how one might drape his arm casually around the other's neck, or how one might rest his hand on the other's knee when they sat side by side. This behaviour wasn't like horseplay. It was more delicate than that. Most people probably didn't even notice it, the youth thought, but he did. The odd thing was that whenever he became aware of those gestures or touches or glances, he felt a flutter of yearning. Sometimes the yearning made him want to get the White Book out and gaze desperately at Sweetheart. Other times it made him want to make friends with Simon and Patrick somehow, and be around them. And there were times when it was a mixture of the two. They were the oddest times. He would see some gesture of Simon or Patrick's—a walk, a turn of the head, a lift of the hand—and he would imagine Sweetheart doing it and feel all choked and stirred and tingling. And the more he had the Tunnel of Love dream, the more his thoughts of Sweetheart had a dark and scary side that also now applied to Simon and Patrick. In the dream now he often had a sense that Simon and Patrick were in the grotto with the spider ("They aren't *with* it!") making jokes about how succulent peons were if you could get at the marrow of their bones. He knew that Diestl despised Simon and Patrick even more than he did Sweetheart. It was all very confusing. Sometimes he felt brimming with love for Sweetheart, and other times he could hardly bear to bring her to mind. Sometimes he found Simon and Patrick so fascinating he couldn't take his eyes off them, and then the next minute he'd relish the thought of them being hoiked off the place on the toe of Denny's boot.

THE YOUTH's shoulder and arm were so sore and stiff one Friday that he could hardly move them. He'd got through the previous few days of work only by controlling the hoe with his left hand a lot of the time. This put new strain on the left hand and arm and they became almost as sore as the other side. Denny noticed how awkward his movements were and asked him what was wrong. The youth replied that it was just an old football injury that he occasionally had trouble with, but that a weekend's rest would set it right. He tried to sound cheery, as though it wasn't any big deal, as though he'd be going like steam shortly. Denny was giving him a long estimating look and the youth could hear how much his own voice sounded the way Long John's had. Denny didn't push it. The youth thought that perhaps a weekend of rest really might help. On the other hand, he knew, a break from the routine might give his body a chance to seize up more. *One time a man would've breezed along these rows like a two year old . . .*

Long John was still at the base hospital in Weegun. Alf, who had known him slightly from years before, had paid him one or two visits.

"He's tryin' to keep cheerful," Alf reported. "He says to give all the fellas his regards, and tell 'em not to do anythin' he wouldn't do."

"Well, that gives us a fair amount of leeway," the youth answered. That was what you were supposed to answer whenever anyone said not to do anything they wouldn't do. The youth felt they owed it to him to make the proper reply, to make it sound as though they were a bunch of pals who went out on the town every night, and were just waiting for their sick mate to return for more mad escapades.

"So what's actually wrong with him?" he asked.

"There's problems with the stump of his leg," Alf said. "But they're more concerned about his ticker now, accordin' to the nurse I spoke to."

The youth wondered whether *he* should've paid a visit, being the former room-mate and everything. Perhaps he'd left it too late and now wouldn't be welcome. And what would they talk about? The youth could say that the fellas all sent their regards, but after that it'd just be awkward, probably.

THE NEXT evening he went across to where Simon and Patrick were sitting on the step of Errol's caravan. He had rehearsed his words.

"I was wondering if you might have something to read," he said.

"*Read*?" said Simon, as though he wasn't sure what the word meant.

"Yeah. I've finished the book I brought with me, and I thought you might have something I could borrow."

Simon turned to Patrick. "*Do* we have any reading material to lend to the needy?"

"I've really no idea," said Patrick.

"I dare say one could go and look," said Simon.

"I dare say one could, if one was inclined to."

"And is one inclined to?"

"It might depend on the inducement offered."

"Yes, it might."

The youth kept an appreciative smile on his lips, to show how amused he was.

"Why are you bent like the Hunchback of Notre Dame?" Patrick demanded.

"Sore shoulder," said the youth, trying to ignore the pain when he straightened up.

"How sad," said Simon.

"How poignant," said Patrick.

"Just a bird with a broken wing," said Simon in a sing-song voice.

"They like their peons hale and hearty, you know," said Patrick. "They'll send you the way of old Pegleg if you don't watch out."

The youth kept smiling, to show he was on their level.

Errol came along then. He'd been at the ablutions block, showering, and was wearing a white flannel dressing-gown and carrying a plastic bag with shampoo and soap in it. His dark hair was wet and tousled.

"Hello," said Errol to the youth. "What a nice surprise to see *you* here." He sounded very sincere and the youth felt a pang of gratitude. Errol stood with one hand on his hip and the other smoothing his wet hair. "We'd been hoping that you weren't going to stay utterly aloof from absolutely everyone," he said, looking straight at the youth and giving him a smile.

The way Errol was standing, the way he smoothed his wet hair with a little fluttery motion of his fingers, made the youth think of Sweetheart. He was getting the choky feeling. Simon and Patrick were now looking at him as though they suddenly found him interesting.

"He's looking for something to read," Simon told Errol. "Do you have anything for him?"

"In the *reading* department, that is," Patrick added.

"Shoo! Shoo!" Errol said, waving them off the steps so that he could enter. "Let me see what I've got." He fished about in the caravan and came up with a battered paperback.

"Thanks," said the youth. "I'll return it in a couple of days."

"Oh, we're leaving," said Errol, "so keep it."

"How do you mean, leaving?"

"Leaving here. Leaving the job. I'd only planned to stay three weeks anyway, and these two are fed up to their little back teeth. So it's the Yellow Brick Road for all three of us."

"When are you going?"

"Oh, in the morning sometime."

"That's a shame."

"The shame is that we didn't get to know *you* sooner," said Errol. "Such a lost opportunity." He touched the youth very lightly on the arm. "You really shouldn't be such a loner, you know, going about all closed up the way you do."

"Is that what I do?" asked the youth, hoping Errol would say more. It was fascinating to hear how you seemed to others.

"Sweetie, you might as well carry a placard saying 'PRIVATE PERSON—KEEP OUT.'"

"Really?"

"Yes, really. And apart from it not being the best thing for yourself, it makes it awfully frustrating for people who can see your, um, *possibilities*, let's call them."

"Where are you heading?" the youth asked, absently. He was trying to register the idea of having possibilities.

"Back to where one has civilised asphalt under one's feet."

"And a *life*!" cried Simon.

"And not a cotton plant in sight," added Patrick. "Or a cowboy hat."

"Now let's not be judgemental," Simon said. "A cowboy hat can have its charms—not to mention leather chaps and a lasso—but just not here!"

"It'll be sad to see you go," said the youth.

"You could come with us, if you want," said Patrick.

"What do you think, Errol?" Simon asked.

Errol gave the youth a long look before he spoke. "Yes, think about coming with us. If nothing else it's a free ride back to the land of the living."

The youth left them and went back round the campfire to

his room. There were murmurs of conversation still going on, but Keith was strumming his guitar with increasing firmness, getting focused, putting himself into a mood to sing. The youth understood that Keith sang on emotion. It was only when he got stirred up that his shyness fell away and he began to surge on the power of songs like "Deportee." Right now his face was shadowed and flickery from the glow of the fire. It made him look like more than just a normal bloke. He looked like the spirit of Anger and Pity, preparing to speak.

KEITH WAS in his best-ever form that night and the youth lay listening for a long time with tears on his face and his heart thumping. The songs made you feel sad and angry and brave all at once. They made you feel that you were in touch with the spirit of all the people in the world, and that you loved them all as your brothers and sisters. You loved them not because they were necessarily good or nice, but because they were all going through the same hard mill. The details might vary, but the mill was the same one in every time and place—for King Harold, and for Harry Dale the Drover, for the friends like dry leaves at Los Gatos, for Gus Gordler's wife caught in a hail of bullets like the Bushranger a hundred years back, and for Long John lying alone a few miles away with a raw stump and a bad ticker.

The youth drifted to sleep a long time after the campfire had been left to itself and had sunk down to embers. He had a vivid sense of blood-red roses turning dark, and a black-haired, olive-skinned girl . . . Goodbye Rosalita . . . Goodbye Rosalita . . .

In the light of morning he had to decide what he would do.

Half his mind told him that going with Errol and Simon and Patrick was an opportunity to get out of the old groove of his life. He could take the Yellow Brick Road with them. The thought of it made him feel tingly and excited. He knew that something was being offered, something beyond a mere lift

232 - PETER KOCAN

back to the city. It was like the Pleasures of India thing that he thought about sometimes—the sense of being in an exotic street full of mysterious perfumes and alluring doorways. It was very scary though. It meant opening yourself up and being vulnerable. Who knew what might happen? But that risk was the price of the pleasure. He wasn't stupid. He knew that nothing comes for free.

There were practical aspects to consider, too. His arm and shoulder and back were troubling him so much that he'd be struggling to get through the remaining fortnight of the job. He had three weeks pay in his pocket now, and could afford to just up and go if he chose.

He wondered what Diestl would advise, but knew the answer already. Do anything, as long as you fundamentally don't care. If you start caring, you start wanting to survive for the wrong reason—you start wanting to savour life, and then the world has you where it wants you. You have surrendered then. The only good reason to survive a bit longer is to get closer to the point of striking one good blow, of hitting the enemy hardest as you go down. But now the youth was toying with hopefulness.

"I thought you were one of my kind," Diestl would say. "That's why I've kept saving you in the Tunnel of Love. But it seems not. You want strudel instead of steel."

The bit about the strudel was the worst insult you could get from Diestl. The youth wasn't completely sure what strudel was, but he knew that wanting it more than the steel of the Schmeisser, or more than the long empty road, made you the weakest of the weak. And yet "weak" wasn't the right word. Diestl didn't despise anyone for being weak. He knew too well how cruel the world was and how it could frighten a person to their very core. What Diestl despised was a person who wasn't entirely weak, who had the potential to hit back, to make the world grin on the other side of its face, but who shirks the duty.

It wasn't cowards he hated but turncoats, those who *could* choose steel before strudel but decide not to.

Just before breakfast the youth went across to Errol's van. The door was open. Errol was lounging on one of the seats with his hands behind his head and his feet up on a bench-top. At first he didn't notice the youth looking in. He wore only a pair of shorts and the youth could see how fit and muscled he was. He looked like a lightweight boxer. For a moment the youth felt scared.

Errol told him not to make any fuss about their departure, but to just bring his bag quietly across and stow it in the back of the car. Simon and Patrick had already put their bags in.

"Strictly speaking," he explained, "we signed up for the full five weeks work. If you shoot through they blacklist you for the future. I couldn't care less, and I don't suppose you do either, but I'd rather avoid a scene with the Great White Hat if possible."

The youth nodded agreement. He hadn't known he'd be barring himself from working here again. It gave him a pang of misgiving. He'd liked it, really. It was just his line of work. It would've been good to know he could come back another time, even have it as a regular thing each year. But he'd made his decision. Besides, with his sore arm and shoulder . . .

They left while breakfast was being served.

"Right," said Errol as he closed the boot. "Let's move."

The car was already hooked up to the caravan. Errol only had to disconnect the van from the camp electricity, turn off the gas cylinder and hop into the driver's seat. A few blokes around the camp looked, but no-one seemed interested.

As he and Simon and Patrick went to get in, the youth felt a moment of confusion.

"Um, who's sitting in front?" he asked.

"Well, *you* are, silly!" Simon replied.

"Talk about coy!" said Patrick.

The youth got in beside Errol, who was tapping a gauge with his finger.

"We'll need to stop in Weegun for petrol," he said.

They drove out of the camp and then out beneath the Continental Cotton sign onto the public road. They drove beside the cotton fields for several minutes and the youth gazed over the endless pattern of green and brown. There was already a slight heat haze and the huge machines in the far-off compound shimmered. Errol had his eyes on the road and was fiddling with the car radio with one hand. Simon and Patrick were talking in the back. The road began to veer away until the cotton fields couldn't be seen anymore.

Simon and Patrick were discussing places in the city, especially somewhere called "Ricky Rascal's." It was a nightclub or dancehall or something.

"We met at Ricky's," Simon said, clutching Patrick's arm. "Didn't we, chook?"

"Yes," Patrick replied. "I was cradle-snatched at Ricky's."

"I thought you'd probably met at uni," the youth said.

"Nah," said Simon. "We'd been at the same campus for two years without clapping eyes on each other."

"I suppose you would've studied 1066 at uni?" the youth said.

"What?"

"1066."

"What's 1066?"

"King Harold and all that."

"Who's King Harold?"

"Hastings and all the rest of it."

"Who's Hastings?"

The youth figured they were having a joke, so he turned and grinned at them, to show he was enjoying it.

"Actually," said Simon, "1066 has a delicious ring to it. Sounds like something you'd get at Ricky's."

"Yes," agreed Patrick. "I can just picture some slutty little baggage sidling up and saying, 'Hello. I'm into 1066. Are you?'"

"And 'King Harold' hardly bears thinking about!" cried Simon.

They clutched each other, giggling.

The youth forced himself to chuckle, while Errol looked ahead at the road with a preoccupied air.

"Actually," said Simon, when they'd recovered, "you'll have to get Errol to take you to Ricky's. We couldn't live without it."

"Or without the Green Door," said Patrick.

"Or the Passion Pit."

"Or the Velveteen."

"Get him to take you to all of them!"

"Hear that, Errol?" said Simon. "We're getting you organised."

"Good," Errol replied. "I need organising."

"And for God's sake get him some clothes!"

"Right," said Errol. "Any more instructions?"

"No," said Patrick. "But stay alert. We may think of something."

The youth was trying to figure out exactly what the talk meant, what the joke of it was. Why would Errol take him to places? Why would Errol buy him clothes? It dawned on him that Simon and Patrick thought he was going to be Errol's boyfriend, the way they were boyfriends with each other. The youth wasn't stupid. He knew now that they were on together, though it had taken a while for the penny to drop. But they were wrong if they thought he was like that too. Or Errol. Errol didn't giggle and clutch arms, or roll his eyes and make pouty faces. And he never mentioned *sar-tra* or *nee-cha*. The youth thought of the moment when Errol had come back from the showers and made that gesture of fluttering his fingers through his wet hair. That had reminded the youth of Grace

Kelly somehow, and so he'd got a bit tingly and aroused. But it was Grace Kelly he'd felt tingly about, not Errol. That was the important thing. It was Sweetheart it loved and yearned for. And if it couldn't be her, if it had to be someone you'd known in real life, well, he had Meredith Blackett to remember. He'd always have the sweetness of their time together. Nothing could ever take that away. But in fact he had Sweetheart herself, ever-present and ever-lovely, and as long as he had one photo of her, or one image of her in his mind, the world would be alright for him. Except when he was having the Tunnel of Love dream . . . The youth did not want to think of the Tunnel of Love dream just then, so he brought his mind back to Errol. You could tell how silly Simon and Patrick's chatter was by the way Errol half-ignored it, as though he couldn't be bothered even setting them straight about such nonsense.

The youth felt *he* should say something to Simon and Patrick. He should be the one to set them straight. Just a brief comment would do. Something like: "Gee, you blokes have got wild imaginations. All Errol's doing is giving me a lift back to civilisation." And no doubt Errol would appreciate having it cleared up as well. After all, they were going to be in the car together for a few hours, and they didn't want any awkwardness. But just as he was getting ready to speak they arrived at Weegun and pulled in beside a petrol pump at the garage.

"I'm going for a pee," Simon announced.

"Need any help?" Patrick asked.

"Could be."

"Lead on then."

The garage attendant came out and Errol told him to fill the tank, then started to check the oil under the bonnet. The youth felt he should offer to pay a share of the petrol. He took a couple of notes from his wallet, unsure of how much he should offer but anxious not to offer too little. He went over to Errol, bent under the bonnet, and bent beside him.

"Um, let me contribute towards the petrol," he muttered awkwardly, proffering the two notes.

"Oh don't *you* worry," Errol said, pushing them away. "It's those other two who'll need to kick in."

"No, really," the youth insisted, proffering the notes again, wanting to get the embarrassment over.

Errol made as though to push his hand away again, but then he closed his own hand over it and held it shut. The youth felt how strong a grip he had, but it was gentle, too. He looked up, into Errol's eyes. Errol moved his face closer and tilted his head to bring his lips level for a kiss. The youth could not move his head away because of the car bonnet, so he closed his eyes and held his own lips firmly together and stayed still, telling himself not to panic. He was surprised how cool and soft and pleasant Errol's lips felt on his. It lasted only a moment, then came the voices of Simon and Patrick returning.

The youth stepped quickly out from under the bonnet, his heart pounding, but feeling that he'd coped rather well. He knew his face had gone a bit flushed and he saw Patrick giving him a smirky look.

"And what have our two little grease-monkeys been doing under that big naughty bonnet, do you suppose?" he asked Simon.

At that moment a big-finned American car came gliding along the street. It slowed right down and the youth saw someone looking across at them from behind the wheel. The car looked familiar, but the youth was too full of confused feelings to think. He turned away and went round to the Gents to give himself a minute alone to get calm.

As he stood at the basin he heard a challenging voice outside, then other voices responding. He realised that the American car was Alf's big Pontiac, and that it was Alf's voice he could hear. He went out of the Gents and cautiously approached the corner of the building and peeked around the edge. The Pontiac was pulled up across the driveway with the front wheels slewed to one side and the driver's door open, and Alf was confronting Errol and the other two in front of the open bonnet of Errol's car.

"Who are *you* to be so high and mighty?" Simon was asking.

"Yes, what gives *you* the right?" Patrick demanded.

Alf ignored them and kept talking to Errol in a low intense voice. The youth heard the words "underage kid" being repeated.

Errol didn't reply. After a moment of silence he turned and put the bonnet down with a clunk and waved Simon and Patrick to get into the car.

The youth pulled back from the corner and stood against the wall of the building. He heard the car start up and saw the back end of the caravan glide forward and out of sight. He took deep breaths. After a minute he went round the corner and found Alf leaning against the Pontiac, rolling a cigarette.

"Ah," Alf said. "How ya goin'?"

The youth nodded distractedly. He'd just remembered his bag had been in the boot of Errol's car.

"Um, them friends o' yours said to tell ya they had ta go. They was runnin' late, or somethin'."

The youth was thinking of his bag, his White Book, his few belongings.

"Anythin' wrong?" Alf wanted to know.

"My bag's in their car."

"Nah, it's here," Alf replied, indicating the Pontiac.

The youth sighed with relief.

"I'm just headin' back to camp, if ya want a lift."

"No, I'm okay," the youth said. "I think I'll hang around in town for a while."

Alf finished rolling his cigarette, lit it and blew out a long stream of smoke. He didn't seem in any hurry to go. He kept on smoking and gazed away at the sky. The youth gazed at the sky too.

"Ah well," said Alf after a minute. "I better get back to me cookin', I s'pose."

"Okay."

"I just made a quick run into town to see how Teddy Bennett was doin'."

"Ah," murmured the youth, wondering who Teddy Bennett was.

"The news ain't too good. He had a bad turn last night. The doctor said he's goin' downhill fast and there's not much they can do except keep him comfortable. He's dopey from the drugs they're givin him and I don't think he's got much idea of what's goin' on."

"Sorry to hear that," said the youth, having realised it was Long John.

"Yeah. And he seemed so chirpy on Wednesday when I saw him. He asked after you. I think I told ya that, didn't I?"

"Yes. Thanks."

"He's got no relatives, apparently. I been droppin' in ta see him because I knew him a bit round the shearin' sheds years ago. Before he lost his leg."

"Yes, you mentioned knowing him."

Alf flicked his butt sharply away.

"Ah, well, it's what we're all gonna fuckinwell come to, sometime!" he said, as though to himself. Then he seemed to remember the youth was there. "Blokes o' mine and Teddy's vintage, I mean. Blokes who've let it all slip by 'em somehow. But you still got the chance of havin' a life."

He looked as if he might say more, but a big truck nosed into the drive and he had to move the Pontiac out of the way. He handed the youth's bag out, said, "See ya later," and drove off.

At the railway station the youth was told there was a train to the city in twenty minutes, so he bought a ticket. He sat slumped in his seat, watching the outskirts of Weegun fall away. How sad, he thought, how sad. He called up the words and tune of the song, and wished Keith was there to sing it one last time. The youth hummed it, for a man who was going downhill fast, and who had asked after the room-mate who hadn't even bothered to know his name.

*Goodbye to you Juan, goodbye Rosalita,*
*Adios mis amigos, Jesus and Maria.*
*You won't have a name*
*When you ride the big airplane,*
*All they will call you*
*Will be deportee.*

# 10. Karma

He had rented a room in a converted garage at the back of a big old run-down mansion from the Victorian era. The garage had been divided into three tiny rooms and the youth had the middle one. It contained a bed and a dressing table and a wardrobe and this left hardly enough space to turn around in. The youth didn't mind. The room was cheap and snug and he had no possessions other than what he could keep in his one bag. The lavatory and shower were over in the rear part of the house. There was a large backyard with a sagging clothesline and lots of unruly vines with purplish flowers on them. If you pushed past the tangle of vines you found a back gate and a laneway.

There were occupants in the other two rooms of the garage. One was a young chap named Sunny, from Ceylon. The youth knew this because he heard the chap talking to Delia, the landlady. Sunny and Delia spent a lot of time together in the backyard. Sunny's English wasn't the best but you could get the drift of what he said.

The man on the other side was a night-worker that no-one ever saw. The youth would hear him come in early each morning, and then a few sounds of him moving about, then nothing.

Sunny made a fair bit of noise with his radio. The youth would hear him repeating words and phrases from it, as though he was practising his English. There was a disc jockey who called himself "Mannie the Man" and "Mad Mannie" and "Mannie Wannie" and "Mannie Mabuly Wuly" and other names. Mannie talked a whole crazy lingo of his own. "Mabuly Wuly's Truly Cool, Fool!" he might shout half-hysterically, and then you'd hear Sunny repeating it, but in a tone of formal politeness, the way you'd say, "Hello, I'm very pleased to meet you."

Sometimes the youth felt like knocking on Sunny's door and explaining to him that Mannie was a nitwit and not worth taking notice of, and also that he'd prefer not to have the rubbish inflicted on him through the partition. And God knew what the night-worker bloke on the other side thought. He must be getting a gutful of Mannie too. Sometimes the youth fancied he could feel the irritation coming from that side. But he said nothing. He just wanted to mind his own business. He wanted to be snug and private with his White Book and his magazines and his copy of *Year of Decision*. He wanted to be left to think his own thoughts, a lot of which were now about Delia.

He'd been walking past, that first day, and had heard a tinkle of wind-chimes. He had looked up at the old house and had noted the elaborate verandah, the wrought-iron balcony, the stained-glass panels in the front door, the run-down relaxed look of the whole place. He had thought it would be nice to live there. Then he'd seen the small "Room to Let" notice. He'd wandered up and down the street for a long time, bracing himself for the ordeal of having to front up and act like a normal person who can smile and talk and be pleasant. Finally he went in at the iron gate and approached the front door. There was a discreet sign beside it which said: DELIA'S KARMA CENTRE * BIRTH CHARTS * TAROT * CRYSTALS * AROMATHERAPY * ETC. He rapped with a heavy doorknocker and waited for a longish while, but no-one responded. The sign worried him. He could feel his dredged-up determination draining away. He was heading back towards the gate when she came around the side of the house and called hello.

She looked like a beautiful witch. She had on a long flowing robe, and her hair was flowing too, long and dark and wavy.

She was barefoot and had beads round her neck and bangles on her wrists. There were tiny bells attached to her ankle so that she made a tinkling sound when she walked. The youth was deeply struck from the first instant and would've fled except that her manner was so friendly.

"How *are* you?" she called as she came up to him, as if he was an old pal she was pleased to see.

"Not bad, thanks," he replied, stopping at the gate. It would've been too rude to keep walking away.

She came and looked straight at him. She had hazel-green eyes, and her eyelids were painted a gold-speckled green, so that when she blinked you got two flicks of iridescent colour, as if two green butterflies had instantaneously fluttered and vanished. She had a long nose and pointy chin and very red lips and was perhaps in her thirties.

"How can I help you?" she asked.

He didn't trust his voice at that moment, so he gestured towards the Room to Let notice.

"Ah, lovely," she said, as though the prospect of him coming to live there was just the nicest thing.

She showed him the garage room and within a minute they'd decided that he would take it. He asked if he could pay a month in advance and she agreed. Even though the room was cheap, four weeks would use up most of the money he'd brought back from Weegun. But at least he'd be sure of a whole month of having a roof over his head.

"You'll be one of my outsiders," she said. "But only in the bodily sense, not the spiritual. In spirit we're all *insiders* here."

They went into a front room of the house to organise the payment and the receipt. It was an office or consulting room where she received her clients. The room was full of crystals and charts and beaded curtains and feathery things dangling. And it had a smell that gave you a light, tingling sensation. It was bracing like the air of a high mountain meadow. But there was a heavy, musky, *witchy* feeling about it too, even if the witch was beautiful and had gold-flecked green butterflies for eyelids.

As Delia had leant over a little desk to write the receipt, she'd been outlined against the daylight at the window and her robe had become slightly see-through. The youth had been able to glimpse her breasts, or at least tell that they were bare under the material. After a moment he had averted his eyes, to be polite, and had looked instead at her feet. They were beautifully shaped, the toes long and slender, the nails painted a silvery colour. Then he looked at her hair lying across her back and shoulders, at the rich dark weight of it as it rippled to one side when she moved. The tinkle of the wind-chimes came from the verandah and suddenly the youth had a vivid sense of how much beauty and pleasure there must be in the world. It must be everywhere, just a little out of sight but almost close enough to touch. He had stumbled on a fraction of it, simply because those wind-chimes had prompted him to look up from the footpath. It was as chancy and flukey as that. You might walk the footpath till the end of time and never know what tingling beauty and bracingness was near you at a given moment.

That was part of the way that life toyed with you, he reflected. If the world was completely bleak and barren it would all be very simple. You would just grit your teeth and struggle to the end as best you could. Everyone would, and no-one would have any illusions. It would be like the life he imagined Eskimos have—knowing nothing but ghastly horizons of ice and snow. Never having had meadows and orchards and songbirds, they didn't miss them. But if you allowed them a glimpse of those things, they'd never again be content with everlasting ice. They would be going through the motions of their old true bitter lives, but the thought of the meadows and songbirds would be eating them away, ruining them as Eskimos without giving them the new things in any measure.

That was the insight Diestl had tried to drum into him. The youth understood the point about the strudel. If you think about the strudel—about sitting in some beautiful cafe in Vienna, with Strauss waltzes playing—you are finished as far as the long road of your destiny is concerned. That's what the world wants: for you to glimpse enough of the orchards, enough of the strudel, that you'll be snivelling for it ever afterwards. And yearners and snivellers are no threat. They get stepped on and can't do a damn thing about it. And Delia was a walking orchard, a living plate of strudel.

A phrase suddenly popped into the youth's mind. *The beautiful knife.* The most beautifully made and decorated knife is the one most likely to cut you, because you are drawn to touch and handle it. The most delicious berry is the one most likely to poison you. The most desirable witch is the one most likely to do you evil. He decided to call this the Principle of the Beautiful Knife. He felt he'd gained a new level of understanding. He reminded himself to tell Diestl about it.

By the time he and Delia had finished their transaction, he was in the Diestl mood. He stared blankly past her and said nothing. He felt the solid weight of the Schmeisser and imagined what a burst from it would do to that room and all those knick-knacks of wisdom and sensitivity. She had asked him about his star sign and was chatting pleasantly about whether Earth or Water was his best element. But then she sensed that he'd got very distant. Her flow of talk began to peter out. He left without saying anything more and went out to the garage room and lay on the bed and stared coldly at the ceiling for a long time.

SO HE kept to himself in his room. He always peeked out into the yard before venturing across to the toilet, or if he was on his way out. Mostly he came and went via the backyard gate that connected to the lane. Delia was in the backyard a lot. She did washing for the tenants for a fixed amount per load, so she was often in the laundry at the back of the house, or hanging the washing out. When she did washing she put a big apron on over her billowing robe and tied her flowing hair back and wore rubber gloves of a bright yellow. The youth thought of this as the Working Witch outfit. She also tended a herb garden in a corner of the backyard. Other times she just hung about there with Sunny, the two of them side by side on a couple of deckchairs.

The youth would stand with his eye to the crack of the curtain and watch her as much as he could. Whenever he was watching her he would find himself feeling more alive and happy and somehow grateful to the whole scheme of things. But then he'd think of the Principle of the Beautiful Knife and begin to feel bitter and imagine unslinging the Schmeisser and injecting a burst of reality into it all. Despite his caution he occasionally came face to face with Delia. She would smile at him and say hello, or ask how he was getting on, and he would give a curt nod of the head or a half-wave of the hand to acknowledge her. It would have been rude not to acknowledge her. The youth wasn't one for outright rudeness. Neither was Diestl. No, you remain polite, as long as it doesn't endanger you, and as long as you also make it clear that you don't care. In fact you make it clear that the extent of your not caring would stun people if you chose to reveal it fully. You are walking a different road and have nothing in your heart but the endless ruin of the world.

One day, when he was watching Delia chat with someone in the backyard, his hand accidentally brushed the curtain. He saw her glance across, her eye caught by the movement. She knew that he was there watching. He felt he could never face her again. She now knew that his pretending not to care was just a pathetic act, and that he actually cared so much that he skulked at his window with his eyes bulging for the least glimpse of her. But then he got enraged. Who was *she* to despise *him*? He paid good money for his room and he had a right to glance out of his window once in a while if he wanted to. He had a right to the view from his window without *her* being in his line of sight every two minutes, just as he had a right not to be tormented by Mabuly Wuly nonsense. He felt like storming and shouting that he'd leave, that if he'd known he was going to be stopped from looking out his own window he would never have come there.

But he did nothing except keep more out of sight. He was going to have to leave anyway, when his month was up. Then he'd be homeless on the street again, and there'd be no Delia to look at.

He began leaving his room first thing in the morning and not returning till after dark. He spent his time wandering the city and suburbs, or at the State Library, or in the Botanical Gardens. He kept away from the State Museum, because of the pushbike thing, but he discovered the Technological Museum in another part of town.

The Technological Museum had wonderful things in it. Above all there were the Viking swords. There were half-a-dozen of these in a glass case, blades corroded, and the handgrips rotted away, but otherwise they were the same as when the long-dead people had carried them. Beside each sword was a printed card giving some facts about it, like the period it was from, where it had been made, where it was found. They were all earlier than 1066 and the youth stared at them in wonderment that they had existed when King Harold was alive.

There was one in particular. The card said it was probably Norwegian and that it had been found in Yorkshire. Stamford Bridge was in Yorkshire, the youth reflected, and it had been the Norwegian Vikings that King Harold had defeated there. It all tied in! The youth began coming every day to look at the swords and let his thoughts and feelings run loose. How sad and heroic it all was. He had read in *Year of Decision* that the Vikings' big mistake had been in not guarding the actual bridge more carefully. When King Harold's men came to cross it, a single Norwegian warrior had stood against them. He had been so brave that the Anglo-Saxons remembered his deed for generations. This sword from Yorkshire could be the very one that lone hero had used.

The youth wished he could talk to someone about this. Did the museum authorities know what a sacred treasure they might have here—the very sword that had defended the bridge for those few glorious moments? The more the youth dwelt on this, the more anguish he felt. He had to speak up. This was something incredibly important to the whole world, and he was probably the only person who'd ever thought of it. He would gaze into the glass case until the emotion got too much. Then he'd go into the toilet and wash his face and dry it with a paper towel, then return to the display for another while. Once a uniformed attendant came into the toilet and saw him half-sobbing over the basin. The youth tried to pretend he was coughing, but the attendant gave him suspicious looks after that.

One afternoon the attendant came over to him and asked, "No school today?"

The youth understood it wasn't a friendly question. It meant, "I don't like the look of you. What are you doing here?"

He made an effort to look and sound normal. He said that he'd left school last year and was a jackeroo in the bush, that he was on holiday in the city, and that his hobby was learning about the Vikings and their swords and stuff. The attendant was a heavy man and wore an expression of contempt. The youth had an awful feeling that he might not be speaking properly, that the words might be coming out as gibberish. He sounded normal to himself, or half-normal anyway, but his mouth felt like it was working strangely.

The attendant's expression became more hostile and he seemed to be looking the youth up and down, taking note of his shabby appearance. The youth felt he had to assert himself, had to make it clear he was a proper person with important information. He forced himself to look the man right in the eyes and to speak very clearly, although his mouth still felt as though it was moving in a peculiar way.

"Who's in charge of the swords?" he asked.

"What?"

"The swords."

"What about them?"

"Who's the person I should speak to?"

"What?"

"The person."

"What person?"

"I need to talk to someone."

"What about?"

"I need to talk to them about one of the swords."

"Talk to who?"

"That's what I'm asking."

"What are you asking?"

"I need to talk to someone."

"Yeah, I reckon you do. But this is a museum. There's no-one here to tell your troubles to. Don't you have a family? What about your local minister? Come back when you've got yourself sorted out."

The youth left the area where the swords were. The attendant followed him until he was on the stairs, then stood and watched him descend. "You aren't on mara-u-ana, are you?" the man called. The youth did not reply. He reached the entrance lobby and went out into the street.

It was late afternoon and he felt too downcast to do anything but go back to his room. He crept in through the garden gate without being seen, then lay on his bed and thought about how

stupid he'd been. He'd made himself conspicuous. He'd hung
about in the museum in a way that the attendant couldn't help
noticing. He'd let his emotions get out of hand. He'd broken
every one of the basic rules. Diestl would disown him. The
worst part was that he was barred from seeing the swords, now
that the attendant had marked him out. To return would be
like walking into the cross-hairs of a rifle sight. The whole
principle of survival was to stay out of the cross-hairs, to keep
a bit in the shadows, a bit indistinct, a bit side-on. Diestl had
taught him that, but apparently it hadn't sunk in. The youth
was angry and disgusted with himself. It was proper that he
was barred from seeing the swords. That was his fitting punishment. But he felt he deserved something more physical and
immediate too. He stood up and got a heavy wooden coat-
hanger from the wardrobe and hit himself on the shin as hard
as he could. It hurt a lot, and for a long time. He thought
maybe he had cracked the shinbone.

The next day he bought a TV magazine because it had an
article about Grace Kelly. There was to be a festival of her films
on one of the channels. It wasn't a very interesting piece, and
the photo of her was a poor-quality one hardly worth keeping,
but there was something else at the back of the magazine. It
was a half-page advertisement for the Technological Museum.
At the bottom of the panel were three small pictures. One was
of a robot, another was of a ship's sextant from Captain Cook's
time, and the third showed the six Viking swords in their glass
case. He took the magazine home and carefully cut out the little picture of the swords and pasted it into the White Book. He
threw the rest of the magazine away, including the bad picture
of Sweetheart.

It seemed to him that fate had sent the picture of the swords
as a consolation. He was sure it was because he had accepted
the need to be punished and had hit himself with the coat-
hanger. It had really hurt, that was the main thing. It hadn't

been just a pretend hit. Fate knows when you are only pretending.

The youth felt more cheerful. He reflected that even if you've made a serious mistake and behaved like an idiot, as he had with the swords, you could redeem yourself by doing the appropriate thing, and that fate could accept that you'd made amends and were sorry. It made you feel you had a bit of leeway. You could make a mistake now and then—as long as it was just once in a while and wasn't *too* serious—and it wouldn't necessarily be the end. The thing was, fate knew you were on your empty road through the ruined world. It knew you had a destiny, and fate was always on the side of those who had a destiny, as long as they themselves kept faithful. It wasn't the odd stupidity that angered fate against you, but unfaithfulness.

With this more cheerful outlook, the youth had more energy for walking, and for looking at people and things, and for thinking how stimulating a place the world was. He sat for hours on park benches or on bus-stop seats, gazing into the sky. Cloud formations now struck him as especially interesting and somehow stirring and calming at the same time. They were these huge, beautiful, slow panoramas moving endlessly over the world. They were witnesses to all the dramas of human fate. No doubt they'd been rolling over Stamford Bridge that day and had seen the lone Norwegian barring the passage for those few moments before he was overwhelmed. No doubt that Viking's whole life had been going down the long road towards that point. And fate had helped him reach it because it was meant to be. And so the very people who killed him remembered his courage and his faithfulness, and wrote it down in their chronicles.

Yes, the youth felt better about things than he had for a long while.

WALKING NEAR Telford Square one evening, on his way home, he paused to look into the window of a shop that sold fishing rods and penknives and tents and tomahawks and various other outdoor things. It was a very small shop, and the window display looked flyblown and faded, as though it hadn't been changed for years—the cardboard price tags were bleached and curled from the sun, and even the fishing rods and penknives looked as though all their freshness had gone. The youth had never been into that shop, but he often paused outside it. It was just the sort of window display he liked. It was settled and predictable. You approached it with the comfortable feeling of knowing what was there. You could always see the shopkeeper inside, behind his counter. He was a fat man who wore a woollen beanie in red-and-black football colours. The red-and-blacks were Ronnie Robson's team, the best team in the world. The youth had got interested in the idea of football again, now that he was feeling more cheerful. He kept telling himself he must start going to the games, to support Ronnie and the great red-and-blacks.

As the youth turned to walk on, he saw a rifle hanging up in a corner of the window. He turned back. He'd never noticed the rifle there before. Maybe he'd missed it because it was up high. Or maybe it was a new addition to the window. The rifle had a neat, compact, chunky appearance. He thought he should buy it. Not right now, this minute. He hadn't nearly enough money. But sometime. He would buy it sometime. The youth had a very strong feeling that he was *meant* to buy that rifle, that it would still be there whenever he came for it, and that this moment of his first seeing it was somehow profound. He glanced up at the clouds lit red by the setting sun. He thought that perhaps at this moment they were looking down at him particularly.

He had no idea why he felt so strongly that he was destined to buy the rifle. He just knew he should, and would.

He sensed Diestl beside him, nodding gravely in confirmation and saying, "Yes."

THE YOUTH'S new confidence even extended to his attitude to Delia. He began to come and go from his room a bit less stealthily. He would use the front gate and this meant going along the disused driveway at the side of the house. It meant passing the window of Delia's lounge room, and because of the gravel on the ground it was hard to walk past in silence. A couple of times she was in the lounge room when he passed and they exchanged glances and she smiled at him. Another couple of times he came upon her and Sunny together in the backyard, lolling on the deckchairs on the grass. Delia called to him to join the conversation. Sunny needed to talk to as many different people as possible, she said, to improve his English. So the youth stopped and talked a little. He mentioned the cotton-chipping and Delia asked him to tell them more about it because it sounded so fascinating. The youth noticed that Delia reached over and touched Sunny lightly on the thigh and that Sunny responded by placing his hand over hers for a brief moment. It looked so casual that maybe they were hardly aware of doing it. But there was something powerful and exciting about the two of them together, the youth thought, the beautiful witch and the golden-skinned young man from a land of spices and temples and cobras and elephants. The youth couldn't think of anything else to say just then. They seemed to have gone into another mood where talking wasn't needed. He figured he should leave them and go into his room, but he was feeling a tingle from just being near them. It was as though the two of them together created an energy greater than either of them had on their own. Or maybe it was him. Maybe he was just so aroused by Delia that he was extra-sensitive to any flirty, lovey stuff that she was part of. Right now he felt so stirred and tingling that he was even excited by the thought that Delia knew he'd been watching her from behind the curtain that time. He had hardly ever felt that way before—of being so stirred that you *want* it to be gross and shameless and for the person to be completely aware of it.

The strange thing was that Delia didn't really arouse him all that much. At least he didn't think so. Her flowing robes and dark hair and amulets and ankle bells weren't really his cup of tea. Glimpsing the outline of her breasts that first day had been nice, but so would have been a glimpse of any woman's breasts. It was the gold-flecked green eye make-up that had got his attention. He had never met anyone who had green butterflies startle on her face whenever she blinked. But that didn't mean he was keen on her as a general thing. She wasn't like Sweetheart in the slightest. She had none of that cool containedness, none of the Ice Maiden about her. Of course there was that other darker side of Sweetheart now, the Tunnel of Love thing, but the youth tried to keep that out of his mind as much as possible. No, it was hard to imagine Delia in jodhpurs and high polished boots, or in a fencing costume with rapier poised, like in that superb photo of Sweetheart he'd pasted in the White Book.

Anyway, the youth had gone into his room and left the two of them there on their deckchairs on the grass. He'd lain down on his bed and closed his eyes and the delicious tingly feeling had stayed with him for a long while.

A few mornings later the youth saw a young woman in the yard as he was on his way out. She wore jeans and a white blouse and lace-up black shoes, and her hair was neatly tied back. He thought she must be a new tenant and went to go past her as quickly as possible. Then she turned towards him and he saw it was Delia. She had none of the usual make-up on and none of the bracelets and bangles. She looked like a fresh country girl, but sort of sophisticated with it. Except for the darker hair and the thinner, sharper nose and chin, she looked just like Grace Kelly would have looked in those clothes. The youth's feelings must have shown in his face.

"You haven't seen me looking like this, have you?" she said. "What do you think? Do I scrub up okay?"

"Yes."

"I'm not always the Witch of Endor. It's just that clients expect a karmic practitioner to look the part. I could read their cards perfectly well in jeans and T-shirt, but they wouldn't feel they'd had their money's worth."

"No."

"The trappings do seem to matter in this life."

"Yes."

"I'm heading into town. Are you going towards the bus stop? We could walk together."

"I'm not catching the bus."

"But you're walking that way, aren't you?"

"Um, yeah."

"Then it won't hurt you to walk along beside me and be sociable for a minute or two, will it?"

She gave him a challenging look that seemed to say: *I know you want to wriggle out of this, but I won't let you.*

They went out to the street and walked along. The youth tried to think of something to talk about. Delia was fishing in her leather shoulder bag, making sure she hadn't forgotten something. Because she was peering down into the bag, he was able to look at her face from the side. All he could think of was how good she looked with her hair tied back, and the contrast of its dark colour with the white of the blouse. There was a Spanish look about her. That was it. Some Spaniards are olive-skinned and some are pale, and Delia was the pale-skinned type. She looked like a Spanish Grace Kelly. She'd look great on a horse, the youth thought, sitting very straight with her chin out and one of those flat-brimmed black hats that Spanish riders wear. Not really arrogant, but knowing how to do that posture with the head back. It was like the way Grace Kelly knew how to do that blue-eyed stare that would destroy you at twenty paces, except that you knew it wasn't actually hostile but just a look she knows how to do, even when she's feeling perfectly friendly. And yet there is a scary element in it because you know this is how she'd look at you if she *was* rejecting you, and so you are always getting a sense of how lucky you are that she *isn't* being hostile. Fear and gratitude mixed up together. It was complicated, the youth thought. It was all bound up with the way your feelings were about women. It was about yearning so much for creatures who had the power at their fingertips to hurt you very badly. That must be the meaning of the Tunnel of Love dream. He wished he understood these things better. Perhaps he should get Delia to read his cards.

It was interesting, he thought, that he'd had feelings about Delia even before today, before he'd seen that there was a Spanish Grace Kelly behind the Witch of Endor. It showed that we know more than we are aware of. *We know more than we know.* He stored that thought away to reflect on later. Right now he was getting the tingling sensation very strongly.

It was so good to be walking along with Delia. They had fallen into step and seemed to stay in step without any effort. The shared movement felt wonderful. It was as though his body and Delia's were joined in the rhythm of their steps, as though the rhythm was a single heartbeat for the two of them, as though they were sharing each other's body and breath and life. The youth had never felt such a sense of oneness with anyone before. He could go on walking beside Delia forever. Then he realised he was by himself. She'd stopped some distance back to talk to someone over a fence.

"So, how are things?" she asked when she caught up.

"Okay," he replied. The tingling sensation had begun to fade.

"Do you like being one of our jolly band?"

"Yes."

"Good. *What* do you like about it?"

"Oh, um, I don't know," he muttered.

"You'd be happier, wouldn't you, if I gave you that question a week in advance, and in writing, so that you could think it through in ten different ways before having to answer."

"I would, yes."

"Ah, that's the Gatekeeper answering."

"Who's the Gatekeeper?"

"The side of you that deals with other people in all the everyday, practical matters that can't be evaded or postponed or denied. The side of you that I'm having this conversation with at the purely verbal level."

"Is there another side then?"

"Another side, or another self. The terminology isn't important. There's the other you that's mostly off in its cave, or forest, or fortress, or Arctic tundra, or whatever. That's the one who just signalled to the Gatekeeper to 'evade' or 'stall.' That's the one I'm talking to on the emotional plane. That's the one that really matters."

"And what is this other self like, the one in the Arctic tundra?"

"I don't really know," she said, stopping and looking into his eyes. "But I think it's significant that you picked up on the 'Arctic tundra' rather than something else."

"It was the last thing you mentioned, after forest and fortress. I just picked up on the last thing. If you'd said 'cave' last, I would've picked up on that."

"Now the Gatekeeper has orders to procrastinate."

"Possibly."

"I think you picked up on 'Arctic tundra' not because it was the last thing but because it was closest to the truth of your emotional landscape. An Arctic tundra is, let's see, cold . . .

bleak . . . hostile . . . exposed. That landscape is all about a bitter struggle to get survival needs met." She peered harder into
his eyes. "An Arctic waste has powerful symbolic meaning for
you, doesn't it?"

"I s'pose so."

"If you'd picked up on 'cave' the implications would be different. A cave can be a place of fear and darkness, but it's just
as likely to signify being snug and safe and hidden. At any rate,
a cave-dweller is quite another thing from a figure in an Arctic
landscape."

"I see."

"Do you feel pissed off by all this?"

"No, I'm enjoying it . . . But of course that might just be the
Gatekeeper with orders to lie."

"Good on you," she said, patting him on the cheek. "I *knew*
you had a sense of humour. I told Sunny so."

They resumed walking.

"Does Sunny have a Gatekeeper too?"

"No doubt. But Sunny is full of spiritual and cultural reso-
nances that elude me, although I catch on to more every day.
The archetypes are universal, but a lot of the detail is cultural-
ly specific. And Sunny is very steeped in his own culture. He's
a poet. Actually, he's known at home as the best young poet of
his generation. He's as sensitive as a harp string."

"Ah," said the youth, recalling Mannie Wannie's Mabuly
Wuly.

"Don't be fooled by that stuff he listens to on the radio. He's
trying to fathom the vibes of Western culture, that's all."

"I'd never have known."

"He and I have talked quite a lot about you. Sunny says
you're . . ." She stopped.

"Go on."

"I'm talking too much, as usual."

"You can't stop now. What does he say about me?"

"He says you're very young and very divided."

"Is that all?"

"He put it more poetically."

"How poetically?"

"He says you don't know whether to be angry at yourself or at the world."

"Is that poetical?"

"The poetical thing is the simile he used."

"Tell me."

"He says you're a young tiger that doesn't know whether to hide or kill."

The youth thought about this. Delia saw her bus coming and fished in her bag again.

"This is an invitation," she said, handing him a card. "In writing, and well in advance, to give the Gatekeeper time to get his orders. It's Sunny's birthday, and I want to give him a bang-up party. Do come. You don't have to socialise, if you don't want to. Just be there for a slice of cake. Okay?"

The bus came and Delia waved through the window at him as it pulled away.

Afterwards he marvelled at how well he'd got through the conversation. He'd held his end up like a real person. He'd never had such an interesting talk with anyone, not even the times with Meredith Blackett. How lucky to have met Delia in the yard at that moment. How interesting to know that there was this other version of her who wore jeans and a white blouse and lace-up shoes and neat hair and no bangles or make-up. It made him think again how full of possibility life was. You hear wind-chimes and look up, and you meet a Beautiful Witch with green butterflies for eyelids. You go out of your room at a given moment, and you meet a Spanish Grace Kelly who tells you that you're like a young tiger that doesn't know whether to hide or kill.

The youth knew there was a point to this, an insight that

floated just beyond the mind's reach. Then it darted in and he caught it. It was about the whole Pleasures of India thing. You take it for granted that the thrill is necessarily in far-off exotic places, and that you perceive it—if you ever do—by learning to fathom peculiar signs and signals. You assume that it only comes wrapped in outlandish foreign perfumes and weird foreign music. But the truth is that it is all around you wherever you are, and its thrillingness can be ordinary as well as exotic. Not ordinary in the sense of being humdrum or cheap, but in the sense of being of the common world. It was like flowers, the youth thought. Rare orchids in a hothouse at the Botanical Gardens might be beautiful, but a ragged patch of daisies beside the footpath is no less beautiful. You might even like the daisies better. You start out thinking that the flowers of this world are unapproachable hothouse rarities, and only later do you start to see that they are also simple and friendly things you can come across round the next corner.

It was enough to lift you right up and make you feel extra happy and optimistic.

He understood that these insights also related to the rifle in the shop window. You assume an instrument of fate must be wrapped in a special aura, must be sealed off in a protected hush, like a hothouse orchid, when in fact it could be as unpretentious as a daisy, there in a common window among penknives and fishing tackle. The youth hadn't thought of the rifle as precisely "an instrument of fate" until now, but that's what it was of course. It was a real advance to have cottoned on to that.

He strode onto a pedestrian crossing and a car stopped abruptly within a few inches of him and he saw an angry face mouthing words at him through a windscreen. He was in a daze and needed to pull himself together. He was beginning to get the sweaty, headachy sensation and wasn't entirely sure, now, whether the conversation with Delia had really hap-

pened. Maybe he had imagined it, the way he so often imagined Delia lying on his bed with him. He knew that he had
many conversations that weren't exactly real, and that he spent
a good deal of time with people who weren't strictly there.
Maybe there wasn't really any Delia in jeans and a white
blouse. He stopped and tried to think what he'd done with the
invitation she'd given him—*if* she had. He searched his pockets, then walked back to the bus stop, examining the ground
the whole way. There was no sign of it. He sat down on the
bus-stop seat. He was glad there was nobody else there and
that no bus came for a long time, and he was able to stare off
at the sky.

He let himself go into the Diestl mood. He made the motion
of unslinging the Schmeisser and sat like someone utterly tired
and blank and uncaring. When he had let that mood drive
everything else out, he could think clearly.

"All that stuff is shit," he was able to decide. "Whether she's
in jeans and blouse, or witch's robes, or a fucking clown-suit,
it doesn't matter. Whether she even exists is beside the point.
You know now what the focus is. It's hanging up in that window, waiting for the practical details to fall into place, waiting
for you to see the Assignment clearly."

The youth got that vivid image of the city skyline burning
and falling.

HE HAD promised to keep in touch with his mother in the
northern town so one evening he called from a phone box near
the State Library. The cranky old lady answered and again
began to dispute with the operator, but the phone was snatched
away from her in mid-sentence. He heard his mother accepting
the reverse charge, then asking him to hang on a minute. Then
he heard the old lady's protesting voice fading away.

"I've wheeled her out of the room," the woman said when
she came back to the phone, "so I can have a minute's peace."

She sighed that she was very fed up with the job.

"She keeps complaining to her daughter about the way I look after her, and the daughter keeps ringing up to query what I'm doing. Mind you, the daughter doesn't want a bar of the old bat herself, and lives a hundred miles away, but she likes to play the Virtuous by taking the silly old cow's part against whoever's doing the actual dirty work."

And it *was* dirty work, the woman went on. The old lady had a palatial house and a solid silver tea-service, but would spit on the floor if she felt like it. That appeared to sum up for her all the unreasonableness of life and the world and other people. Also, the old lady picked on the boy. She had it firmly in mind that the boy was the young former self of her estranged grandson, who was now a man in his forties, and she would rebuke him about his failed marriages and shady business deals. The boy was a kind of phantom to her, and it was a bit eerie, the woman said, because you knew the old lady was at times addressing him as a figure in her mind rather than as someone really standing there. It could be quite funny, she added, but you had to be in the mood for it.

She asked the youth what he'd been doing with himself, whether he had another job yet, whether he'd made any nice friends. He mumbled evasive replies. She did not press very hard for answers, and he got the feeling she was stalling somehow. There was a long pause.

"I've been in touch with Vladimir," she said. "Or rather, he got in touch with me, through Georgie, and I wrote back to him."

"I see," said the youth.

There was another longish pause. Georgie and her husband Earle were the closest things to friends they'd ever had. They'd been the next-door neighbours for a few years. Georgie had made it clear that she didn't like Vladimir, and if Vladimir was drunk and being a bit scary the woman would whisper to the

youth to take his brother and "go to Auntie Georgie's."
Georgie would sit them down and give them some ice-cream
or jelly and then go out to her front gate and keep an ear
cocked. A few times she had hurried back in and said to Earle,
"Quick, go and show your face in there, love!" Earle was a thin
wheezing man on a disabled soldier's pension, but he'd go
straight in through the backyard and into the house via the
kitchen. The youth remembered how Earle would come back
after a couple of minutes and say, "She reckons she's alright,
and I'm willin' to take her word for it." But another time he'd
not come back for quite a while. Georgie had called out worriedly across the fence to him and he'd put his head out the
kitchen door to let her know he was okay, then he'd gone back
in. Later the youth heard his mother telling Georgie how Earle
had stood between her and Vladimir and said to him, "If you
raise a hand, you'll raise it to *me!*" While the woman was
telling it, Earle was sitting beside Vladimir in the backyard.
Vladimir was crying and Earle was patting him on the shoulder and telling him that he was too decent a man to be a standover merchant, specially with a woman, and that it was the
grog that was doing it, and that he needed to knock it off.
They'd moved from that suburb, and later they heard that
Earle had passed away, but the woman had stayed friends with
Georgie. She'd got the youth to memorise the phone number
and would say, "If anything ever happens, call Georgie." She
never spelt out what she meant by anything happening, but the
youth understood it to be something like, "If you ever find me
dead on the floor and don't know what to do." Even now he
could reel the number off by heart, and it sometimes popped
into his mind in moments of stress.

Everything gradually got worse without Georgie and Earle
next door. The youth sometimes thought it was because
Vladimir no longer had anyone to remind him that he was too
decent a man to be a standover merchant.

So now Vladimir had got a letter to the woman through Georgie. He must've sounded sincere, the youth thought, for Georgie to have even given him the time of day.

"We had a long talk over the phone two nights ago," the woman said, at the end of the pause.

"You and him?"

"Yes."

"So what does that mean?"

"It doesn't automatically mean anything. I just wanted to tell you that we've been talking to each other."

"Okay. You've told me."

"Do you object?"

"Why should I object?"

"Well, it concerns all of us."

"What does?"

"The fact that Vladimir and I are communicating. I just want to know how you feel about it."

"I'm not in charge of what you do."

"Don't get angry."

"I'm not angry."

"Alright, you're not angry."

"Can I ask a question?"

"Of course."

"Did the two of you discuss *me*?"

"He asked how you were getting on, and I answered as best I could, that's all."

"Well, would you please not discuss me anymore. Just leave me out of it."

"There wasn't any 'discussion' about you. He just wanted to know how you were, the same as he asked about your brother and about me. It was only a brief conversation."

"You said it was a long one."

"It was a medium one."

"Was it the *only* time?"

"Well, no. We've talked a few times, actually."

"The story changes each time you tell it."

"We've spoken three times on the phone, and exchanged one letter each. Is that exact enough?"

"Did you discuss me the other times?"

"He was curious to know whether you're alive or dead, so I told him. I'm sorry if that's classified as a national secret!"

"I have to hang up now. Someone else is waiting to use the phone."

"Look, don't start acting like a brat! I won't put up with it!"

"There's someone waiting."

"Let them wait. We need to talk about the future."

"Why?"

"Because things are happening."

"You mean getting all chummy with him again?"

"Not just that."

"What else?"

"I've given my notice here. That means we need to work out what the next move is going to be for all of us."

"The person is banging on the phone box. I have to hang up."

"Is there *really* someone there?"

"Yes, really," he lied. "Shall I put them on the line so you can ask their name?"

He heard the woman sigh.

"Well, hang up if you must. But phone again tomorrow night, reverse charges, so we can talk more. Will you promise to do that? Or will I phone you where you're living?"

"No," he said hurriedly. "Let me phone you."

The last thing he wanted was to have her knowing where he lived. All he'd told her was the name of the street, and that he had a nice garage room. Thank God he hadn't given her an exact address or the phone number. She might even have told Vladimir what it was, now that they were getting so pally again.

266 · PETER KOCAN

The youth got a sudden chilling image of Vladimir coming along the driveway, a looming figure in the dark, heading for his door. In his mind's ear he could almost hear the sudden loud knock. It gave him the awful stomach-churning, going-to-water feeling.

"By the way," the woman said, "do you need any money?"

"Um, sort of," he replied. "Why do you ask?"

"Vladimir has sent me some. Quite a lot, actually. To help us out, and to show his good faith. You have a right to some of it."

The youth would have snapped back that he didn't want anything that came from Vladimir, but the thought of being able to keep his rent paid at Delia's, of being able to stay with her, was too much of a relief.

"Well, I do need to pay some rent shortly . . ."

"I'll wire you a couple of hundred tomorrow, to the GPO," she said quickly. "Is that convenient?" She sounded pleased. His accepting Vladimir's money was obviously a promising first step. "Is that okay?" she repeated.

"Yes," he said, knowing he'd given ground.

"Right then," she said, her voice rising with confidence. "Talk to you tomorrow night, around this same time. I'll have the old duck out of the way. And your brother will want to say hello, too."

"Right."

"Bye then."

"Just one thing," said the youth, "so I know what we're really talking about."

"Yes?"

"Do you want to go back to him?"

"More or less."

"I see."

"We need to start being a family again."

"Is that what you call it?"

"He wants to change."

"Does he?"

"He's had a bad fright, us walking out like we did. And so
have I, in a way. The world's a hard place, and after you reach
a certain point in life there aren't a lot of options. There aren't
any fresh fields beckoning anymore. You have to make the best
of what you've got."

"Stand or fall where you are, you mean?"

"Yes, that's a way of putting it, I suppose."

There was a silence.

"Have *you* found fresh fields, these past few months?" she
asked.

"I have to hang up."

"Is the person still waiting for the phone?"

"Yes."

"Till tomorrow then."

The youth hung up the receiver, left the phone box, and
went round past the front steps of the library and into the
park. The statue of Henry Lawson loomed against the dark
sky. He sat on a bench for a long while, thinking of what she'd
said about not having options, and having to make the best of
what you've got. It was the first time he'd understood that her
life was poignant too, and that there was a bravery in what she
had done and been through, and in her idea now of going back
to stand or fall with Vladimir. It was like the lone Viking on the
bridge. He must've wished he had other options, wished he
didn't have to make his stand that very day on that particular
bridge. But he did have to. The youth looked up again at the
dark shape of the statue and it made him think of young Harry
Dale the Drover. Another case of having to do or die where
fate had placed you. Harry Dale must've wished in his heart
that he didn't have to swim that particular river, with its deadly flood tide running. But that was the river that ran between
him and his homestead and his people. He could've turned
away and found another river that was safer to swim, but it

would've been utterly beside the point. Fate had allotted him *that* river on *that* day.

Yes, he could see how going back to Vladimir, going back to being a "family" again, might be the allotted thing for her. But he knew it wasn't meant for him. He had some other bridge, some other river.

The money came through to the GPO next day. The youth collected it and went to a cafe and had a slap-up meal of fried eggs and sausages and a big brimming milkshake. It was lovely to be sitting there, looking at the people, feeling well-fed, with money in your pocket, knowing you weren't going to be homeless for a while yet. "This is happiness," he said to himself, as though recognising it for the first time. He could pay another month's rent now, and go on having Delia in his life.

He phoned the woman the next evening. She was back in her old brisk manner and her plans had firmed a lot in twenty-four hours. She and the boy would be leaving the northern town in three weeks, on their way back to Vladimir, and they'd be stopping for a day or so in the city to see the youth and find out what his intentions were. He knew this bit about finding out his "intentions" was a trick to pretend she understood how grown up he was. In fact she took it completely for granted he'd be going back south with them. This assumption on her part was the price he'd known he would have to pay for accepting Vladimir's money. He had tamely taken the money, so of course he must be a tame creature all round. This was what had always hurt and enraged him, though he hadn't put it properly into words until now—you never got credit for having any *honour*.

He began to protest about this on the phone, but then the woman really frightened him by saying that Vladimir was prepared to come from interstate, if necessary, so that all four of them could meet and talk it through. So already it was back to the old system: your life ruled by fear of Vladimir. Maybe the woman had always been able to use that fear as a lever, just as she was using it now.

He decided not to argue the point. He would never go back to that system, never. Whether she knew it or not was *her* problem.

IN HIS daily wanderings in the city, the youth had found the offices of the *Rural Times* newspaper. It had occurred to him that he might need to get another job in the country one day, if things became desperate, and it'd be handy to know where the paper was located. It turned out to be a nice old building in a crooked street in the business area. He had been attracted along that street by a lit-up sign saying "McQuigan's Military Models" and had found the *Rural Times* almost opposite. McQuigan's was a quaint-looking shop with small green-painted windows. When you entered, though, you found a well-lit, air-conditioned space with counters and display cases and a number of large tables with model battlefields on them.

The first table the youth looked at showed the battle of Pharsalia. He had never heard of it and felt no interest, though there was a printed card giving the key information. Then he thought of something and felt his heart beating harder. Maybe there was a model of Hastings here. He approached the next table, almost holding his breath, and found that it showed Bosworth. He paused to read the card. King Richard III had been brave and resolute, but had lost the battle because of treachery when some of his nobles had changed sides at a crucial moment. The youth felt emotion well in him. Another hero who'd gone down. He gazed at the display. It was very detailed and complete and it made it seem as though you were looking down at the real thing from the sky. According to the card, it depicted that moment of the battle when King Richard led the main charge of his knights. There they were, strung out along the slope with their banners rippling and the manes and tails of their horses flying. They must've known, at that moment, about the treachery, and that the battle of Bosworth was already lost, and that most of them would die that day with the King.

Ah well, the youth thought to himself, his eyes hot with tears, ah well, never mind: they were winning the Battle of Honour instead.

The phrase had come unbidden into his mind and he felt a tremor through him and he gave a kind of sob. That was it! That was exactly it! He sighed deeply. How wonderful it was when you found the exact words to express a whole enormity of meaning! "The Battle of Honour" summed everything up, made everything clear, the whole of history and the whole of life. It was so simple, so obvious, that you might have thought of it years ago, except that these things come when they are *meant* to come, and that's only when you are ready for them, and when they won't be wasted on you like pearls before swine.

He turned from the Bosworth table and saw two young men behind a counter. They were looking at him with worried expressions. He wondered vaguely what was wrong with them. Then he glimpsed his own face in a section of mirror. For a moment he did not know who it was. The face was distorted with emotion, the eyes staring and the mouth pulled down in a grimace of misery or something, and tears were running down the cheeks. He ran his sleeve over his eyes and cheeks and took a couple of deep breaths and tried to straighten his mouth from its downward grimace. He looked back at the two shop assistants and they looked awkwardly away.

Walking towards the door, he knew the embarrassment didn't matter. All that mattered was that he'd found the phrase, the meaning, the message of the world. The Battle of Honour. He stood outside McQuigan's for a couple of minutes, breathing deeply and trying to contain his sense of having just been filled with a great truth. He felt like walking for miles, and it was nearly midnight when, tired out and calm in his mind, he tiptoed along Delia's driveway to his room.

The youth never went into McQuigan's Military Models again. It wasn't because he felt embarrassed. He cared nothing about that. It was simply that there are places you never need to return to, because you've already gained the special thing that was there for you. Not returning was a kind of homage to the place, a salute to its significance.

He did go back along the street though, whenever he was nearby. On the side of the *Rural Times* building were glassed-in noticeboards with pages of the current edition of the paper displayed. He went to browse over the pages, to look at photos of prize bulls, advertisements for tractors, scenes of harvesting, reports about wool prices. He found that browsing there set off trains of thought.

How interesting, he reflected, that this paper goes out over the whole countryside, goes to every town and hamlet, into every general store and corner shop and service station. And it worked the other way as well. Every happening in every part of the country was taken notice of in this building. In this building they knew the cattle prices at Bindialla, and what the river level was at Connaweal, and how the wheat was looking in the Gungamai district.

And this paper had classified ads full of poignant details about human lives. You'd learn, for example, that out at Tullibar a "recently separated grazier with two children under eight" wanted a housekeeper, and you'd wonder what those people were like and what the whole story of it was. You'd think how there were thousands and thousands of stories going on every moment all over the country. At times it gave the youth a peculiar shock to remember that he had actually been in the bush and had first-hand knowledge of a few stories. It was startling because it reminded him that those people and places had been real, not just figments of his own thought.

The *Rural Times* noticeboards gave the youth the same feeling he used to get from listening to *Country Calling* on the radio at Clem and Gladys's. He felt the romance of it, the grandeur, the sense of it going on over generations. A lot of it was tragic, of course, but tragedy was part of the tide of life, like with Romeo and Juliet. He had been determined to read

that play ever since Meredith Blackett had talked about it.
He'd sought it out at the State Library and, when he'd got used
to the old-fashioned language, had become absorbed. He saw
how the sadness of it was a proper part of its power and meaning. He saw that if the lovers had not had it in them to meet
such drastic ends, they would not have been capable of powerful love in the first place. It was a kind of trade-off that lay at
the centre of existence: you can only have the joy if you accept
the misery as well.

It gave him a shudder to grasp that the whole country was
packed with that intensity of life, from rabbits in burrows to
eagles on cliffs, from insects teeming in the grass to farm fam-
ilies laughing or weeping in their kitchens. The shudder was of
mingled pleasure and dismay that life was so vibrant, so *insis-
tent*. A lot of the time it felt reassuring. If you spent your time
being conscious of all that surging life across the generations it
would sustain you. You would take some of the vibrancy into
yourself just by the fact of your sympathy with it. There were
moments when the youth yearned to work for the *Rural Times*,
to come to this building each day and dwell on the eternal
surge of life.

Of course he understood there was no chance of that, since
he himself had only the bitter road of ruination to tread. But
now he saw that the ruination did not cancel out the beauty,
any more than Romeo and Juliet's grief cancelled out their
love. It was just the two sides of that trade-off. The point was
to keep faith with the side of the equation you found yourself
dealing with.

It was Bosworth and the idea of the Battle of Honour that
had given him the key. It was to do with the difference between
choosing and accepting. The traitors had made a choice at
Bosworth, to be on the winning side, whereas the loyal hearts
had simply accepted that their post was with the King, whatever the outcome. Honour was in acceptance rather than in

choosing. If you start doing your own choosing you are on a slippery slope. It was not for the lone Viking to choose his bridge, or Harry Dale his river, or the Bushranger his town, any more than for the true knights at Bosworth to choose the winning side. It was for each of them to accept his given post, the site at which the Battle of Honour was his to wage.

What excited the youth about this idea of choosing or accepting was its implication: the Battle of Honour wasn't only a matter of lonely roads and bitter ruin. It could equally apply to the happy side of life. It could be in accepting joy with as much courage as one would accept despair. Romeo and Juliet had to face both joy and despair in equal measure, but most lives aren't set in such a balance. The profound element in most lives is usually more on one side than the other. Person A is called on to have a happy marriage and to raise a family, whereas Person B is called on to die of leukaemia at eighteen. Each of them is at their post, and each is engaged in the Battle of Honour. And somehow each of them is fulfilling something for the other.

He walked for hours through the city and suburbs, his head down, going over and over the same ideas, trying to phrase them in the exact way that would make them clear. If you could stumble on the right way to say a thing, the whole idea would click for you, as in that pure moment when the words "The Battle of Honour" had come unbidden. At the edge of his mind another insight floated. It was about human beings doing things or fulfilling things for each other, and about acceptance rather than choice being the basis of it.

It darted in as a thought about Romeo and Juliet. They had more passion and anguish than most people ever have. And therefore . . . they *provide* it for those people! Then he thought of Ronnie Robson. Why did it always make you feel better in yourself to recall that Ronnie was the world's greatest, and always gave a hundred and ten per cent? Because most people can't do what Ronnie does, and so he does it *for* them. And again, most human beings are not enchantingly beautiful, so Grace Kelly embodies that for them, and an element of that beauty is brought into all their lives. And hardly anyone is a doomed leader going down with his people in a saga of heroism, so King Harold is that on everyone's behalf.

Things like passion and skill and beauty and heroism are granted to individual people, the youth reasoned, because the thing needs a person to embody it. In a much more important sense, though, those things belong to the entire human race. It was like someone being an excellent gardener and having gorgeous flowers in their yard. That the flowers are in *their* yard is just a kind of technicality, but that those flowers exist in the world is a splendour of nature and a joy of the human spirit.

And the acceptance is in the gardener's willingness to *be* the gardener. If he or she could choose, they'd probably rather be a great sports champion, or a world-famous beauty. But for better or worse those sites of the Battle of Honour are allotted to others. Being the champion is Ronnie Robson's bridge to defend, being the beauty is Grace Kelly's river to swim. The post that is actually *there*, to be accepted rather than chosen, is that of growing gorgeous flowers in a suburban yard. And though Ronnie Robson and Grace Kelly may never see those flowers, they are of the world made sweeter by them. And equally, though the gardener might never see Ronnie on the field, or Sweetheart on the screen, he or she is of the world made finer by the prowess of the one and the enchantingness of the other.

The youth was sipping a milkshake in a cafe as he mulled for the fiftieth time over this notion of people in the world *doing* things for each other. It was, he told himself with the clarity of truth, The Great Reciprocation. He knew the word "reciprocation" because he'd come across it a few days earlier and had looked it up in a dictionary: "mutual giving and receiving," it said. How amazing, to find that word just when it was needed to click everything into place! But of course he knew it wasn't amazing at all. It was fate providing what was needed.

These concepts of The Battle of Honour and The Great Reciprocation had armed him in a way he'd never known before. He began to see what a crude implement a Schmeisser was by comparison. He would have liked to confer with Diestl about it all, but he feared Diestl would be suspicious—especially of the bit about accepting joy as readily as disaster.

A FEW nights later the youth came home to Delia's house after dark and went to walk along the driveway to his room. There was a strong breeze that made the leaves rustle at the front, and he could hear it stirring and sighing in the tangles of vine down in the backyard. There were clouds moving fast in the sky, so that the moon kept going bright and dark as they swept across it.

The sounds of the breeze were loud enough that the youth did not feel he had to tiptoe on the gravel. And besides, it was only about ten o'clock. In fact he had started getting out of the habit of tiptoeing past Delia's lounge-room window. He'd decided that he had to live up to his new idea of accepting the good as readily as the bad. Delia's presence in his life was about as good as a thing gets, and he knew he must try to be open to it. He must allow things to happen, to unfold, to "blossom" even. "Blossom" was a nice word and the youth had it in his mind a lot. It came, he supposed, from those thoughts about the flowers and the gardener. Acceptance was allowing things to bloom as they are meant to. Like at that walk they'd had to the bus stop. Look what had blossomed from that, and all because he'd *accepted* that Delia wasn't going to let him wriggle free. And now, too, because of his insight about The Great Reciprocation, he could imagine that maybe Delia being in his life wasn't totally one-sided. If she was in his life, he was also in hers, and surely that meant there was reciprocation. He must be doing something for her, even if it was only the tiniest fraction of what she did for him by just existing. She'd said that she and Sunny had talked about him quite a lot. That was a scrap of reciprocation. He'd been a topic, a talking point, a help to her in occupying an idle moment.

As he came near Delia's window, he heard a faint sound of music from inside. It was the old-fashioned New Orleans jazz that she loved. She and Sunny and the youth had had a little conversation about it the morning before when the youth had come on them lounging in their deckchairs in the backyard. The old-fashioned New Orleans jazz was the real thing, Delia said, because it had melody and was based on tunes that people knew and could sing along with or dance to. All that got thrown away later, and jazz turned demonic, like so much else in the world. All the good karma was in the old style. Louis Armstrong was a great karmic force, Delia declared, and one that she often recommended to clients as an antidote to demonic energies. The youth had enjoyed the conversation and had promised himself he'd get into old-style jazz and Louis Armstrong and all that. Maybe he could even buy himself a record-player. It was another bit of the reciprocation system—Delia giving him guidance about something that could enrich his life. There was no doubt about it: once you cottoned on to a profound insight like The Great Reciprocation, you saw it constantly at work.

He paused near the window to try to catch the music properly above the noises of the breeze. The window was shut and the blind drawn, but the blind had a crease or curl at one edge, and this opened a space you could see through. The youth peered in. He could only see one side of the room, with the gramophone and the back of the sofa, and there was no sign of anyone there. The music was slow and sensuous. It was a saxophone playing, he thought. The youth looked up at the clouds

and the moon, and listened to the faint, slow saxophone min-
gling with the rustling and sighings all around him. It all
seemed to flow together and he felt calm and happy.

Then Delia came into sight. She had on an Oriental silk
dressing-gown. It was shimmery and clung to her body, and
her hair was flowing loose. She was looking across the sofa at
someone and speaking to them. She smiled and gave whoever
it was a long level gaze. Sunny came around the sofa into view.
He had on only a pair of white shorts. They kissed. It was a
very long and slow kiss, and the youth thought he could see
their tongues working at each other's mouths. Suddenly he felt
hot and excited and leant closer to the glass.

As they drew apart, Delia lifted her hands and drew her
dressing-gown from her shoulders and it fell with a motion as
quick and smooth as water. She gave a shake of her hair and it
moved like water too, but darker and heavier. She stood there
naked, smiling at Sunny, and he smiled back. Delia put her
hands on the band of Sunny's shorts and began to pull them
down off his hips. The shorts were bulging at the front and she
eased them gently over the bulge and then let them drop on
the floor. They kissed again, with Delia stroking the erection
with her hand. The youth was erect too, inside his pants, and
his throat felt so tight he could hardly breathe. He pressed
closer to the glass. When the long kiss ended, Delia leant her
bottom against the back of the sofa and moved her legs apart,
then Sunny bent and began to position the end of his erection
between her legs. Delia took it in her hand again, to guide it.
She looked up and said something and Sunny gave her face a
reassuring touch. Then they got their positions right and he
slid into her and began to move quite slowly and gently.

They both smiled again and gave each other more of the
reassuring touches. Even half-choking with excitement, the
youth thought how sweet of them to be so *friendly*. He knew
about lovers being sweet and tender when they cuddled. He'd

had lots of sweet and gentle times with Sweetheart, cuddling his pillow. But he'd always imagined that actual fucking was abrupt and frantic, that you got it over quickly because it wasn't fair to the woman to make her put up with it. The sweet friendliness of *this* fucking was unlike anything he'd imagined. So was the fact that you could do it in a position other than lying down. And that the man got between the woman's legs. The youth had vaguely assumed the man lay astride with his legs outside hers. He had assumed a woman's opening was right up in front, but now he could tell, from the angle of the thrusting, that it must be further down between her legs. So that was how it worked. The woman held her legs apart to let the man in.

How sweet, he was thinking, how sweet . . .

He heard the crunch of gravel a split second before he felt the hand grab him by the shoulder.

"What are ya fuckin' doin'?" a voice bawled in his ear. "Ya fuckin' pervin', aren't ya!"

"No," the youth said weakly, half-collapsed with fright.

"Yes ya fuckin' are, ya dirty little bastard!"

The youth tried to step away but the man grabbed him by the front of the shirt and held him. It was all happening very fast, but to the youth it felt like horrible slow motion.

"You're not goin' anywhere, ya dirty little hoon!" the man snarled, his face so close that the youth could feel the spit.

The man rapped loudly on the glass with his knuckles.

"Hey, there's somebody pervin' out here!" he bellowed. "Hey, I've caught a fuckin' perve!"

The youth made another effort to pull away, but the man shoved him against the wall and pinned him there while he banged his fist against the window frame.

"Hey, I've caught a perve! Phone the fuckin' Jacks!"

The blind went up and light spilled out. Sunny peered anxiously through the glass.

"Hoy!" the man yelled to him. "Phone the fuckin' Jacks!"

Sunny peered harder.

"Here he is!" the man said, pulling the youth away from the wall and into the light.

Sunny was still adjusting his shorts with one hand. Behind him in the room Delia was clutching her dressing-gown tightly round her and looking shocked and frightened.

It was obvious that Sunny couldn't quite see who was outside. The man tapped on the window and made a gesture to him to open it. Sunny fumbled with the catch.

"What is this kerfuffle occurring?" the youth heard Sunny ask as the window went up. And he saw Delia coming cautiously forward. In a moment they would be able to see who was there.

He pulled away hard and got free of the man's grip, then turned and ran.

"Hey, you fuckin' . . .!" the man yelled after him.

The youth felt too weak in the knees to run properly and expected to feel himself being grabbed again. But he wasn't. He heard Delia's voice saying, "Is that you, Dave?" and, "What on earth's going on?" He realised the man who'd grabbed him was the bloke from the end garage room, the night-shift worker, and he sensed that the bloke had vaguely realised who he was just as he'd pulled free.

"The little bastard was pervin' through the window!" he heard the man tell them. "Getting a good eyeful of *somethin'*, he was!"

The youth had not known which direction he'd run. It turned out to have been towards the backyard. He got to the tangle of vines and paused, ready to make for the back gate. He listened carefully above the sighing of the breeze in the foliage. There was no-one coming. He could tell from the voices that the man was still at the window, explaining what had happened.

From being like slow motion, everything turned to a rapid blur. His mind sped. He might just have a minute before they came down to the backyard. They might be taking a minute to phone the police or whatever. He must try to get his things from his room, right now. He ran to his door and fumbled in his pocket for his key, then grappled frantically to get it into the lock. He ordered himself to stop the panic. The door flew open and he flicked the light on and went in. If they came now they'd have him like a rat in a trap. He began to count the seconds under his breath and as he counted he got his bag and laid it open on the bed and put the few important things into it—the White Book, the old broken spurs of Clem's, a couple of pieces of clothing. He tried to think what else, but panic was rising again: the words "get out, get out, get out" were chiming with the seconds as he counted them off. He was up to twenty-something seconds now. Or had he lost count and got confused? Where was his money? He couldn't think. In his pocket? Yes! Go then!

He shouldered the bag and went out, half-expecting to find them standing by the door. He could no longer hear voices along the driveway. Where were they? He ran to the back gate and entered the lane, then scurried as fast as he could along it, his ears pricked for any sound behind him. At the end of the lane he paused and looked along the street in both directions. He bolted down the street to the next corner, then turned left and ran to the corner after that. He stopped, out of breath. The police would be alerted by now. He didn't know what the cops did when they got word of a perve. Did they arrive with sirens and flashing lights? Or did they creep up stealthily? Should he focus on being quick, or being careful? He was standing there too long. He began counting seconds again, to give himself a time frame. The panic was rising once more. The cops hate perves. That was common knowledge. The police probably give perves a good bashing when they catch them.

And perves get bashed up in prison too. That was a well-known fact.

Then a voice in his head said very clearly and calmly: "Start walking in a normal manner, and keep going till you're out of the area."

He supposed it was Diestl, but wasn't sure.

He did what the voice said.

HE HAD walked solidly for about an hour. The energy that shock and fear had given him had drained away and he felt exhausted, hardly able to keep lifting his feet. The breeze had gone and the air hung heavy and warm. The youth stopped for a minute to think. There were no people in the dark streets and only an occasional car went by. One of them was a taxi with its "For Hire" sign lit. He half-thought to flag it down, but he had nowhere in particular to go and would not know what to tell the driver. He wanted more than anything to lie down and was wondering where he might find a sheltered spot.

"Good evening," a voice said beside him.

He jumped with fright. He was next to someone's front fence and an old chap was standing in the shadows with a sprinkler hose in his hand. The youth had not heard the faint sound of the water.

"They like a bit of a drink after dark," the old chap said, swishing the spray onto some broad leaves so that it made a soft pattering sound. "Do any gardening yourself?"

The youth had recovered enough to mutter, "No."

"I took it up when I retired," the old chap said. "To give myself an interest. And then I got hooked on it. Wouldn't be without my plants now. The thing of it is, they stay with you when everything else has gone—the job, the family. That all goes, one way and another. But the plants are always there."

The old chap didn't seem to mind that a strange youth had come to stand at his front fence in the middle of the night.

Suddenly the youth yearned to be like this old chap, to be seventy or eighty, to be on the pension and finished with everything except the plants that like a drink after dark and are always there. And to know that sometime in your sleep you'll probably just drift away without even knowing it. Life was too hard and too complicated. And the complication, the youth saw, was in the moment-to-moment detail rather than in the larger scheme of it. You could think your way through the big scheme—or try to, at least—but the devil is in the detail. That phrase had popped into his head. He'd heard or read it somewhere. Yes, that summed it up: *The devil's in the detail.* The devil suddenly jumps out of some casual-seeming moment, out of a trivial detail—like whether there's a crease in the blind of a window—and before you know it a disaster has happened and can never be made to *un*happen.

He half-thought to ask the old chap whether he'd found life very complicated, and whether the devil had kept leaping out of the detail at him, and how he had coped with the whole tangle of it. After seventy or eighty years a person must know a thing or two.

The youth wished someone would tell him, for instance, whether his life was the way it was because he was doing it wrong, or whether life just happened in certain ways no matter what you did. Was "life" more inside yourself, in the form of thoughts and feelings and dreads and decisions, or was it more outside, like weather conditions that you have to put up with or adapt to. He thought of Lawson's "Faces in the Street." Do the faces make themselves miserable, or is it the street that does it to them? A bit of both, he supposed. You do the best you can inside yourself, and you cope with the outside weather as best you can too.

He might have asked the old chap about it, but he had walked on and the old chap was a couple of streets back.

But of course he didn't need the old chap's advice. He had

Diestl. Diestl had merged into step with him. The youth felt the weight of the Schmeisser, the roughness of the torn tunic, the rhythm of the limping walk. How familiar and comforting it was.

"Where have you been?" the youth asked in his mind.

"I've been with you all the way."

"I didn't realise."

"Your mind wanders."

"Yes, I know. But I've been thinking about interesting things. About The Battle of Honour and about The Great Reciprocation."

"They were good ideas. They'll help you do what you need to do."

"Will they?"

"Of course. That's why those ideas came to you. Did you think it was all unconnected?"

"I wasn't sure."

"But now the situation's laid out."

"Like it was for the lone Viking, and for Harry Dale, and for the Bushranger?"

"That's it."

"So everything is as it should be?"

"Pretty much."

"Is it very close now?"

"You know the answer to that. You know the instrument is at hand."

"What if it gets sold? Anyone could walk into that shop and buy it any time."

"You know that won't happen. You know it is meant for you."

"Yes."

"All the same, don't get careless. Even if a thing is meant to be, it still has to be *done*. You might let them off the hook if you get sloppy about it."

"I won't get sloppy."

"Good."

"I won't let them off the hook."

"I know. If I hadn't been sure of that I wouldn't have stayed with you all this time."

"Thanks for believing in me."

"You're welcome."

"And for always coming to help me in that dream. The Tunnel of Love one. I still don't quite understand what all that meant."

"It doesn't matter."

"I know you never liked her."

"It was never a matter of liking or not liking. She helped you through. She was necessary, but only up to a point."

"I see that now."

"That's it then."

"I've got money. I'll go and buy it first thing."

"It'll be there."

The Diestl mood began to break up and fade, as it always did, but the youth limped on down empty streets and the hours of the night went by.

IT WAS nine days later. He had a blue airline bag with a shoulder strap. The bag was cheap and had a nasty synthetic feel, but that didn't matter because he only needed a few hours use from it. He'd bought it at Woolworths and taken it back to the room he'd rented in an inner-city residential. He'd left it on the bed while he sawed the barrel and stock off the rifle. Then he'd put the cut-down rifle and the box of bullets into the bag and had zipped it up. He had walked back and forth across the room with the bag first in one hand and then in the other, to accustom himself to the weight and feel of it. Then he had tried it with the strap over one shoulder and then the other. It was okay.

He carried the bag along a city street. It was three o'clock in the afternoon and at around eight o'clock that night he had to be at a certain location where all would be revealed. That phrase kept running through his mind: *All will be revealed*. Oh yes, he was thinking, I have the bag of tricks right here. Actually it's just the one trick, but it's a bobby-dazzler. You'll read all about it tomorrow. He kept his eyes level and didn't mind exchanging glances with the oncoming people. He felt as confident and cheerful as he ever had in his life.

He could keep on walking, but it was a cold and windy day and he didn't want to wear himself out. He had to be fresh for later. He came to a cinema and stopped to look at the posters and photos outside. The film was called *Summer Island* and the poster said it was a breathless tale of young love. He felt for the money in his pocket. He had just enough left for a ticket into the movie, with a bit over for a sandwich later on. He had to be sure to eat something later. It wouldn't do to bungle things because he was shaking with hunger. He went into the foyer and to the ticket box and asked for a seat in the stalls. The woman watched him count the coins out. This would normally have withered him with embarrassment, and he would have wanted to slink away, but now he felt above all that.

The session was just about to begin. He went past the usherette at the door and down the aisle. He took a seat in the middle of the stalls and put the bag on the seat beside him. There were perhaps a dozen people in the theatre. He slumped in his seat and rested his neck against the back of it and stared at the red velvet curtains. There was muted organ music coming through the speakers. A uniformed boy came down the aisle carrying a tray of sweets and ice-creams, but no-one bought anything.

The lights dimmed and a short item about hydro-electric power came on. Then there were previews of a couple of upcoming features. Then it was interval. The boy came with the tray again. Two or three men went down the aisle to a door with "Gentlemen" lit above it. The youth wished the main film would start. He was starting to feel a bit aimless, sitting there, as though the momentum was faltering. That mustn't happen. It might be hard to get it going again later. Then the lights went down.

*Summer Island* started with a scene of the sea crashing on rocks behind the opening titles, the theme music swelling and receding in time with the waves. The story of the young lovers was very touching and as it unfolded his emotions responded. He sat with his eyes wet and a lump in his throat. It came to a scene in a summery glade where the boy and girl lie naked in each other's arms. There are beams of sunlight slanting down through the trees and the camera is right on their faces as they kiss and you can hear their tender sighs and murmurs.

How sweet life was, the youth thought. Not real life, but life in a movie or a book or a song, or in the pages of history. Life in those was truer because it brought out your feelings in the purest way. He'd had so many pure moments like that. He'd had moments so sweet it gave him a pang of despair to realise there'd be no more of them after tonight.

But the scene of the lovers in the glade had helped him. It had reminded him about The Great Reciprocation and the way it works, the endless interaction of the light and the dark. Happiness is precious only because there is tragedy in the world, and tragedy is profound only because there is happiness. The kiss of lovers is sweet because other people are bereft and lonely. The plight of the loveless is poignant because others are kissing. Pain and joy, death and life, gain and loss, and all of it bound in the great circle of reciprocation.

Because a certain dark thing happens tonight at eight o'clock, the light will be truer. And since the side of dark and pain and loss is the harder station in the Battle of Honour, and the harder to keep faith with, it is assigned only to the truest hearts.

On a sudden impulse he stood up and went along the row of seats and down the aisle to the Gents. It was empty. He went to the urinal and opened his fly and stood there. He could hear the soundtrack of the movie. He stayed at the urinal for what seemed like a long time, then he closed his fly and went to the washbasin and spent a long time washing his hands. He heard the movie ending and the theme music welling up to its finale, then silence. He heard the outer door of the Gents open and he darted into a cubicle and sat on the edge of the toilet until he heard whoever it was finish and go out. He leant forward with his elbows on his knees and his hands under his chin and stared at a bit of graffiti on the cubicle door. Then he decided he'd given it enough time. He got up and went out of the Gents. The lights were on and the theatre was empty.

The blue bag was still there on the seat. Nobody had taken it.

"So be it," he said to himself. "So be it."

## About the Author

Peter Kocan was born in Newcastle, New South Wales, in 1947 and grew up in Melbourne. He left school at fourteen to work on country New South Wales properties and in factory jobs. He served a decade in custody for a shooting offence and it was then that he began to write. He has published three previous novels and five collections of verse.

## AVAILABLE NOW FROM EUROPA EDITIONS

### The Days of Abandonment
*Elena Ferrante*
Fiction - 192 pp - $14.95 - isbn 978-1-933372-00-6

"Stunning . . . The raging, torrential voice of the author is something rare."—*The New York Times*

"I could not put this novel down. Elena Ferrante will blow you away."
—ALICE SEBOLD, author of *The Lovely Bones*

Rarely have the foundations upon which our ideas of motherhood and womanhood rest been so candidly questioned. This compelling novel tells the story of one woman's headlong descent into what she calls an "absence of sense" after being abandoned by her husband. Olga's "days of abandonment" become a desperate, dangerous freefall into the darkest places of the soul as she roams the empty streets of a city that she has never learned to love. When she finds herself trapped inside the four walls of her apartment in the middle of a summer heat wave, Olga is forced to confront her ghosts, the potential loss of her own identity, and the possibility that life may never return to normal again.

**Troubling Love**
*Elena Ferrante*
Fiction - 144 pp - $14.95 - isbn 978-1-933372-16-7

"It's the first time a novel ever made me get physical, and it was the first good mood I'd been in for weeks."—*The New York Times*

"Like Joyce's *Ulysses*, this journey draws vigorously on its cityscape. Naples is one of those sun-drenched spooky cities, thrumming with life and populated by ghosts, spastic with impermeable local culture."—*Time Out New York*

Following her mother's untimely and mysterious death, Delia embarks on a voyage of discovery through the streets of her native Naples searching for the truth about her family. Reality is buried somewhere in the fertile soil of memory, and Delia is determined to find it. This stylish fiction from the author of *The Days of Abandonment* is set in a beguiling but often hostile Naples, whose chaotic, suffocating streets become one of the book's central motifs. A story about mothers and daughters, and the complicated knot of lies and emotions that binds them.

www.europaeditions.com

**Cooking with Fernet Branca**
*James Hamilton-Paterson*
Fiction - 288 pp - $14.95 - isbn 978-1-933372-01-3

"A work of comic genius."—*The Independent*

"Provokes the sort of indecorous involuntary laughter that has more in common with sneezing than chuckling. Imagine a British John Waters crossed with David Sedaris."—*The New York Times*

Gerald Samper, an effete English snob, has his own private hilltop in Tuscany where he wiles away his time working as a ghostwriter for celebrities and inventing wholly original culinary concoctions—including ice-cream made with garlic and the bitter, herb-based liqueur of the book's title. Gerald's idyll is shattered by the arrival of Marta, on the run from a crime-riddled former Soviet republic. A series of hilarious misunderstands brings this odd couple into ever closer and more disastrous proximity.

www.europaeditions.com

**Minotaur**
*Benjamin Tammuz*
Fiction/Noir - 192 pp - $14.95 - isbn 1-933372-02-0

"A novel about the expectations and compromises that humans
create for themselves . . . Very much in the manner of William
Faulkner and Lawrence Durrell."—*The New York Times*

An Israeli secret agent falls hopelessly in love with a young English
girl. Using his network of contacts and his professional expertise,
he takes control of her life without ever revealing his identity.
*Minotaur* is a complex and utterly original story about a solitary
man driven from one side of Europe to the other by his obsession.

**Total Chaos**
*Jean-Claude Izzo*
Fiction/Noir - 256 pp - $14.95 - isbn 978-1-933372-04-4

"Rich, ambitious and passionate . . . his sad, loving portrait of his native city is amazing."—*The Washington Post*

"Full of fascinating characters, tersely brought to life in a prose style that is (thanks to Howard Curtis' shrewd translation) traditionally dark and completely original."—*The Chicago Tribune*

This first installment in the legendary *Marseilles Trilogy* sees Fabio Montale turning his back on a police force marred by corruption and racism and taking the fight against the mafia into his own hands.

**Chourmo**
*Jean-Claude Izzo*
Fiction/Noir - 256 pp - $14.95 - isbn 978-1-933372-17-4

"This hard-hitting series captures all the world-weariness of the contemporary European crime novel, but Izzo mixes it with a hero who is as virile as he is burned out."—*Booklist*

"Chourmo . . . the rowers in a galley. In Marseilles, you weren't just from one neighborhood, one project. You were chourmo. In the same galley, rowing! Trying to get out. Together." In this second installment of Izzo's legendary Marseilles Trilogy (*Total Chaos, Chourmo, Solea*) Fabio Montale has left a police force riddled with corruption, racism and greed to follow the ancient rhythms of his native town: the sea, fishing, the local bar, hotly contested games of belote. But his cousin's son has gone missing and Montale is dragged back onto the mean streets of a violent, crime-infested Marseilles.

www.europaeditions.com

**The Big Question**
*Wolf Erlbruch*
Children's Illustrated Fiction - 52 pp - $14.95 - isbn 978-1-933372-03-7

Named Best Book at the 2004 Children's Book Fair in
Bologna.

"[*The Big Question*] offers more open-ended answers than the likes
of Shel Silverstein's *Giving Tree* (1964) and is certain to leave even
younger readers in a reflective mood."—*Kirkus Reviews*

A stunningly beautiful and poetic illustrated book for children that
poses the biggest of all big questions: why am I here? A chorus of
voices—including the cat's, the baker's, the pilot's and the
soldier's—offers us some answers. But nothing is certain, except
that as we grow each one of us will pose the question differently
and be privy to different answers.

www.europaeditions.com

**The Butterfly Workshop**
*Wolf Erlbruch*
Children's Illustrated Fiction - 40 pp - $14.95 - isbn 978-1-933372-12-9

Illustrated by the winner of the 2006 Hans Christian Andersen
Award.

For children and adults alike . . . Odair, one of the Designers of All
Things and grandson of the esteemed inventor of the rainbow, has
been banished to the insect laboratory as punishment for his
overactive imagination. But he still dreams of one day creating a
cross between a bird and a flower. Then, after a helpful chat with a
dog . . .

**The Goodbye Kiss**
*Massimo Carlotto*
Fiction/Noir - 192 pp - $14.95 - isbn 978--933372-05-1

"The best living Italian crime writer."—*Il Manifesto*

"A nasty, explosive little tome warmly recommended to fans of James M. Cain for its casual amorality and truly astonishing speed."—*Kirkus Reviews*

An unscrupulous womanizer, as devoid of morals now as he once was full of idealistic fervor, returns to Italy where he is wanted for a series of crimes. To avoid prison he sells out his old friends, turns his back on his former ideals, and cuts deals with crooked cops. To earn himself the guise of respectability he is willing to go even further, maybe even as far as murder.

**Death's Dark Abyss**
*Massimo Carlotto*
Fiction/Noir - 192 pp - $14.95 - isbn 978-1-933372-18-1

"Beneath the conventions of Continental noir is a remarkable study of corruption and redemption in a world where revenge is best served ice-cold."—*Kirkus* (starred review)

"Dark and, in part, extremely brutal stuff, but an interesting game of taking action and responsibility, of being able to—and not being able to—forgive and make sacrifices."—*The Complete Review*

A riveting drama of guilt, revenge, and justice, Massimo Carlotto's *Death's Dark Abyss* tells the story of two men and the savage crime that binds them. During a robbery, Raffaello Beggiato takes a young woman and her child hostage and later murders them. Beggiato is arrested, tried, and sentenced to life. The victims' father and husband, Silvano, plunges into an ever-deepening abyss until the day, years later, when the murderer seeks his pardon and Silvano turns predator as he ruthlessly plots his revenge.

**Hangover Square**
*Patrick Hamilton*
Fiction/Noir - 280 pp - $14.95 - isbn 978-1-933372-06-8

"Hamilton is a sort of urban Thomas Hardy: always a pleasure to read, and as social historian he is unparalleled."—NICK HORNBY

Adrift in the grimy pubs of London at the outbreak of World War II, George Harvey Bone is hopelessly infatuated with Netta, a cold, contemptuous, small-time actress. George also suffers from occasional blackouts. During these moments one thing is horribly clear: he must murder Netta.

www.europaeditions.com

**I Loved You for Your Voice**
*Sélim Nassib*
Fiction - 256 pp - $14.95 - isbn 978-1-933372-07-5

"Om Kalthoum is great. She really is."—BOB DYLAN

"In rapt, lyrical prose, Paris-based writer and journalist Nassib
spins a rhapsodic narrative out of the indissoluble connection
between two creative souls inextricably bound by their art."
—*Kirkus Reviews* (starred)

Love, desire, and song set against the colorful backdrop of modern
Egypt. The story of the Arab world's greatest and most popular
singer, Om Kalthoum, told through the eyes of the poet Ahmad
Rami, who wrote her lyrics and loved her in vain all his life.
Spanning over five decades in the history of modern Egypt, this
passionate tale of love and longing provides a key to understanding
the soul, the aspirations and the disappointments of the Arab
world.

**Love Burns**
*Edna Mazya*
Fiction/Noir - 192 pp - $14.95 - isbn 978-1-933372-08-2

"This book, which has Woody Allen overtones, should be of great interest to readers of black humor and psychological thrillers."
—*Library Journal* (starred)

"Starts out as a psychological drama and becomes a strange, funny, unexpected hybrid: a farce thriller. A great book."—*Ma'ariv*

Ilan, a middle-aged professor of astrophysics, discovers that his young wife is having an affair. Terrified of losing her, he decides to confront her lover instead. Their meeting ends in the latter's murder—the unlikely murder weapon being Ilan's pipe—and in desperation, Ilan disposes of the body in the fresh grave of his kindergarten teacher. But when the body is discovered . . .

**Departure Lounge**
*Chad Taylor*
Fiction/Noir - 176 pp - $14.95 - isbn 978-1-933372-09-9

"Smart, original, surprising and just about as cool as a novel can get . . . Taylor can flat out write."—*The Washington Post*

"Entropy noir . . . The hypnotic pull lies in the zigzag dance of its forlorn characters, casting a murky, uneasy sense of doom."
—*The Guardian*

A young woman mysteriously disappears. The lives of those she has left behind—family, acquaintances, and strangers intrigued by her disappearance—intersect to form a captivating latticework of coincidences and surprising twists of fate. Urban noir at its stylish and intelligent best.